EMERALD EYE

EDITED BY

FRANK LUDLOW & ROELOF GOUDRIAAN

DUBLIN, 2005

Acknowledgements

Thomas Crumlesh 1960 - 1992: A Retrospective from Getting It In The Head by Mike McCormack, published by Jonathan Cape. Reprinted by permission of The Random House Group Ltd.

Hello Darkness copyright Mike O'Driscoll, first published in The Third Alternative and reprinted by kind permission of the author.

Encore copyright John Kenny, first published in Albedo One and reprinted by kind permission of the author.

Pleasing Mister Ross copyright Robert Neilson, first published in Fear and reprinted by kind permission of the author.

The Giaconda Caper copyright Bob Shaw, first published in Cosmic Kaleidoscope from Victor Gollancz Ltd. and reprinted by kind permission of the author's estate and its agent, Barry N. Malzberg.

Something Occurred; Bennie on the Loose copyright Seán MacRoibin, first published in Albedo Showcase No. 3 and reprinted by kind permission of the author.

Everyone This, Nobody That copyright David Murphy, first published in his story collection Lost Notes and reprinted by kind permission of the author.

Miss Smith reprinted by permission of PDF on behalf of William Trevor (C) 1967.

In Dublin's Veracity copyright Michael Carroll, first published in Albedo One and reprinted by kind permission of the author.

Velvet Fields (copyright (c) 1973, 2001 by Anne McCaffrey; first appeared in Worlds of IF) from The Girl Who Heard Dragons and Other Stories (Corgi Adult, 1996) is reproduced by kind permission of the author.

The Burnished Egg copyright Dermot Ryan, first published in Albedo One and reprinted by kind permission of the author.

Skin-Tight copyright James Lecky, first published in Albedo One and reprinted by kind permission of the author.

The Invisible Man Game copyright Nigel Quinlan, first published in the story collection This Way Up and reprinted by kind permission of the author.

The moral right of the authors has been asserted
First published in the Republic of Ireland in 2005 by Aeon Press, 8 Bachelors Walk, Dublin 1, Republic of Ireland.
ISBN 0-9534784-4-0. Set in 10.5 pt Berkeley Book. Printed in Ireland by Colour Books Ltd. All rights reserved. Without the prior consent of the publisher:
1. no part of this publication my be reproduced or transmitted by any means, electronic, mechanical, photocopying or otherwise
2. this book may not be lent, re-sold, hired out, or otherwise circulated in any form of binding or cover other than that in which it is published and without a similar condition including this condition being imposed on the subsequent purchaser.
Produced and promoted for The Meath Leader Project by Frank Ludlow and Roelof Goudriaan.

CONTENTS

Introduction

Forget imagination for a moment, forget the time most of us have spent wasting our young impressionable eyes on thrilling stories of wonder and speculation. All that aside: even when we write about the future or imaginary places, we write about what we know.

Do not expect stories about cowboys in space in Emerald Eye, that genre of story originated in, and belongs to, the US pulp magazines. No, the backdrop to stories in this collection are the landscapes that have harboured and nourished fantasy and legend throughout Irish history. The hills of Elfland shimmer through the green mounds of Meath and its ancient sites, and with such influence, no wonder that modern high fantasy to this day pays tribute to the pioneering work of Irish writers such as Lord Dunsany (1878-1957).

But Ireland is more, much more, than green hills, rainbows and romanticized pots of gold. Ireland is a melting-pot of modern and ancient, rural and urban, English and Gaelic, emigrant and immigrant, Protestant, Catholic and agnostic, often at conflict. The true essence of Ireland lies more in its people, their past and their experiences. Stoker's vampires grew up in Ireland as much as faeries did. And the simple tall tale is as close and true to the Irish tradition of story as is Celtic High Fantasy. Dermot Ryan's 'The Burnished Egg' in this collection is one of the tallest tales you'll ever read, Irish or otherwise, as well as a fine fable about character.

In selecting stories for this collection, we have let ourselves be guided only by a tale's ability to move, disturb and entertain. Nothing more, nothing less. We have not attempted to include only stories that readers might instantly identify with being "Irish", nor have we limited ourselves to stories that probe the nature of existence and the human condition, though speculative fiction, despite the comments of its detractors, is as suited to such an endeavour as any other genre, be it mainstream or literary. For our choices we make no apologies.

These stories, all from modern writers, reflect a myriad of influences, from traditional Irish fantasy to influences of modern life, alongside the writer's individual imagination of future or alternate worlds and nightmares. Not all are set in Ireland, and you will not find any mentions of leprechauns here. Yet these stories are Irish nonetheless, more purely so than stories of the 'little people' that are now mostly the province of Hollywood (or bad Star Trek episodes).

But perhaps a couple of unifying threads might be identified from the mix. Wit and black humour have become synonymous with Irish writing and Irish character. In this collection, that wit is mixed with the strong tradition of fantastic storytelling present and recorded in Ireland since the early Christian period and before. Writers like Oscar Wilde have used razor-sharp wit to slice through the foibles of Victorian society. Other authors similarly cut through rural environs, as William Trevor's story in this collection about the ordinary evil in small-town Ireland illustrates. And Bob Shaw's story, 'The Giaconda Caper', is in our eyes a truly great - and funny - tale of hoaxers and chancers.

One reason modern Irish authors have found an international audience is because they have engaged with the doubts and suspense of change. Modern Irish writing, for us, started when the Irish political failures of the 19th century left a gap of aspiration to be filled by the arts. Some of the authors in this collection grew up in the middle of the Troubles in Northern Ireland: Catholic in a Protestant society, or Protestant in Catholic. Alongside the deep vein of wit, some of the most intense stories in this collection deal with division in society, alienation, the quest for identity, with power and the struggle to shape one's own fate.

These topics are not only the tropes of speculative fiction, they are all intimately dear to people in Ireland. Yes, we are back where we started: we write about what we know. Perhaps you will know us a little better after reading this collection.

Frank Ludlow and Roelof Goudriaan,
Navan, 2005.

Mike McCormack was born in Sligo in 1965, and now lives in Galway. He is the author of two novels *Crowe's Requiem* (1998) and *Notes from a Coma* (2005), which both achieve a rare blend of small-town rural Ireland and dark, near-death fantasy.

This understated story from his first collection, *Getting It In The Head* (1996), for which McCormack won the Rooney Prize, redefines the concept of cutting edge art.

Thomas Crumlesh 1960-1992:
A Retrospective

Mike McCormack

My first contact with Thomas Crumlesh was in 1984 when he exhibited with a small artists' collective in the Temple Bar area of the city. His was one of the many fringe exhibitions hoping to draw the attention of the international buyers who were in Dublin for the official Rosc Exhibition at the Guinness Hops Store. It was July, just four months after Thomas had been expelled from the National College of Art and Design for persevering with work that, in the opinion of his tutors, dealt obscenely and obsessively with themes of gratuitous violence.

His exhibition, Notes Towards an Autobiography, had been hanging less than three days and already word had got out and excited quite a bit of outraged comment. It consisted of four box frames with black silk backgrounds on which were mounted his left lung, the thumb of his left hand, his right ear and the middle toe of his left foot. Crumlesh was present also and easily recognisable - he was standing by the invigilator's desk with his head and left hand swathed in white and not-too-clean bandages. He was deathly pale and carrying himself delicately; like most young bohemians he was badly in need of a shave. After I got over my initial shock I ventured a few words of congratulations, more by way of curiosity than from any heartfelt belief in his work's merit. He surprised me with a lavish smile and a resolute handshake, contradicting completely his frail appearance. This was my first experience of the central paradox in his personality - the palpably gruesome nature of his work set against his unfailing good spirits and optimism. He surprised me further by telling me in conspiratorial tones that he planned to leave the country that very evening. Some criticism of his work had found its way into the national press and already a few people with placards had picketed the exhibition. He had even heard word that the police were pressing for warrants to arrest him under the obscenity laws. He confided further that what really worried him was that he might fall foul of Ireland's notoriously lax committal laws; he quoted an impressive array of statistics on secondary committals in the Republic.

I ended that encounter by buying his lung. His enthusiasm and verve convinced me of its worth and his whole appearance told me that he was in need of the money. Before I left he outlined the programme of work he had laid out for himself - a programme that would take him up to 1992, the year he hoped to retire. I offered to check his wounds - his bandages looked like they had not been changed in a few days.

He declined the offer saying that he did not have the time, he needed to cash the cheque and he was afraid of missing the ferry to Holyhead. We shook hands before parting and I did not expect to see him ever again.

Our paths crossed again two years later. I was in London, attending a symposium on trauma and phantom pains in amputees at the Royal College of Surgeons. By chance, in a Crouch End pub, I picked up a flyer advertising the upcoming festival of Irish culture and music in Finsbury Park. Near the bottom of a list of rock bands and comedians was mention of a small exhibition of avant-garde work to be shown at a tiny gallery in Birchington Road. Thomas' name was mentioned second from the bottom. When I eventually found the gallery it was nothing more than two rooms knocked together on the third floor over a Chinese restaurant. Among the second-rate paintings and sculptures Thomas' work was not difficult to recognise. It stood in the middle of the floor, mounted on a black metal stand, a single human arm stripped of skin and musculature leaning at an obtuse angle to the floor. The bleached bones of the hand were closed in a half fist and the whole thing looked like the arm of some nightmare robot. As I approached it the arm jerked into life, the fingers contracted completely and the thumb bone stood vertical. It looked eerily like a ghost hitching a lift from some passing phantom car. It was untitled but carried a price of two thousand pounds.

Thomas entered the room and recognised me instantly. I attempted to shake hands - an embarrassing blunder since I had to withdraw my right hand when I saw the stump near his shoulder. As before, he was in good spirits and he entered quickly into a detailed explanation of what he called his 'technique'. He had bleached the bone in an acid formula of his own devising to give it its luminous whiteness and then wired it to electrical switches concealed beneath the carpet which would be unwittingly activated by the viewer whenever he got within a certain radius - he admitted borrowing this subterfuge from the work of Jean

Tinguely. He then circled the arm and put it through its motions, four in all.

Firstly, a snake pose that turned the palm downwards from the elbow and extended the fingers fearsomely, then the hitching gesture, then a foppish, disowning gesture that swivelled the forearm at the elbow and threw the hand forward, palm upwards, and lastly and most comically an 'up yours' middle finger gesture that faced the viewer head on. He grinned like a child when I expressed my genuine admiration. I had no doubt but that I was looking at a postmodern masterpiece. I little suspected at the time that this piece would enter into the popular imagery of the late twentieth century, reaching iconic status through exposure on album covers, T-shirts and posters.

I only regretted at the time that I had not the means to acquire it.

But Thomas was not without worries. He confided that he had found it extremely difficult to find a surgeon who would carry out the amputations, he had to be extremely careful to whom he even voiced the idea - the terror of committal again. It had taken him three months to track down an ex-army medic with shellshock who had been discharged from the parachute regiment after the Falklands War to where he ran a covert abortion clinic in Holloway. In a fugue of anaesthesia and marijuana Thomas had undergone his operation, a traumatic affair that had left him so pained and unnerved he doubted he would be able to undergo the experience again. This fright had put his life's work in jeopardy, he pointed out. He was looking me straight in the eye as he said this; I sensed that he was putting me on the spot. Then he came out straight with his request. What I need is a skilled surgeon I can rely on, not some strung-out psycho. He spoke evenly, without the least hint of hysteria in his voice. He will of course be paid, he added coyly. I told him that I needed time to think on it - it was an unusual request. He nodded his agreement, he understood fully the difficulties of his request and he would not blame me if I refused him outright. We shook hands before we parted and I promised to contact him the following day after I had given his request some thought.

In fact I had little to think about. I very quickly resolved my fundamental dilemma: the healing ethic of my craft set against the demands of Thomas' talents. One parting glance at the arm convinced me that I had encountered a fiercely committed genius who it seemed to me had already made a crucial contribution to the imagery of the late twentieth century. It was obvious to me that I had an obligation to put my skills at his disposal; the century could not be denied his singular vision on grounds of arbitrary scruples. My problem was how exactly I was to make my skills available. That evening in my hotel room I gave the problem much thought and I returned the following day with my plans.

I found Thomas in high spirits. The lead singer of a famous heavy metal band had just bought the arm and Thomas was celebrating with champagne, drinking it from a mug, trying to get the feel of his new-found wealth, as he laconically put it.

He poured me a similar mug when I declared my intention to help him. I explained my plan quickly. Before every operation he should forward to me exact details of what he needed, then give me two weeks to put in place the necessary logistics and paperwork at the clinic where I worked. I believed I would be able to perform two operations a year without arousing suspicion. He thanked me profusely, pumping my left hand with his, telling me he could rest easy now that his future was secure. In a magniloquent moment that was not without truth he assured me that I had made a friend for life.

He contacted me for the first time in November of that year telling me that he planned to exhibit a piece during the Paris Biennale. He needed six ribs removed: when would be the most convenient time for me? I wrote in reply that I had pencilled in the operation for Christmas Eve and that he could stay with me over the festive season and into the New Year while he recovered. The operation itself, an elaborate thoracotomy carried out in the witching hour of Christmas Eve, was a complete success and when, on New Year's Day, I presented him with the bundle of curved, washed bones he was thrilled; it was good to be back at work, he said.

It was during these days of convalescence that our relationship moved onto a more intimate footing. Mostly they were days of silence, days spent reading or listening to music in the conservatory that looked out over Howth to the sea beyond.

Sometimes a whole day would go by without any word passing between us. Neither of us was awkward in this. The looming, inexorable conclusion of his art ridiculed any attempts at a deeper enquiry into each other's past. He simply gave me his trust and I gave him his bones and internal organs.

That was enough for both of us.

On the third of January he returned to London, he wanted to get to work as quickly as possible. Five months later he sent me a photograph from a gallery in Paris, a black and white close-up of a piece called The Bonemobile, an abstract, lantern-shaped structure suspended by wire. His letter informed me that although the piece had excited the inevitable outrage among the more hidebound critics it had also generated some appreciative but furtive praise. Nevertheless, he doubted that any buyer would rise to the fifty thousand franc price tag he had placed upon it. He understood the fear of a buyer ruining his reputation by buying into what some were already calling apocalyptic voyeurism. Still, he lived in hope.

That was the first of twelve operations I performed on Thomas between 1986 and 1992. In all I removed twenty-three bones and four internal organs, eighteen inches of his digestive tract, seven teeth, four toes, his left eye and his right leg. He exhibited work on the fringe of most major European art festivals, narrowly escaping arrest in several countries and jumping bail in four. In his lifetime he sold eight pieces worth a total of fifty thousand pounds, by no means riches, but enough to fund his spartan existence.

Inevitably, by 1989 his work had taken a toll on his body. After the removal of a section of digestive tract in 1988 his body slumped badly and following the amputation of his right leg in 1989 he spent his remaining years in a wheelchair.

Despite this his spirits never sank nor did his courage fail him; he was undoubtedly sustained by the tentative acclaim that greeted his work in avant-garde circles. For the first time also he was being sought out for interviews. He declined them all, pointing out simply that the spoken word was not his medium.

His deterioration could not go on indefinitely. In March 1992 he wrote telling me he planned to exhibit his final piece at the Kassel Documenta. He travelled to Dublin the following month and spent a week at my house where he outlined the procedure I was to follow after the operation. On the night of the tenth, after shaking hands with appropriate solemnity for the last time, I administered him a massive dose of morphine, a euthanasia injection. He died painlessly within four minutes. Then, following his instructions, I removed his remaining left arm and head - messy, dispiriting work. I then boiled the flesh from the arm and skull in a huge bath and using a solution of bleach and furniture polish brought the bone to a luminous whiteness. I fixed the skull in the hand and set the whole thing on a wall mount; Alas, Poor Thomas he had told me to call it. Then I sent it to Kassel at the end of the month, Thomas already having informed the gallery as to the kind of work they were to expect. In critical terms it was his most successful piece and when Kiefer singled him out as the genius specific to the jaded tenor of this brutal and fantastic century his reputation was cemented. This last piece sold for twenty-five thousand Deutschmarks.

When, as executor of the Thomas Crumlesh Estate, I was approached with the idea of this retrospective I welcomed it on two accounts. Firstly, it is past time that a major exhibition of his work be held in his native country, a country that does not own a single piece of work by her only artist to have made a contribution to the popular imagery of the late twentieth century - a prophet in his own land indeed. Secondly, I welcomed the opportunity to assemble together for the first time his entire oeuvre. My belief is that the cumulative effect of its technical brilliance, its humour and undeniable beauty will dispel the comfortable notion that Thomas was nothing more than a mental deviant with a classy suicide plan. The rigour and terminal logic of his art leaves no room for such easy platitudes.

Several people have speculated that I would use this introduction to the catalogue to justify my activities or, worse, as an opportunity to bewail the consequences. Some have gone so far as to hope that I would repent. I propose to do neither of these. Yet a debt of gratitude is outstanding. It falls to very few of us to be able to put our skills at the disposal of genius: most of us are doomed to ply our trades within the horizons of the blind, the realm of drones. But I was one of the few, one of the rescued. Sheer chance allowed me to have a hand in the works of art that proceeded from the body of my friend, works of art that in the last years of this century draw down the curtain on an entire tradition. His work is before us now and we should see it as an end. All that remains for me to say is, Thomas, dear friend, it was my privilege.

Dr. Frank Caulfield
Arbour Hill Prison
Dublin

Mike O"Driscoll was born in London, 1959, to Irish parents who returned to Cork when he was ten. Mike's work often crosses between horror and science fiction. He's had work published in *The Third Alternative*, *Crime Wave*, *Interzone* and *Albedo One*, amongst others. He's also had stories in the anthologies *Off Limits* and *Lethal Kisses*, edited by Ellen Datlow (1996), and all three of the acclaimed *Cold Cuts* horror anthologies (the first, 1993), edited by Steve Lockley and Paul Lewis. Not satisfied only with fiction, Mike contributed a regular column, 'Night's Plutonium Shore', sometimes controversial, always entertaining, to *The Alien Online* until early 2004, now to be found in *Interzone*. The following story shows Mike's characteristic ability and intelligence in exploring the darker needs inherent in the human condition, and was influenced by a chaotic mix of themes, from obsession, celebrity and violence, to the works of Max Ernst, David Lynch and a Simon & Garfunkel song.

Hello Darkness

Mike O'Driscoll

I feel the life slipping from her like shedded skin. She is still now, all her protests ended. I'm envious of her absence of emotion, and curious as to what she sees in the place where she now exists. But she is almost beyond speaking, and the silence itself seems enough to bring us closer.

When she does make a sound I prop myself up on one elbow and study her porcelain face. Her eyes are empty, and she has a rare smile on her face that touches me deeply. She seems grateful when I wipe saliva from her lips, not like before, all those demands she made. "That wasn't really you, Hopi," I tell her. "This is who you were meant to be."

Dolores sits in the corner by the window, touched by neon, waiting for Hopi to join her in plastic aloofness. She is our silent witness, her permanent smile hinting at qualities to which I can only aspire.

Hopi's lips move so I lean closer but can't decipher her words. I kiss her gently, and notice a tear in the corner of one eye. This evidence of lingering emotion unnerves me and quickly I wipe it away. "No more need for that."

The desert of her being arouses me. I pull back the sheets to reveal her pallid, naked body, then touch the taut flesh that clothes her ribcage. Beads of sweat shine there, jewels embedded in skin. I lick her nipples, tasting the unreality of her being, wanting to share it. But I'm still wary of the dark place, and of the dreadful emotions that lurk there. Even though I have become adept at not feeling, I know that if I come too close I risk ceding her the power to hurt me. Gently, I guide my hand through the tangle of her pubic hair, down to her cunt where I part the labia and insert two fingers into her dryness. I pull them out and wet them on my tongue, then part her flesh again, easing them inside her, tenderly greasing her working parts. I whisper her name, afraid to say it aloud in case I bring her back. "What can you see, Hopi?" I ask, as I move on top of her. Her flesh is touched by frost and as I slide into her, I feel it melt beneath me. Now that she's almost gone, I feel so connected to her that I want to extend the moment. Her eyes have fallen closed so I open them, and feel her self-absorption enveloping me, sucking me into cold and empty expanse of her new world. I move inside her like a voyager on a sea of darkness, and as I navigate the small moments of her dying, feeling the bond between us tighten, I try to outrun the pale light of dawn that I know will wipe out our beautiful intimacy.

In the light I reach for her and find nothing there, not even an imprint in the place where she had lain. I search the room and find nothing of hers, no clothes or jewels or other signs of her existence. I sit on the edge of the bed, dazed, not understanding what has happened. Hopi was dead, I was sure of that. All that tequila and nembutal. In the corner Dolores leans against the wall, haughty and impassive. I carry her to the bed and lay her down in Hopi's place. I found her in New Orleans, legs sticking out of a dumpster in an alley, like some corpse. Her right arm from the elbow down is missing and she has no hair, but she has other charms that more than compensate: she never condemns.

There are two pills on the bedside cabinet. I wash them down with tequila, hoping they'll do something to my punch-drunk brain to make it work. My racing heart begins to slow and Hopi skips out of my mind. I turn on the television and flick through the channels till I come across an episode of Santa Barbara. Ronald Reagan lives there, I think, along with all these charming, beautiful people, whose unblemished bodies radiate an unreality that I once possessed.

It's past midnight and Hopi hasn't returned. Maybe she's had enough of Albuquerque. I try to manufacture some hostility toward her but it doesn't come off - the truth is I feel nothing at all, just a raw emptiness in the place I thought she filled.

I pull on my cleanest dirty clothes and check my wallet. A grand or more in cash. The Hopi I knew would have taken it for drugs. I step outside the room and hurry along the walkway to the office where Xabier is watching a porno movie behind the check-in desk. He's unshaven again, which I don't like, and he pretends not to notice me, which I do.

"Hopi?" I ask him. "You seen her today?"

A shake of the head, nothing more.

"This morning," I persist. "You saw her go out?"

"Ain't seen her, man," Xabier says, without looking at me. He leans forward and turns up the volume, allowing the fake sexual moans to pre-empt anything else I might have to say.

I stand in the doorway, hesitant, afraid of what the outside contains. The old Thunderbird I bought in Abilene three months

24

ago, just before I met Hopi, sits outside in the parking lot. I might be safe in there. Taking a deep breath, I stumble toward it, not exhaling till I'm in the driver's seat. I try not to look at the stars as their sheer number tends to overwhelm me. I picture Hopi instead, sitting in the corner of that truckers' bar, a stoned Barbie-doll whose glazed eyes scanned every corner like closed circuit cameras. I asked the bartender about her. Said she'd showed up about two weeks before with some biker. He'd hung around a day or two then had run out on her. She came to the bar most days, shot a little pool, drank a little beer. He figured she was in some sort of transitional phase.

I watched her for awhile, fascinated by her stoned indifference, the way she seemed to exist almost in another world, one that seemed a step or two beyond my own. When I got talking to her, her detachment, her emotionlessness, was immediately apparent, which made her all the more attractive. When I asked if she wanted to head west with me, she came along as if she really had no other option. In time, she became my conduit to reality, sparing me unnecessary contact with the outside. It isn't exactly agoraphobia, it isn't the open spaces that scare me; it's more an uncertainty about who occupies those spaces. Her indifference to the world gave her a natural immunity to its horrors. She could connect without risk, getting whatever it was we needed to survive. Except, of course, that they did finally get to her.

I clasp the wheel firmly as I turn on to the road, trying to subdue it to my will. I head downtown with no clear notion of where I'm headed. Normally, I'm a nervous driver, but not tonight. The city is washed clean of life and the pools of light spilling from the department stores act like candle flames, drawing me into their spheres of influence. I stop in one such pool, caught by the disdainful gaze of three timeless women. Sitting in lighted windows in exotic lingerie, they remind me of Amsterdam's red light hookers. Except I'm certain these three have a clearer understanding of where I want to be.

I wait, allowing them to attune their rhythms to my own. When I'm ready I reverse out into the centre of the road, turn towards the plate glass window and hit the accelerator. I crash through into another world, but before I can join them, the cops have arrived and have dragged me back to where I don't want to be.

"Well, Cicero, I useta watch High School Blues, but you don't look like Casey," the cop says, and I guess he's checked out my story. He's young, about my age, and has a small blond moustache that blights his otherwise good looks.

"It was fifteen years ago," I remind him.

"Ran three seasons, right?"

"Four."

He nods. "You know, you're the first ex-child star I ever busted."

"I did other stuff after Blues," I tell him, defensively, even though I don't feel any real connection to that Cecil Cicero. "I did Frighteners for three years."

"Yeah, I remember the show. Can't place you though."

"I did guest slots."

"So what happened - the offers dried up?"

I point at his notes. "I guess it says right there what happened."

"Well, you wouldn't be the first young actor to get a habit. How'd you get out of the jam?"

"I had a good lawyer."

"Well, I guess your old man has done it again. Got a hot shot Albuquerque lawyer waiting outside for you. Your father was your agent, right?"

"He wires me money to stay away. I guess that's what an agent does."

"Tough break. One minute you're king, next thing your new pilot show is shit."

"You a critic?"

"I guess that's L.A. So much bullshit and people promising you the world, by the time you're sixteen or seventeen, you're in some detox clinic along with the old pros."

He's beginning to piss me off so I ask him if we're done.

"You're positive for barbiturates and booze."

"I was depressed. My girlfriend walked out on me."

"Where is she?"

"Just gone."

"And the store, what were you after?"

"Nothing man, I was just out of it."

The cop grins, despite his play at toughness. "Whatever you say. I'll get your lawyer."

"No. I don't want to see him."

"That's up to you. You're out of here for now."

The car is a little beat up but it gets me back to the Lorlodge on Central Avenue. I throw my things into a suitcase, carry Dolores out to the car and head east on Central till I hit the freeway where I double back on myself and check into a shithole off Lomas that rents rooms by the hour. When I show the guy behind the check-in desk a hundred dollar bill, he grins and says I can have a room for three days. His teeth are yellowing and rat-like and I wonder how such a man can be real. "Number seventeen," he says. "You want anything, just ask. Name's Lennie, okay?"

"Food?"

"We got cable and fuck films. You want food, nearest place is a Taco Bell down the road. Oh, and the ice machine's fucked."

When I was eleven my father and three friends of his took me out on the ocean in a launch to show me what being a man was all about. I had just finished the first series of High School Blues and it was about to go nationwide on NBC. We were going after marlin, my father said, worthy opponents. He scared me, even then, but I hadn't yet grown to hate him. Truth was, I was excited about the trip. The men drank beer and offered me a bottle. Father frowned, but when the others joshed him, he told me to go ahead. I drank it and afterwards felt light-headed and a little sick. But I didn't want to let my father down, so I bit my lip and held on tight to my guts. Finally, my father hooked something and after a tremendous battle, he hauled a dolphin alongside the boat. It thrashed frenziedly in the crimson-foaming water. I'd seen on television that dolphins weren't fish at all, but mammals, like humans. They were intelligent and felt things the same way we did. Things like pain and terror. I screamed at them to cut it loose but they laughed and told me not to act like a kid. Finally, my old man drove a metal spike into the creature's brain and cut the line. Appalled, I stood by the rail, watching its dead eyes stare at me, as it sank below the swell.

Tonight it's not a dolphin we hook but a mermaid. The men drag her up on to the deck where she pleads with them in a language they don't understand. They have clubs with which they begin beating her, the way I've seen Canadian hunters battering seal cubs on television. But she has no fur, only scales that cover her long, graceful tail which thrashes about on the deck, spattering blood everywhere. When she is still, the men open their trousers and piss on her. But all the time her eyes are focused on me, as if she recognises the fact that I am no part of this at all.

I wake with horror's fists at my throat, my screams lost in the darkness. I flail wildly till I grab the cord above the bed and drown the dream in light. The breath rasps in and out of my lungs and I almost hate Hopi for abandoning me. I put my arms around immutable Dolores, hoping she'll keep the darkness at bay.

I play a porn video I've rented from Lennie. It's a cheap, grainy piece of work, filmed with a jerky hand-held camera. The soundtrack is indecipherable but the actors fuck and suck each other as if they really mean it. The performance is disconcerting, made more vivid by the total lack of artifice. I don't recall it ever being like that. I kneel in front of the television, curious, but can feel no connection to the actors whatsoever. "I'm not like you," I whisper. "I don't feel what you feel." But they simply go on fucking and pay me no heed. I retreat to the bed and watch them out of the corner of one eye. What makes them this way? What triggers these terrible needs? They demand the right to participate in this and experience that, to indulge themselves in so many different ways I can't see how they can appreciate any of it. Though I have no recollection of ever being like them, I think that I must once have been.

And then I see the girl in the background, her quiescent body sprawled across a sofa. The camera zooms in on her face which is animated by nothing stronger than profound disinterest as a skinny kid ejaculates over her face, her breasts. She neither smiles nor frowns nor gives any indication that she is even aware of his presence. She is a ghost on the screen, her white face framed by black, bobbed hair, somewhat less than real. I watch the clip again and again, unable to take my eyes from her, until, some time round dawn, exhaustion does it for me.

It's the ferocious New Mexico heat which finally brings me round, that and the failure of the A/C machine. I crawl into the shower and share it with a huge cockroach. He fights a losing battle to climb the lip of the tray but I give him ten for effort. I shave and leave him to it. I pull on jeans and a t-shirt, grab the videocassette and wander down to Lennie's office. I'm still thinking about that girl, thinking how much she reminds me of Hopi back when Hopi was dead.

Lennie asks if I dug the movie and I tell him no, just one girl.

"That right? His eyes light up like he thinks we're on the same wavelength. "Which one is that?"

"You know them?"

29

"Could be I know a guy who does."

"I want to talk to him."

Lennie hisses, exposing his rat-teeth, signifying a memory lapse. I put a twenty on the counter which prompts total recall. "There's a place across town. Guy there distributes these movies."

"They made local?"

"Out on Montano towards Almeda, place called Triple X. Ask for Newton and tell him I sent ya."

It's in a one-storey adobe building with a painted sign above the entrance, three neon X's and a naked woman. Discreet. Inside there's a few johns checking out the videos and sex toys, while a Mexican kid slouches behind the counter. There's a corridor to the left of the counter above which is a sign saying Video Booths & Live Girls. I push through the hanging drapes into the darkened space and step into the first available booth, close the door behind me and slip a couple of quarters into a slot in the wall. There's a control panel set into the wall below the screen. I press the first button and the screen comes to life, showing two women, licking each other on a bed while a guy stands over them, jerking off. I press the next button and the screen changes; this time it's a young girl being fucked by two guys, one in the mouth and one in the ass. The third channel has more of the same. I see her in the fourth sequence, her bobbed hair half-obscuring her profile as she's getting fucked from behind by some heavily muscled ape. A brief glimpse of her lifeless face reveals that she's not really there.

I leave the booth and head further down the corridor till I'm stopped by a tall, bearded guy in leather who puts a hand on my chest. "Sorry bud, no babes till eight."

I step back, recoiling from his touch. "I'm looking for Newton."

"Why?" He walks towards me, so I keep moving backwards. I bump into someone and flinch. Turning, I see it's the Mexican kid with a bucket and mop.

"Lennie sent me."

The bearded guy stops and says, "Who the fuck is Lennie?" He lets the Mexican kid step past. "That's Miguel," he says. "Best workers in the world. Who else is gonna wipe the come off the floor for less than a dollar an hour." He laughs, but all I can manage is a weak smile.

"Runs a motel out on Lomas. Gets movies from here."

"I sell videos all over the place."

"You're Newton?"

"Yeah."

"There's a girl in one of them," I explain, trying to stay cool, but knowing he sees right through me. People can do that, since I became less real. "I'd like to meet her."

"Let's talk in my office," he says and he beckons me to follow him along the corridor to a cramped room behind the counter. He sits in a chair at a desk, waves me to a plastic packing crate. "So, who we talking about?"

"Pale girl with the Louise Brooks hair."

"Lulu, huh. You think she's gonna open Pandora's box for you?"

"No, I just -"

"Forget it. All I'm saying is, she's special. She don't talk much, but I guess you already know that. She's more expensive too."

"That doesn't matter."

"Okay, come back about ten," he says, scratching his beard. "But fella, just one thing - if she does say anything, don't go believing it."

I don't know what he means but I say, "Sure," and leave before he sees that I don't really fit in.

High School Blues was a top rated sitcom for three years, before audiences slumped in its fourth and final year. Frighteners ran for three seasons before the revamped Twilight Zone killed us off. In one episode I played a kid who has wild fantasies about an unobtainable prom queen. She gets killed in a car wreck that was some-how my character's fault. But he kept fantasizing about her until, one night, she came to him in the form of a succubus and sucked the life out of him. It was a good show, ahead of its time.

I sit in the car outside the Triple X, waiting for it to be ten o'clock, thinking about that episode because it reminds me of Dolores, the first Dolores, who was the first flesh girl I ever really loved. When I was fifteen, with High School Blues already in my past, my mother employed a seventeen year old Mexican maid as an accoutrement to our Hollywood lives.

After the sitcom had ended, my father lined up auditions and screen tests but, apart from three television movies, it was to little avail. He took it out on me, accusing me of a lack of commitment. He couldn't see hate's scar tissue hardening on my heart. To escape his bullying I took to spending as much time away from our Bel Air home as I could. I hung with a pack of other rich kids and we spent our time doing booze and coke and dope and, just occasionally, making out. One night, my head full of vodka and barbiturates, I found myself staggering alone in our grounds off Stone Canyon. I crawled as far as the pool before passing out. When I came to I was on a sofa in the house, a blanket thrown over me and Dolores urging me to drink coffee. My parents were away, she said. She smiled and I saw genuine concern in her eyes. I guess it was the first time I'd really noticed her, and doing so, I saw how beautiful she was.

She stayed with me, talking, for half the night. When she finally got up to go, I grabbed her arm and pulled her close. She resisted at first, then let herself be drawn into the kiss. What I felt then, and what I knew she had the potential to make me feel, put all my adolescent gropings into perspective. We made love that night, and afterwards, the more time we spent together, the more permanent and unbreakable it seemed, was the connection between us.

How little I knew of the workings of reality. How stupid I was not to see that its rules were not the same as those of my onscreen world.

It ended one evening when Dolores failed to meet me after finishing her shift. She avoided me for the next two days until finally I cornered her in the kitchen. Tears welled in her eyes as she told me it was over. I told her she wasn't thinking straight but she insisted it had been a mistake. I pleaded with her, begged her not to abandon me, but when I saw the traces of terror etched in her face, I knew my father had discovered our relationship.

I confronted him that night. "What have you said to Dolores?"

He looked up from his paper, stubbed his cigarette out in the ashtray and frowned. He was a cold, cruel man, the virus of whose ambition had never really taken root in me. Finally, he spoke. "I can't let you jeopardise your future, Cecil. The business with the whore has to stop."

Rage boiled up inside me and I lunged at him. He swatted me aside like the child I was.

"You just don't think for yourself," he went on, standing over me. "If the trades got hold of it, it would ruin your career."

"But I love her," I cried. "She's special."

"Love?" he sneered. "No, Cecil, she's using you. It's her nature, just like any other illegal spic bitch." He smiled in that superior way he had and touched my face like I was some errant child. "I'll take care of it, the way I always do."

Two days later, I saw what he wanted me to see. In his bedroom, the door open, Dolores on her knees in front of him, sucking his cock, his face a mask of boredom and disgust, showing me that what I had thought was mine was really his.

She left us shortly after, but it was only when I had started work on the first series of Frighteners that I heard she'd been deported. Slowly I came to see how fatal the touch of emotion really was, saw how it fuels betrayal and pain, and came to recognise that it was only through withdrawal and disconnection that I could safely navigate a path through existence.

The store is busy with hungry men whose realities intrude on my own. I rush past them to the cubicles that look in on the live show. Most are occupied but the eighth one is free. I feed money into the slot that causes a small panel to slide back in the wall. I'm looking into a room where recessed lamps in the ceiling give off a subdued red light. On a podium in the centre of the room, a naked girl lays motionless on her back. She has black hair, but her face is turned away from me. A thin beam of light moves across her opalescent flesh, like a laser, exposing hidden parts, leaving a trail of thin vapour to curl into the air. For one horrible moment I imagine the internal organs, broiling beneath her skin, and I feel a small yearning inside the mechanism of my heart.

A leather-clad man steps out of the shadows and looms over her. He bends to suck each nipple in turn, then pulls a nightstick from his trousers. I shudder, recalling an ancient dream, but he doesn't beat her, just caresses her with it, running it down her body to her crotch where it nestles in her pubic hair. Then he retreats and fades back into the shadows. She hasn't moved at all. Presently, a trolley laden with strange machinery appears, a masked man in surgical robes wheeling it up to the podium. He flicks buttons on a machine and an electronic hum fills the room. He picks up a gleaming metal implement and prods at the girl. Satisfied, he attaches two cables to her nipples, stands away and throws a switch. There's no sound but her body convulses. The man leans forward to examine her again, then removes the cables and lifts up his robe. Beneath it he's naked. He crawls on to the podium and loops his hands beneath her buttocks, raising them, then plunges his cock into her. He fucks her for ten minutes till he comes, then he wheels his trolley back into the darkness. And still the girl has neither moved nor made a sound of her own volition. Blood pounds in my temples and I'm filled with concern, though I don't yet recognise her as unreal.

After a minute, the first guy returns and stands over her. He unzips his jeans, pulls out his cock and strokes it till it's hard. Then he takes her unresisting head, cradles it and forces her mouth open with his thumbs. He proceeds to fuck her in the mouth, occasionally muttering the single word, "feed." He withdraws from her before he comes, to let his hidden audience verify the authenticity of his performance. In the gloom, the semen drips into her mouth like blood.

When she stirs, I rock back in my seat, stunned. I lean forward again, in time to catch her face, a Lulu who is even more perfect than onscreen, as she rises from the podium and moves around the room, head bobbing like a mechanical doll, acknowledging her silent voyeurs without condemnation. Then the red light fades and darkness swallows our dreams.

In the store, Newton is waiting. I give him three hundred dollars. For that she will stay with me the night.

I'm sitting in the Thunderbird as she shuffles across the parking lot in stilettos and stockings, a black microskirt and black denim jacket. Her lips are smeared with red and her eyes are dark and empty. She sits in beside me without a word of greeting. I thrill to the silence that swamps us both, making verbal communication unnecessary.

When we arrive at the motel, she follows me unsteadily to my room, seats herself on the bed and uses the remote to switch on the television. I turn the sound down, which she doesn't seem to mind, and pour two drinks. She takes hers like a machine performing a task, running on autopilot. When I see she's noticed Dolores by the window, I lead her across the room and place her hand on Dolores' face. She keeps it there, stroking the plastic, then lays her own face where her hand had been. I feel good about their closeness, and sense the approach of some revelation.

Something strange and wild, a place of darkness reaching out towards me.

Lulu returns to the bed and says, "She sees things differently."

"You like her?"

She begins to undress and, giggling, she says, "She's like me."

But I already know this, and, noticing the track marks in her arms for the first time, I know what it takes for her to be this way. I carry Dolores across the room and place her at the bottom of the bed, so she can share our secrets. Lulu waits, laying on the bed, her eyes turned to the television, as if to emphasise the completeness of her disconnection from the world. I strip off and lay atop her brutalized flesh, searching her eyes, trying to find the courage to follow her into the darkness.

"What are you doing?" I ask, waking to find her going through my things.

Naked, she turns toward me, hesitantly. She seems agitated. "I feel like ... I, this doesn't mean anything." Grey morning light streams through the blinds, mottling her flesh.

"No," I agree. "It means nothing."

She shakes her head and wipes a hand across her face. "But you want it to," she says. "You just act out the emptiness instead of making it real.

Her words unsettle me, make me consider my motives. "You think this is an act with me?"

"Isn't that usually the case?" she says. Her junkie eyes are restless, moving ceaselessly round the room. This new animation concerns me. "You look at me and you think you understand how it feels. You have no fucking conception."

"You don't want to feel anything, right?"

"You think it's the junk? You're dead wrong," she sneers. "It's just a tool."

I get out of bed and grab her arms. "I can help you, Lulu. Stay here, I'll get whatever you need."

"Lulu? She isn't me," She pulls free of my grip and begins to get dressed. "She belongs to Newton."

"But you want to be her. All the time."

She shrugs, slipping on her shoes. "I can make that happen," I tell her, trying to hide an unfamiliar anxiety.

"Sure," she says, moving towards the door. "I heard that so many times."

"Wait," I cry, frantic for her to stay with me.

She hesitates, smiling with anticipation as I dig some notes from my jacket. I fight down an impulse to tell her to go. "Good," she says, holding out her hand. I place two fifties in it and try not to look in her eyes because the need in them seems too real.

"Newton won't let you be in that place," I tell her. "He wants to keep you real. Remember who I am, Cecil, and remember I want to be there too."

"It's a fucking act, don't you see?" she says, turning her back on unreality.

For two days I try to convince myself that she was wrong. I watch soaps and game shows and Oprah but don't feel the old connection. It's like the horrors have infected them all. Even when I try and picture Hopi, she's wearing Lulu's face. But I'm certain she belongs more in my world than in theirs. Finally I make a decision. I shave till my face looks smooth in the mirror and if I try real hard, I can see only emptiness in my eyes. Not as good as Dolores, but getting there. I get a take-out from Taco Bell, my first meal in three days, and leave it behind on the bathroom floor. Time is altering almost imperceptibly, becoming slower. When I reach the Triple X my watch says mid-afternoon but it could be yesterday. The sweat that glues the shirt to my back serves as a reminder of dreadful reality.

In the store, I hide among the racks of fuck-books. Just the kid at the counter, no sign of Newton. I slip into the corridor and make my way to a door at the far end. It opens and I step into some kind of changing room; there's mirrors on the walls and costumes hung over the backs of chairs. I can feel something of Lulu here, the scent of her machine oil. I pick up items of leather underwear off the dressing table and sniff them, wondering which is hers.

"Cecil," says a voice behind me. "Kinda fucking name is that?"

I turn and see Newton blocking the doorway, a baseball bat hanging from a meaty fist. He smiles but it is cold and hard, mirroring his diamond eyes.

"I want Lulu," I tell him.

"I told you she's special."

"She needs my help."

"Only thing she needs is me. Playing dead ain't easy. I got a lotta time and money invested in that cunt. And you want to steal her away?"

"You don't understand, it isn't just an act."

"You got a jones for her," Newton laughs. "That's too bad."

"Why not just let her -" I don't get to finish what I'm saying because he hits me in the stomach, driving the air from my body. I go down on my knees like a dead man praying. The bat explodes repeatedly against my head. For some time I exist only in a world of pain. Then there's nothing. Later, it comes back but different, somehow. I'm laying in a darkened alley, between the wall and a dumpster. It's a while before I can move even a finger, longer before I can stand. I try to puke up some internal organs but only blood comes. Finally, I manage to stagger round to the parking lot where the Thunderbird waits. It takes a night and more for the car to slip through the gleaming city, as I look for the place where the dark used to be.

This scar tissue signifies my readiness to cross over; it says I 'm almost unreal. As if to confirm this, I don't feel much, which is good, and certainly I don't feel any pain. When Lennie asks me what happened I tell him that I had a bust up with a redneck at a bar. He shakes his head and makes sympathetic noises but I know he's secretly pleased. He sees me as capable of feeling pain; like all real people he takes please in the suffering of others. He smiles knowingly when I ask him about a piece. I put a twenty on the counter and he says he'll make a call and get back to me. About two, he calls my room and gives me the address of a bar in the Old Town and says there'll be a black dude there who can get me what I need.

I pack all my stuff and put some clothes on Dolores and a baseball cap on her head, and sit her in the backseat of the car. They only serve to emphasize her unreality, which pleases me greatly.

I stop at a bank and withdraw two thousand dollars, then call into a liquor store. I'm at Kennedy's Irish Bar in the Old Town by five and find Lennie's friend waiting for me. I know it's him because he's the only black guy in the place. He doesn't ask my name so I don't offer it. Out in his car he shows me a Saturday night special. Nothing fancy he says, but get close enough and it will do the job. Two hundred dollars and he'll throw in some extra rounds.

Afterwards I head north to the Triple X and park across the street. I take a pull on a bottle, imagining the tequila lubricating my working parts, fine-tuning a precision machine. I practice still-ness, which comes easier now I'm on slow time.

He comes out of the store just before midnight, climbs into his Chevrolet Jeep and heads downtown. I follow him to a hotel on the Eastside. It's a fuckshack called The Palace. I wait a few seconds then follow him into the lobby. There's a worn-out look-ing guy at the reception desk and I nod to him like I'm a regular.

No elevator, only a stairwell off to the left. I take it, afraid I might lose Newton. When I hear him on the third floor, one flight above me, I remember to breathe. He leaves the stairwell and when I stick my head round the wall, I see him fumbling with a key outside the second door on the left. I take the gun out now, to give it time to get where it needs to be, then step into the corridor and call his name. He turns, reaching inside his jacket.

"Don't," I tell him.

Seeing the gun, he drops his hand and asks me what I want.

"I want Lulu."

He opens the door and I follow him in. Lulu in her underwear, is strapped to the bed, her mouth gagged. Her body seems to hum with tension and the need to escape this awful reality. "What have you done to her?"

"Stopped her hurting herself, asshole."

"Set her loose," I tell him.

"You picked the wrong guy to fuck with," he assures me.

"Just do it." He moves to the bed and starts untying her hands and legs, making a meal of it. I wave him out the way and finish the job. With the gag removed, Lulu whimpers like a sick animal. Sweat burns on her face and the need in her dark eyes fills me with uncertainty. I back away from her, telling her to get dressed. As if sensing my unease, Newton makes his move. But the round I fired minutes ago catches him in the arm. As he falls, the second one explodes in his guts. He screams but doesn't die. I lean over and remove the gun from his jacket, then help Lulu dress. As we're leaving, Newton spits and fumes, forcing himself up on an elbow. "I won't forget this," he says. "I'll fucking find you, you cocksucker." I don't have anything to say to him so I pull the trigger again. When it finally connects, I see I've done for him, because there's a lot of blood and no more screaming. Lulu sobs at this brutal reality. As I grab the keys from Newton's pocket, we lock eyes. I feel the strength of his hatred and realise the extent to which the world feeds on our collective pain. I half drag, half carry Lulu downstairs out to the street and put her in his Chevrolet. She's shivering violently and keeps biting her lips. "Not anymore," she says, "please, no more," repeating it, like some kind of mantra.

"No more what?" I ask her.

"No more anything," she screams, lashing out at me with her skinny hands.

"Listen, Lulu," I say, holding her wrists. "I'll make you what you want to be."

She sinks back into her seat, her suspicion fading. "You're the man," she giggles, slyly. "I told Newton, said you're gonna make it all go away."

"That's right, no more Newton."

"Seh-sill?" she says and I think maybe she does understand.

"Stay quiet now," I tell her. When she nods her head and closes her bleary eyes, I start the car and pretty soon we're heading south on I-25. An hour out of Albuquerque, I leave the freeway and join route 54, heading towards El Paso.

We run into the border patrol just south of Alamogordo and my heart slows to a clockwork beat while we wait in line behind a truck. But the cop who leans in my window is bored. "Where ya headed?" he says, disinterestedly.

"Las Cruces," I say.

He yawns and says, "Well, pal, you're on the wrong road." Pissed off.

"Must've gone wrong back in Alamogordo."

He gives me a look that says I'm a moron. "You want route 70," he says, finally waving us on.

We reach El Paso a little after four and abandon the jeep in an underground parking lot. I get a cab to take us over the border into Juarez. It takes a while to find a hotel, a while longer to buy the heroin.

41

The blinds lay slats of shadow across Lulu's cold, unyielding flesh. Outside, Juarez has come to life while in here, we're winding down. She's been out since we made love, after I had prepared her fix. Like sex with Hopi the last time, I had almost experienced the moment of revelation but something unseen had deterred me from entering the darkness. Something more than feeling, when all I want is no feeling at all. I watch her sleeping, wishing Dolores were here to help me take that last step.

About midday, Lulu wakes. We don't talk at all - there's no need. She watches as I prepare the fix, and sighs with pleasure as I slip the needle into a vein in her throat. "I'll be coming soon," I say, painfully aware of my own fear of letting go. She slumps back into her stupor, leaving me alone to find the courage to accept the dark's embrace.

Hours pass while I practice my stillness, shallowing my breath to the faintest murmur. Shadows lengthen as darkness crawls across the floor. A shimmer of tension spoils my mechanical poise. I get up and prepare the last of the heroin. It's a massive dose which I draw up into two syringes. I slide into the bed and, placing my head against her waist, I listen to the noises that come from inside her, no longer organic but mechanical. I kiss her navel, her ribs, her breasts, reviving her one last time. As if by instinct she reaches for me but I tell her no, not quite yet. I show her one hypodermic and she nods. "So quiet in here," she says, and I know she's almost there.

She shudders and a small gasp escapes her lips as the smack enters her bloodstream. I extend the moment, savouring it for as long as I can. When it's all gone, I smother her ghostly face with kisses. "Wait for me," I say. I put an ear against her mouth, feel the faintest murmur of breath and hear "Cecil," though it is hardly a sound. And then something that might be, "I'm waiting," and then nothing at all. I pull back her eyelids, searching for meaning, but find nothing there.

I lean close to her lips but feel no whisper of breath. This confirmation of her having moved on thrills me to the very core. I feel no fear as I reach for the second hypodermic and stick it in my arm. Nothing counters the rush that fills my brain. I raise myself over Lulu, stunned by the pale moonlight that glistens on her glacial breasts. I reach between her legs, feeling the chill that has taken root inside her, while my tongue savours the hardness of her erect nipples. As my cock stiffens and I sink into the hollow space of her being, I feel my skin toughening, becoming hard and pristine, like steel, as our bodies mesh like machines working in perfect unison.

And even as I welcome the embrace of darkness, sensing the strange climax gather inside me, drawing me ever closer to a state of absolute unreality, even then, I can hear the screech of tyres outside, car doors slamming and angry commands. But I'm not afraid because those footsteps rattling along the corridors, those guns being prepped for action, those people coming for me, won't find me here at all, nor in any world they know.

John Kenny lives in Dublin in a tiny cottage by a wee babbling brook. His main claim to fame is playing the part of Padraig Pearse in Neil Jordan's 1996 film *Michael Collins*, and being stabbed on-stage by the Guinness Man. Since then he has disappeared from the acting front, and turned his attention to writing. He has published stories in Irish magazines *Albedo One*, *First Contact* and *FTL* and abroad. He has recently completed a children's book, which is currently doing the rounds with agents.

'Encore' will strike a chord with everyone who has ever wished for a second chance.

Encore

John Kenny

The hot sun beat upon the head of Fermino Salousse as he hobbled on his crutches up Avenida da Marginal from his shack on the outskirts of Maputo proper. There was little mercy in that sun, the palm trees stretching along the avenue that hugged the wide bay offering tiny, isolated islands of shade.

He offered up a prayer that a minibus would appear along the avenue soon, that it would be Paulo Mucavele driving, the only bastard son who would stop for him these days. As he pushed his emaciated, dying body along with the crutches, he passed through a group of small stalls selling beer, fruit and CDs by the roadside. It faced the Costa do Sol restaurant on the other side of the road, packed with aid workers and the more well-to-do in the city.

Just as Fermino was sending a silent avowal of hatred towards those eating the finest of prawns and crabmeat, he spotted from the corner of his eye a minibus hurtling down the avenue. Quickly he turned, stuck out a crutch to halt the bus. The driver, spotting the telltale signs of Fermino's diseased body, his skeletal frame, the crutches, swerved and pelted past, gathering even more speed, throwing up an immense cloud of dust, the bus' occupants jammed sardine-like swaying from left to right.

He tried to quell the anger inside of him, tried to focus on his destination, prayed that Paulo would come by soon, before the sun had its final way with him. On and on he went in the sweltering heat. Hard to believe this was all under water little more than a year ago, although the damage to the roads and pathways was still evident enough.

He was coming up to a turn on the right when he saw another minibus. This time it was Paulo, this time the bus stopped.

"Bon dia, Fermino, what are you doing out this far?" Paulo enquired.

"On my way to Parque José Cabral," Fermino replied, reaching for the sliding door on the side of the bus.

There was an outcry from some of the occupants. They were convinced they would become tainted, wither away and die.

"Hey, Fermino, get in front with me, don't worry about them," Paulo said, casting a look of disgust at the people piled in the back. "Mariamo! Shut up! Sergio, the rest of you!"

Amid grumbles, the bus turned right and took off down the avenue at speed. As they were passing the prison, heading towards the centre of the city, Paulo asked, "What do you want with that freak show?"

The word 'freak' touched something in Fermino, and he adopted a look of defiant dignity tinged with shame. "I..." he started.

It suddenly dawned on Paulo what it was that Fermino was interested in seeing at that 'freak show'.

"Ah... sorry. Sorry. I didn't mean..."

"It's okay. Don't worry about it. I'm just curious is all. Just curious."

Turning on to the main boulevard of the city, Fermino looked out at the high-rise office blocks and apartments lining the avenue, crumbling and dilapidated from all those years of war. The detritus of the war machines lay strewn not far from here on the grounds of the old military hospital.

Fermino's wandering thoughts were interrupted by the minibus skidding to a halt at the corner of Avenida dos Martires da Machava. He got out, as did most of the other occupants; the show was attracting anybody and everybody. There was a carnival atmosphere surrounding the park.

"Obrigado, Paulo, bon dia."

"Bon dia. You look after yourself, my friend."

The bus disappeared in a roar of exhaust and fumes.

The heat reasserted itself and a burst of sweat covered Fermino as he made his way along the broken path towards the centre of activity in the park.

In the distance he could hear a loudspeaker announce that the show had just returned from a tour of Cabo Delgado Province and the towns of Nampula, Beira and Inhambane.

"Roll up! Roll up!" the loudspeaker barked. "See the oldest man alive! See the heaviest woman in the world! Test your skill at the rifle range! Prizes! Prizes! Transform yourself in the Hall of Mirrors! Roll up! Roll up!"

It was a mad, crazy freak show all right; like something from a century ago. But it had caught the public's imagination, starved as it was of diversion from the daily routine.

Fermino cast about, looking for the particular attraction he had heard about. The heat was finally getting to him. He began to feel a little queasy. As if by some kind of radar sense, or perhaps an affinity with the man he had come to see, Fermino found himself drawn to a knot of people gathered around a red and white striped tent pitched by the children's playground.

He joined the queue, some of the people nearest him glancing warily at him, and fished out a handful of meticais to gain entrance. The shade of the trees around the tent offered sanctuary from the sun but was also a haven for mosquitoes, which buzzed angrily in Fermino's ears.

Looking ahead he saw a batch of people emerge from the tent with dazed expressions on their faces. They wandered off in different directions, intent on nothing and nowhere. The queue shortened a little.

Suddenly everything became still, an air of expectancy in the air. Long moments passed followed by a sudden gasp from the people in the tent. As if on cue, Fermino's guts started to churn. Pain lanced through his midriff causing him to stumble on his crutches. Sweat was now pumping from him; his shirt and trousers stuck to him wetly.

Now there were startled cries of disbelief and wonder issuing from the tent. The pain in Fermino's body increased, almost doubling him over. A groan escaped his lips. People in front and behind moved a little away.

Now the people were leaving the tent with the same look on their faces as the last batch. The queue moved up and Fermino reached the tent flap and paid a man who stood by a small fold-up table.

He was in, and a dark coolness enveloped him. There was total silence. People crowded against Fermino, unmindful of his state, curiosity overcoming any fear of infection. All eyes were on a small, elevated stage and a dark velvet curtain.

When the jostling subsided, a man arrived in front of the curtain and announced the event, reminding people to please not panic. There was mute acceptance of what their host said and he withdrew, pulling the curtain across with him.

On stage was a gallows with a spotlight trained on it. There was a collective intake of breath. Moments later a man was lead by the Master of Ceremonies to the steps adjoining the gallows. They slowly climbed the steps and the man positioned himself over the trapdoor. The MC took the noose of the rope hanging by the man's head and, with great solemnity, placed it over the man's head securing it around his neck. He then stepped to the side of the gallows and placed his hand on a large wooden lever. With his free hand, he pressed the play button of a tape recorder that rested on a pedestal beside him and a loud drum roll filled the tent.

Fermino watched. The pain renewing itself in his body, he watched. The MC pulled the lever. The trapdoor dropped open. The man plummeted. The rope snapped tight. A sharp crack echoed through the tent. Everyone gasped. The man's eyes bugged out a little. His tongue was forced out through his lips. He kicked slightly, a nervous response; he was instantly dead.

The crowd in the tent were appalled and fascinated in equal measure. Feet shuffled; there were curses and oaths and startled cries, a general jostling and the temperature increased, becoming noticeable again to Fermino.

He stared at the face of death. The open, bulging eyes were now glassy, the face flooded with trapped blood. The lolling tongue was comical; any dignity the man could have held on to was replaced by a shameful injustice.

This was what Fermino had to look forward to. This was to be his fate, waiting for him in the months, perhaps only weeks, ahead. His eyes were wide open, the pupils fully dilated; he sought to take it all in, staring, looking for the slightest movement, expecting evidence of some kind of continuance, here, or in the hereafter.

But there was none.

Silence reigned again as the MC arrived from the wings of the stage. He walked to the steps leading up to the gallows, ascended, and lowered the dead man to the ground below.

Descending again, the MC dipped his head beneath the gallows platform to kneel beside the body. All pain was gone from Fermino as he watched attentively, banished to another realm by adrenaline.

The man began to loosen the noose from about the dead man's neck. When it had been removed, he stepped back. The air assumed an electric quality as the crowd insinuated itself a little closer.

The dead man's face began to change; it lost its angry demeanour. The swollen eyes receded slowly. A sort of low moan began to issue from the throat, matched by something similar from the crowd.

But it was when the tongue moved that a kind of panic seemed to gather in the closely pressed people. The tongue moved back into the mouth, the lips closed. The eyes closed, followed by an intake of air.

Fermino also took a deep breath, sharing this moment of renewal with the man on the ground.

When the eyes opened, there was a light in them; they refocused on the man's surroundings. They looked at the audience. In that instant there was a collective cry of astonishment. The heat in the tent increased. Fermino's heart raced like a jackrabbit; sweat ran freely down his whole body. He felt faint and sick with an elation that transcended his awful predicament.

And then the man sat up. The MC moved in again and helped him to his feet. The crowd shouted in wonder and dismay. The MC pronounced the end of the show and quickly pulled the curtain closed again, leaving the spectators to make their stunned way out into the blazing sun, abandoned as if in an unknown country without even a map or a compass or the time of day.

Fermino was quaking as he hit the bright sun outside. He wandered about trying to rerun the event on the retinas of his eyes. Was that real? Did that man die and return to life? Or was it some kind of trick? He could not begin to imagine that the whole show had been a conjuror's illusion. And yet, the alternative... Fermino lost his footing and quickly righted himself with the help of his crutches. He brought his head up to look at the queue patiently awaiting their turn.

Oh, to have that second chance. Or to at least know what awaited him when the time came. Fermino looked up at the blazing orb in the wide empty sky.

The immensity of that sky, this land, this continent. He imagined that immensity, his tiny place in it as he made his way to the back of the queue. He imagined that immensity as if he were looking from a great height, like a God, a God dispensing justice with an even hand.

Robert Neilson was born in 1954. He lives in Dublin with his wife, two daughters and a son, whom he makes use of to see films of questionable merit in the cinema. His first sale was in 1989 and since then he's had work appear in magazines such as *Roadworks*, *Auguries* and *Andromeda Spaceways Inflight Magazine*, along with several plays written for radio and broadcast in Ireland. His first story collection, *Without Honour*, was published in 1997, along with a collaborative comic, *The Big Fellow*, with Alan Casey. Robert is currently working on a graphic novel, *Spell Maffia*, with Denise O'Moore, and a comic, *Daddy's Rules*, with Carlos Devizia. Robert was heavily involved with *FTL* and other endeavours of the old Irish SF Association, and has been a co-editor of *Albedo One* since its inception in 1993, contributing articles, interviews with highly regarded genre authors, and book reviews, including the occasional famously succinct one-liner. The following story shows us that no matter how bad things seem, they can still get worse.

Pleasing Mister Ross

Robert Neilson

Monique stopped to check her make-up in a shop window. The reflected face looked thirty-five. Lines about the eyes and mouth were plastered over with a heavy layer of foundation. Too much rouge made her appear flushed; as though from exertion or high blood pressure.

Her hair was suicide blonde. Brittle and thin, it fell wispily to meaty freckled shoulders. She tried a few practice smiles. Stepping back, she ran a critical eye over her figure. She smoothed the wrinkles from her simple black sheath dress. It had cost her the equivalent of two months rent but it was worth the expense. It had a touch of class.

Pity it emphasized the bulge of her stomach. She breathed in, turning sideways on.

Not bad, she said to herself. Still worth a hundred a night.

Although the last time she had turned up a punter who could afford to pay her to sleep was less than a memory. Monique turned back to her beat, cursing the heels that cramped the backs of her legs. She clicked along the pavement kicking aside wind-blown detritus. Larger human refuse, she stepped over or avoided. She glanced up at a street light.

At least its light was still welcome. Another couple of years and those pools of reassurance would be shunned. Another couple of years and she would hit the big three oh.

God how she hated this time of night. An hour before the pubs closed. No-one on the street except kids and freaks. The kids who couldn't afford her trade, the freaks too damaged or obsessed to spare a thought for their fellow traveller. Sometimes on nights like this she'd give one of the streetkids a freebie. Just for the company, and the energy. Word had been passed along the grapevine. There were always a handful of youngsters tracking her. Never coming too close. Never pushing. Just available.

Gillick didn't approve, but to hell with him. He wasn't her master, just her pimp. And her connection. She rubbed her arms, shivering. It would be forty minutes before the late rush started. She could make it to his place and back again well within the time. All she'd miss might be a couple of hand jobs. He couldn't begrudge her a jolt on a nothing shift like this. She began to persuade herself, repeating the arguments in her head.

It would be worth the risk, she told herself. What would be the worst Gillick could do? She stopped, remembering a similar night not so long ago. A night that she had worked with two cracked ribs. She smiled ironically. In all the years she had worked for Gillick he had never touched her face. Or her arms. Or legs. He stuck strictly to the torso, efficient businessman that he was. She could see him smiling, hear his litany.

Thou shalt not damage the goods. Thou shalt not endanger thy mealticket. Thou shalt not hospitalize; unless the bitch really needs it. And each commandment punctuated by fist or boot.

She took a deep breath, wishing that the air was sharp. Clean.

Instead it reeked of urine, Chinese food, exhaust fumes, dogshit and stale booze. She shook her head to clear it. Hair blew about her face.

She pushed a lank strand out of her eyes and hovered under a lamp post, smiling professionally at a car drifting slowly past.

She had begun to turn away when she realized the vehicle had pulled in to the kerb. Squaring her shoulders and composing her features, Monique strode to the swinging door. She ducked her head into the cab.

The driver was a small swarthy Mediterranean type. He smelt of cologne and a gentleman's hair preparation that she recognised. Gillick used it.

Some Korean muck for preventing hair loss - much good it did him. A placebo, more than likely. Though this guy appeared to have a full head of thick wiry hair. An ounce of prevention, maybe?

"Hi," she said. "I'm Monique." She slid into the passenger seat. "What can I do for you?" She endeavoured to sound eager.

The driver said nothing. His eyes bored into her, a look of intense concentration on his face. His breathing came hard and shallow.

He's regretting stopping already, she thought. Talk fast you stupid bitch or you'll lose him. "You look like a man with plenty of stamina," she said. "I like that." She was about to reach over and squeeze his arm, remark on his strength. Something in his demeanour made her hesitate.

"I want you to come with me," he said simply.

"Where to?" Monique asked, slightly nervous.

"My flat," he said.

"No," she said. "I have a room. Not far from here."

Distaste showed on his lips. "Please," he said. Almost a whisper. "How much do you charge? A hundred? One fifty?"

"Two hundred all night," she speculated.

"No, no. An hour. No more."

"Your place?"

He nodded. "I'll have you back here within a couple of hours," he said. "Two hundred and you can take the rest of the night off." A tentative smile pushed at his mouth.

"Got your medalert card?" she asked, holding out her hand.

The driver fumbled out his wallet and withdrew the card. Monique pulled the portascan out of her handbag and wiped the card. Handing it back to him she took a sachet from the bag and passed it to him. He gave her a blank look.

"It's two weeks since your last check," she explained, taking the sachet and tearing off a corner. She handed him the small tab it contained. "Stick that under your tongue. If it's still green in a minute, we're in business."

The tab stayed green. "I'll need the money up front," Monique said. "And then I'm yours for the evening. Or whatever portion of it you want."

"Amex?" he enquired.

"Of course," she said.

He passed over his credit card and put the car into gear. She cursed the crumbling inner-city streets as she attempted to complete the transaction. Their route wound through the decaying backstreets of the slumbering city. Everywhere, there was evidence of the poverty of the architecture. The modern buildings crumbled. The slick new facades imposed on older structures, peeled off. Everywhere the veneer of technology cracked, revealing the enduring labours of craftsmen, medieval to Victorian. The abiding power of stone was casting off the fripperies of the petulant generations.

They pulled into a laneway behind a row of warehouses which had been converted into expensive modern apartments. The car halted at a set of double doors. To one side stood a construction that looked like a sentry box. Before it stood a brazier. A pair of hands encircled by over-large cuffs stuck out of the box's gloom. The driver sounded his horn.

A figure bundled in layers of raggy coats scuttled from the watchman's hut and saluted. The hoods of at least two anoraks hid its face. "Sorry, Mr Ross," came a muffled voice. Low, definitely male. "I never seen you there. My mind was miles away."

Mr Ross drummed his fingers impatiently on the steering wheel. He grimaced at the man. The doors were hauled back with some difficulty.

From his movements the watchman was obviously old. Possibly infirm. He didn't limp or stoop or grunt, but he walked as though every joint in his body was lubricated with grit.

As soon as the doors were wide enough to allow the car to pass, Ross drove into the warehouse. Headlights illuminated a forest of concrete columns. At their bases stood row upon row of prestige motor cars. No Fords or Nissans or BMWs here.

They parked a short distance from the lift. It was an old industrial model with cage-like doors that split horizontally rather than vertically. Groaning and juddering, they rose five floors. Standing clear of the unadorned cold steel walls, Monique stared at her client.

Since their initial negotiations not a word had passed between them. He appeared tense, tightly wound.

"We're in Butler's Wharf, aren't we?" she asked, to break the silence hanging between them.

Ross grunted an affirmative, staring directly ahead, hands thrust deep into his trouser pockets.

"I've never been in these apartments," she said. "I'm trying to

picture what yours looks like. Lots of leather, I'll bet. A real batch-
elor place. Decorated in browns and beige and cream." She
glanced at him. "Am I right?"

The lift jerked to a halt. Ross ushered her out along a dimly
lit corridor to his flat. It was not at all as she had expected. It was
all chrome and black teak. Sparsely, functionally furnished. Clean
as an operating theatre. And small. Mirrors had been strategically
placed to give an impression of space. Monique was surprised.
She had been under the impression that places like this were vast.

"Would you like a drink?" Ross asked.

"Got anything of a... chemical nature?" she asked.

"Dust? Scag? Wire? Root?"

"You got wire?"

"When we're finished." He pointed to a door on her right.
"The bedroom's through there. I'll make a call and order your
wire. I'll be there in a minute."

The bedroom was a complete contrast to the rest of the flat. It
was huge. Black and white dominated, with red trimming a recurring motif.

Facing the door was a bed, at least seven feet square. The base
was black. The coverings, satin unless she was badly mistaken,
were an unblemished white. On the pillow cases and the duvet
cover, a hint of red. An outline. The carpet was white, shag pile.
Three walls were matt black with a faint red pinstripe. Gently
ticking hot water pipes low on the walls, blended into the decor,
all but invisible. The effect would have been overpowering but for
the abundance of framed prints. A couple were numbered and
signed. At least one, a pink banana by Warhol, appeared to be an
original.

The complete right-hand wall was given over to a vanity unit,
almost feminine in concept, surrounded by built-in wardrobes
with mirrored doors. Facing the mirrors, against the opposite wall
was a monstrous leather armchair. Several white cushions had

been casually thrown onto its seat. Monique was still standing just inside the doorway when Ross arrived.

"You like it?" he smiled.

"It's a bit imposing," she said.

"Oh!" He sounded disappointed, in a little-boy way.

Crossing to the wardrobes he began to undress, folding his suit neatly onto a hanger.

"Where can I leave my clothes?" Monique asked, wary of disturbing the room's symmetry.

"There's no need for you to... " he said, unbuttoning his shirt. He turned and threw it into the bottom of the wardrobe, stepping out of his shorts and dropping them on top.

He went to another of the wardrobe doors and opened it a crack.

Reaching inside, he produced a thin, bamboo cane. Handing the implement to the girl, he lay face down on the bed.

"Well?" she said.

"You know what to do." There was strain in his voice.

She lightly flicked his buttocks. "Yes," she said. "But you must ask nicely," she smiled.

"What?"

She went to the armchair and sat. "Beg," she said.

He raised himself onto one elbow. "I don't wish to be humiliated, merely beaten."

"Mama knows best," she said in a sugary voice. Then harshly, "Now beg, you fucking pervo, or I walk."

"That was... " Ross groped for the correct word. He shook his head, defeated. "It was better. So much better than I expected. You have... such... such empathy."

Monique ignored him. Her mind was elsewhere. She carefully coiled the entire spool of wire he had procured for her and taped it to the inside of her wrist. She sighed as it punctured her skin. She imagined it coursing through her body.

Ross's voice washed over her. "What?" she asked, langorously.

"Next week," he said. "You must come again. Next week."

There was an edge to his voice. Was he pleading with her or ordering her? She couldn't tell. She could care less.

"Sure," she said. "Next week."

"Answer me. This day week. Ten pm. Two hundred for an hour. Hour and a half maximum."

"Will you have wire?"

"Perhaps," he said.

"I'll come if you've got wire. Or maybe dust."

"No. The drugs are not part of the arrangement. The wire tonight was a gift. You come for the money. If I wish, I may give you another present."

Monique shrugged her shoulders. "Okay!" she said. Even with her thought processes out of whack, she could understand earning two hundred for an hour's work. She grinned at him and giggled. Leaning over the arm of her chair, she vomited onto his pristine carpet.

Gillick was ambivalent about her score. The money was fine, as was the prospect of a regular gig. Particularly with a john who didn't lay a finger on her. Although his sort were never to be trusted. You never knew when they might want to start dishing it out. And when they did, they were out of control. Monique was past her prime, but he wasn't ready to consign her to the scrap heap just yet.

But a john that gave her wire? No. That was dangerous. From what Monique told him the coil must have cost at least fifty. And he just gave it to her. A tip. No. The business was good. He had no problems with that. But feeding her habit was his territory. And his budget didn't stretch to wire. Not for her, anyway.

He decided to accompany her to Mr Ross's place on Butler's Wharf.

Suss him out. Have a little chat. Tell him the score. Have a squint at the apartment while he was at it. He knew a couple of faces that might be interested in a rundown on the premises.

They entered the converted warehouse by the front door. There was a single security guard on duty in the lobby. Monique flashed him a nervous smile and told him they were expected. The bored guard waved them through without a second glance.

That's security? Gillick thought. He grinned at the girl as they stepped into the lift. She was wearing a full length navy-blue over-coat.

Ross would appreciate what she was wearing underneath. He'd picked the outfit out of her wardrobe specially. He wondered momentarily, if it was altogether too clichéd. Red leather mini skirt. Black tank top. Black knee length boots. He almost fancied the cow himself.

Ross showed no signs of surprise when he opened the door to two visitors instead of one. He brought them into the living room and offered them a drink.

"No thanks, Mr Ross," Gillick said. "I won't be stopping. But I would like to have a few words with you in private."

Ross turned to the girl. "Would you mind stepping into the bedroom, my dear?" he said. "It will only be for a moment."

"Sure." She walked slowly from the room and closed the door behind her. The bamboo cane was lying on top of the bed. She was sure she could make out flecks of blood along the shaft. Circling the bed, she slipped out of her coat and dropped it onto the floor. Her eyes kept returning to the cane. She could almost feel Ross's pleasure emanating from it.

The door opened. It was the client. "Your friend Mr Gillick would like a word with you," he said.

Gillick seemed preoccupied when they spoke. His eyes focused on a point just above her left shoulder. "Mr Ross and me," he said. "We've come to an understanding." He paused.

She didn't like the sound of this. No matter how distasteful the jobs he had organized for her in the past, Gillick had always been able to look her in the face. In fact, she had often suspected that he got some sort of perverse charge out of her aversion.

"You'll... be staying here with him," Gillick said. "No more street work. You live here. He pays you a salary. He's your only client."

"Now, wait a minute," she said, her tone brittle, angry. "You're my pimp. You don't own me. You can't give me away."

Ross interrupted. "I'm sorry, my dear. Gillick has explained badly."

"It doesn't matter what sort of sugar coating you put on it. This bastard thinks he can sell me like a piece of meat. White slavery went out of fashion a long time ago. In this country, anyway."

Gillick ignored her. "Thank you, Mr Ross," he said, and walked out of the apartment.

"Jesus Christ!" She stormed across the room. "I'm getting my coat and then I'm out of here."

"Monique. Please." Ross followed her to the bedroom. "Listen to me."

"What? You want to show me how comfortable the servant's quarters are?" She picked up her coat and whirled on him. "I may be a whore, but I've still got some dignity."

"Monique, just listen. For a second. I don't live here. This will be your flat. All I ask is that you entertain me a couple of nights a week. And that you have no other clients. That's all."

"Fuck off!" she said, pushing past him.

She caught Gillick before he got back to his car. "Are you out of your mind?" she screamed at him. "What gives you the right...?"

He backhanded her in the mouth. She tasted blood. Her lip was split.

She was sure he'd loosened a couple of teeth. He stepped in close and punched her in the stomach. His full weight was behind the blow. She doubled over. The pimp twined his fingers in her hair and pulled her head back so that he could look into her face.

"If you don't go back up there straight away, I'm going to break evey bone in your body right here and now. You understand?" he said.

His eyes were wide. He was terrified. She could feel his hand trembling against her scalp. He shook her. "You understand?" he said, his free hand moving to her throat. "And if you leave him, I'll come after you. And I'll find you. I know where to look. And then I'll make you very sorry. And then I'll kill you."

"Why?" was all she could say.

Gillick let her go and she dropped to the pavement. When she stopped crying he was gone. She felt a hand on her shoulder and knew it was Ross. It was the first time that he had actually touched her. She shuddered.

"We'll get you home, my dear," he said, sounding as if he had nothing but her welfare at heart.

Something stung her wrist. She glanced down. Ross was pressing a coil against its pale flesh. She almost thanked him.

Time dragged in her new life. There was no constant struggle to make ends meet. No targets or deadlines. No police to pay off against walls or in the back of squad cars. No hustling drunks for hand jobs. No beatings from Gillick.

So she had nothing to do. For a while she sat around the flat all day and all night, wired. But no matter how slowly the time passed, the gaps between Ross's visits were never long enough.

It wasn't that he treated her badly. He didn't. Twice a week he'd call around, Tuesday and Friday, and she would flog him. That was all.

Sometimes he would ask her to tie him up or handcuff him, but generally all he required was a beating. Of course he introduced a variety of instruments with which she would abuse him: whips, garden hose, sticks, switches, rods and wands of all descriptions, nettles, brambles, gorse (his passion for vegetation was short-lived but intense), leather straps and (once only) a cat of nine tails.

But every night he insisted that she beat him a little more severely and after three months she was seldom permitted to stop while Ross was conscious. She couldn't help but marvel at his powers of recovery. The sessions seemed to drain her more than they did him.

In the beginning she had felt used. Soiled. Now she could hardly bear to look herself in the mirror. And what was worse, Ross insisted that she was straight on the nights he called. No wire for at least twelve hours beforehand. She was careless of the ban in the early days and he warned her that this was one of the few things he would not permit. Then one Friday afternoon she deliberately wired-up prior to the evening's session. Ross sensed it as soon as he arrived. Without a word, he left.

He called unexpectedly the following day. "I didn't want to have to do this, Monique," he said. "But you can't be trusted. I've cancelled your bank account and your credit cards. You may retain your store charge cards, unless, that is, I find that you are making purchaces with the specific intention of selling them or exchanging them for wire. I will supply all your drug needs. But if you attempt to cross me again I shall cut off your supply completely. Is that clear?"

It was very clear. As soon as he left, she packed a bag. Nothing fancy. The best of her clothes and the most expensive of the small pieces which decorated the flat. It was only fair that Ross should fund her until she got back on her feet.

The street felt comfortable. She got herself a hotel room.

Temporary, but cheap. She could cover the cost without even taking out her chewing gum. She hit her old patch. A young chick had staked a claim while she was locked away in Ross's flat. The newcomer was no more than thirteen and about a third lighter than Monique. But she was fired up on reality. Her eyes were clear and her skin was fresh. Her breath actually smelt sweet when she thrust her face into Monique's and spelt out exactly how she was going to tear the older whore's face off.

There were plenty of other streets.

But they were all part of someone's territory. Girls who had been her friends in the old days, warned her off. Most of them wouldn't even talk to her. A couple of them said that when Gillick heard she was back, he'd be looking for her. And not to put her to work, either. One of them, a fat old bird by the name of Chantal, sure that they were alone and in no danger of being overheard, told her to go back to Ross. She hadn't used his name. It wasn't necessary.

"What do you know about him?" Monique asked.

"You're not the first," Chantal said. There was a strange glassy look about her eyes, like a china doll's. Monique had always assumed the grizzled prostitute was retarded, never really listened to anything she had to say. "He's something in the government or the civil service. Big. A colonel maybe. Carries a lot of weight. And he likes a special kind of girl." Her voice was thoughtful, the delivery slow.

"Takes a long time to choose her. Or to find her. And when he's finished with her..."

"What?"

"She's finished."

"Dead?"

"Just... empty."

A car drew up to the kerb. "Beat it," the older woman said to her. "I've got business."

She knew it was Ross, even before the side window slid down.

Gillick might have been preferable.

Monique numbed herself with routine. Each day she showered twice. Once when she arose, and again when she had finished cleaning the flat. She vacuumed, polished, dusted and scrubbed, not that the place needed it.

She cooked herself elaborate meals, not that she ever did more than pick at them. She pressed the wire hard to her vein, its power to occlude the world diminishing steadily with use.

She seldom went out any more. Ross had not forbidden it, but there seemed little point. She no longer felt a part of the life that surrounded her. Watching other people interact, even at the most basic level, made her sad. Mostly, she sat around and waited for her exclusive client. On Tuesdays and Fridays she spent a lot of time in the shower.

Her flesh glowed as if flayed. As the time of his arrival drew near she contented herself with washing her hands.

Monique picked up the newspaper. It was delivered daily, although she hardly ever bothered with it. She scanned the TV page. Something to take her mind off herself, she thought. Fill a half hour, maybe. The newsprint blurred before her eyes. All she could see were black streaks.

She dropped the paper to the floor and examined her hands. Cursing softly she went to the kitchen and ran the hot tap.

She was squeezing thick green washing-up liquid onto her palm when Ross arrived. He joined her in the kitchen. He took a glass from one of the cupboards, filled it with water and emptied a sachet of white crystals into it. The powder effervesced slightly, depositing a rime of tiny bubbles around the sides. He handed her the glass.

"Drink it," he said. "It'll make you feel better."

There was no point in arguing or even in asking what the sachet had contained. She swallowed the draught in one long gulp. He gently prised the glass from her fingers and led her to the bedroom. She did not resist when he pushed her down into the armchair. Her head felt light.

It sparkled, as the water had done. She smiled.

Ross reached into his inside pocket. His hand appeared to move in slow motion. The smile shattered on her lips. She knew what he was going to produce.

The gun was no surprise. She recognised it as an automatic. Ross checked the action and smacked the base of the butt into his palm. He pinned her with his eyes as he crossed to where she sat. Standing over her, his features were almost benign. He placed the gun on the arm of her chair. He stepped backwards and began to loosen his tie.

Monique focused on the weapon. There was a warmth about it. Her fingers caressed it involuntarily. Ross called to her softly.

"Tonight," he whispered, "you will provide me with the ultimate experience."

She took a sharp breath. Her entire body stiffened.

Ross laughed, softly. "No, no," he reassured her. "You won't be harmed, my dear. You're far too precious."

Her tongue felt as if it had been glued to the roof of her mouth.

Swallowing repeatedly she said, "You want me to... shoot you?"

"There are levels of ecstacy to which I have not previously aspired," he said. "But tonight. Ah! tonight."

He rolled onto his stomach and reached for the drawer of the bedside cabinet. He pulled out a brass contrivance that Monique had always assumed was an over-large thumbscrew. He grinned broadly. She could feel him salivating as he described how she should apply it to his genitals.

Spontaneously, her dinner, light as it had been, erupted from her stomach. The back of her throat was seared by liquid heat. She coughed violently and dropped to her knees. The gun slipped from her fingers.

She could hear Ross whispering to himself.

"Yes," he repeated over and over. "Yes, yes, yes."

Monique clamped her eyes tightly shut but nothing could keep his leering face out of her head. She felt his fingers crawling over her.

But it was not her body that was being violated. They were still seperated physically by ten feet of carpet. Something was leaving shiny, white slug trails across her brain. Something soft and clammy was picking through her emotions, trying them on, squeezing them dry. Her loathing, her revulsion, her hatred and her fear were all being sampled.

Ross slithered through her mind like a psychic gourmand, dipping, tasting then flitting onwards only to return and immerse itself in the deepest pools of blackness. She could smell her own putresence.

Her head snapped upright. Ross knelt on the bed facing her. His mouth hung open. A line of spittle ran along his chin. His hips jerked at her spastically. But his eyes...

She showered and vacuumed and showered and dusted and showered and scrubbed. The bedroom showed no evidence of the previous night.

Mechanically, she inspected the hidden corners of the room for traces of the grotesquerie.

The memory would not leave her of that most intimate of violations.

His eyes. Staring. Lascivious. Greedily sucking her dry. The tendrils sliding across her thoughts, depositing their filth on her very core.

The gun in her hand. The noise. The smell of powder. The kick of its recoil jarring her arm. Ross bucking and squirming orgasmically. The blast of exultation that burnt into her frontal lobes. The rapture on his face.

Retching. On the bedroom floor. In the bathroom. Through the small hours. Into the morning.

And Tuesday was only three days away.

Bob Shaw, one of Ireland's best-loved SF authors, was born in Belfast, 1931, and moved to England in the 1970s due to the situation in Northern Ireland. Bob trained as a structural engineer, also working as an aircraft designer and journalist. From the 1950s, Bob was active in SF fandom, and highly regarded for his wit and intelligence. Bob had early pro sales in the 1950s, but feeling these lacked maturity, went in search of world experience. He returned with such notable stories as '... And Isles Where Good Men Lie', *New Worlds* (1965) and the Nebula and Hugo-nominated classic, 'Light of Other Days', *Analog* (1966). His first novel, *Night Walk* (1967), was published to good reception, and his 1975 novel, *Orbitsville*, won the BSFA Best Novel Award. *The Ragged Astronauts* (1986) was also Hugo-nominated and a winner of the BSFA Best Novel Award. Sadly, Bob passed away in 1996. The following is a fine example of his great humour and skill as a storyteller.

The Giaconda Caper

Bob Shaw

It was a Thursday morning in January - stale and dank as last night's cigar butts - and my office phone hadn't rung all week. I was slumped at the desk, waiting out a tequila hangover, when this tall creamy blonde walked in. The way she was dressed whispered of money, and what was inside the dress hinted at my other hobby - but I was feeling too lousy to take much notice.

She set a flat parcel on my desk and said, "Are you Phil Dexter, the private psi?"

I tipped back my hat and gave her a bleak smile. "What does it say on my office door, baby?"

Her smile was equally cool. "It says Glossop's Surgical Corset Company."

70

"I'll *kill* that signwriter," I gritted. "He promised to be here this week for sure. Two months I've been in this office, and. . ."

"Mr. Dexter, do you mind if we set your problems on one side and discuss mine?" She began untying the string on the parcel.

"Not at all." Having lost the initiative, I decided it would be better to improve customer relations. I never saw much sense in private psis trying to talk and act like private eyes, anyway. "How can I help you, Miss. . . ?"

"I'm Carole Colvin." Her brow wrinkled slightly. "I thought you psi people knew all that sort of thing without being told."

"It's a wild talent," I said in a hollow voice, giving my stock response. "There are forces beyond the control of mere humans."

It was always necessary at this point to look sort of fey and hag-ridden, so I stared out through the fanlight and thought about the lawsuit my ex-secretary was bringing against me for non-payment of wages, Carole didn't seem to notice. She finished unwrapping her parcel, took out an unframed oil painting and propped it in front of me.

"What can you tell me about this painting?" she said briskly. "It's a good copy of the Mona Lisa," I replied.

"A very clever imitation, but ..." My voice faded away of its own accord as the full blast from the canvas hit my extra senses.

There was an impression of great age, perhaps five hundred years, and a blurring rush of images - a handsome bearded man in medieval costume, hilly landscapes with dark green vegetation, bronze sculptures, thronged narrow streets of antique cities. Behind this montage, almost obliterated by its brilliance, was the suggestion of a dark place and of a circular wooden frame which might have been part of a large machine.

Carole was regarding me with interest. "It isn't a copy, is it?" I dragged my jaw back up to its normal position. "Miss Colvin, I'm just about certain this painting was done by Leonardo da Vinci himself."

"You mean it's *the* Mona Lisa?"

"Well. . . yes." I gazed at the canvas, paralysed with awe.

"But that isn't possible, is it?"

"We'll soon see." I pressed the button on my computer terminal and said, "Has the Mona Lisa been stolen from the Louvre in Paris?"

The reply came with electronic swiftness. "I cannot answer that question."

"Insufficient data?" I said.

"Insufficient funds," the machine replied. "Until you pay your last three quarterly subscriptions you're getting no more information out of me."

I made a rude sign out through the window in the direction I imagined the central computer to lie. "Who needs you?" I sneered.

"It would have been in all the papers if the Mona Lisa had been stolen."

"Then, more fool you for asking," the machine said. I took my finger off the button and smirked desperately at Carole, wishing I hadn't tried to put on a display of computerized efficiency.

She looked at me with what seemed to be increasing coldness. "If you are quite finished, I'll tell you how I got the painting. Or don't you want to hear?"

"I want to. I want to." Realizing I was in danger of losing her business, I sat up straight, looking poised and alert.

"My father was an art dealer and he had a small gallery up in Sacramento," Carole said, folding herself into a chair with an action like honey flowing from a spoon. "He died two months ago and left the business to me. I don't know much about art, so I decided to sell out the whole thing. It was when the inventory was being made up that I found this painting hidden in a safe."

"Nice stroke of luck.".

"That remains to be seen. The painting might be worth a few

million, or it might be worth a few years in the pen - I want to find out which."

"And so you came to me! Very wise, Miss Colvin."

"I'm beginning to wonder about that. For somebody who's supposed to have a sixth sense you seem a bit deficient in the other five."

I think that was the moment I fell in love with Carole. The reasoning was that if I could enjoy looking at her while being treated like an idiot child, life should get pretty interesting if I could get her to regard me as an intelligent man. I started on that private project there and then.

"Your father never mentioned the painting to anybody?"

"No - that's what makes me wonder if something illegal was going on."

"Have you any idea how he got it?"

"Not really. He was on vacation in Italy last spring, and I remember he seemed rather odd when he got back."

"In what way?"

"Tense. Withdrawn. Not what you'd expect after a vacation."

"Interesting. Let's see if I can pick up something more to go on." I leaned forward and touched the slightly crazed surface of the painting. Once more there was a strong psychic impulse - images of a balding man I knew to be Carole's father, bright glimpses of cities. The latter would have been unknown to me had they not been accompanied by the intuitions which elevate the psi talent and make it roughly equal to a course in chiropody as a viable means of earning a crust.

"Rome," I said. "Your father went to Rome first, but he spent most of his time in and around Milan."

"That's correct." Carole gave me a look of grudging approval. "It appears that you do have some genuine ability."

"Thanks. Some people think I have nice legs, too." Her compliment was partly lost on me because I had again half-seen a dark

73

place, like a cavern, and a circular wooden machine. There were distracting undertones of mystery and centuries-old secrets.

"We're not much further on, though," Carole said.

"I thought we were doing pretty well."

"You haven't answered the big question - did Leonardo paint the Mona Lisa *twice*?"

"That's the way it seems to me, Miss Colvin. I don't know how this will affect the value of the original."

"The original?"

"I mean, the other one." I stared at the painting in awe, letting its sheer presence wash over my senses, then I began to get a feeling there was something not quite right about it, something difficult to put a finger on. The Mona Lisa stared back at me, the famous smile playing about her lips just as I remembered it from all the prints I'd seen. Her face was exactly right, the rich medieval background was exactly right, and yet there was some detail of the picture which seemed out of place. Could it, I wondered, be something to do with those plump smooth hands? To impress Carole, I assumed a look of deep, brooding concentration and tried to decide what it was in the painting which was ringing subconscious alarm bells.

"Have you fallen asleep?" Carole said, rapping the desk with an imperious knuckle.

"Of course not," I replied huffily, and pointed at the Mona Lisa's hands. "Do these look right to you?"

"You think you could have done better?"

"I mean, in the Louvre painting does she not have one hand sort of cradled in the other one? Instead of separated like that?"

"Could be - I told you I don't know anything about art."

"It might explain the existence of two Mona Lisas." I began to warm to my theory. "Perhaps he did this one and then decided it would have been better with the hands in repose."

"In that case," Carole said reasonably, "why didn't he just
paint the hands over again?"

"Ah . . . well. . . yes." I swore at myself for having concocted
such a dumb theory. "You've got a point there."

"Let's go." Carole got to her feet and began wrapping the
painting in its brown paper covering.

"Where to?"

"Italy, of course." A look of impatience flitted across her beautiful features. "I'm employing you to find out if this painting is
legally mine, and it's quite obvious you won't be able to do it sitting here in Los Angeles."

I opened my mouth to protest, then realized that the assertive
Miss Colvin was right in what she said, that I needed some of the
money she so obviously had, and that a spell in the Mediterranean
sun would probably do me a lot of good. There was also a powerful element of curiosity about both the painting itself and that
part of my psi vision I hadn't yet mentioned to her - the dark cavern and its enigmatic wheel-like machine. . .

"Yes?" Carole challenged. "You were going to say something?"

"Not me. I'll be glad to wave good-bye to this place for a few
days. How do you say *arrivaderci* in Italian?"

We caught the noon sub-orbital to Rome, were lucky with a shut-
tle connection, and by early evening had checked into the Hotel
Marco Polo in Milan.

The travelling had made me hungry and I did justice to the
meal which Carole and I had in a discreet corner of the dining
room. A glass of brandy and a good cigar helped me to enjoy the
cabaret, even though most of the singers had to rely on the new-
style tonsil microphones to make their voices carry. I guess it's a
sign of age, but I insist that *real* singers can get along perfectly well
with the old type of mike they used to clip on to their back teeth.
Still, considering how badly the day had started off, there was lit-

tle to complain about. I had a glow of wellbeing, and Carole was looking incredibly feminine in something gauzy and golden. Into the bargain, I was earning money.

"When are you going to start earning your money?" Carole said, eyeing me severely through a small palisade of candle flames.

"I'm already doing it," I assured her, somewhat hurt by her attitude. "This is the hotel your father stayed in while he was in Milan, and there's a good chance this is where he made the connection. If it is, I'll pick up an echo sooner or later."

"Try to make it sooner, will you?"

"There's no controlling a wild talent." Sensing the need for more customer relations work, I introduced a bit of echo chamber into my voice. "Right now, as we sit here, the intangible billowing nets of my mind are spreading outwards, ever out …"

"Yes?"

"Hold on a minute," I said. Quite unexpectedly, the intangible billowing nets of my mind had caught a fish - in the shape of a passing wine waiter. He was a slim dark youth with knowing brown eyes, and my psi faculties told me at once that his recent past was linked in some unusual way with that of Carole's father. I immediately tried to connect him with the Mona Lisa Mk. II. There was no positive response on the intuitive level, and yet I became more certain the wine waiter would be worth questioning. That's the way ESP works.

Carole followed my gaze and shook her head. "I think you've had enough to drink."

"Nonsense - I can still crawl a straight line." I left the table and followed the waiter out through double doors and into a passageway which probably led to the cellars. He glanced back when he heard me, then turned around, his eyes sizing me up like those of a cattle-buyer examining a steer.

"Pardon me," I said. "Do you mind if I speak to you for a moment?"

"I haven't got a moment," he said. "Besides, I don't speak English."

"But ..." I stared at him for a few seconds, baffled, then the message came through, loud and clear. I took out the expense money Carole had given me, peeled off a ten and tucked it into the pocket of his white jacket. "Will that buy you a Linguaphone course?"

"It all comes back to me now." He smiled a tight, crafty smile. "You want a woman? What sort of woman do you want?"

"No. I do not want a woman."

He grew even more shifty-looking. "You mean. . . ?"

"I mean I've got a perfectly good woman with me."

"Ah! Do you want to *sell* a woman? Let me tell you, *signor*, you have come to the right man - I have many connections in the white slave market."

"I don't want to sell a woman, either."

"You are sure? As long as she has got white skin I can get you two thousand for her. It doesn't even matter," he said generously, jiggling cupped hands in front of his chest, "if she hasn't got much accoutrements. As long as she has that flawless white skin ..."

I began to get impatient. "All I want from you, Mario, is some information."

The gleam of avarice in the waiter's eyes was quickly replaced by a look of wariness. "How did you know my name?"

"I have ways of knowing things," I told him mysteriously. Actually, I wasn't sure whether I had esped his name or whether it was the only Italian one I could think of on the spur of the moment.

"Pissy," he said. "That's what you are - pissy."

I grabbed him by the lapels and raised him up on his toes.

"Listen, Mario, any more lip out of you and I'll ..."

"You've got me wrong, *signor*," Mario babbled, and I was relieved to discover he was more of a coward than I am. "I mean,

77

you are one of the pissy ones who know things without being told of them."

"P-S-I is pronounced like sigh," I said, letting go of his jacket. "Try to remember that, will you?"

"Of course, *signor.*" He stood back to let another waiter pass between us with a bottle of wine. "Now, tell me what information you want to buy, and I will tell you the cost. My scale of charges is very reasonable."

"But I've already paid you."

"*Non capisco*," Mario said in a stony voice and began to walk away.

"Come back," I commanded. He kept on walking. I took out the roll of bills and he, displaying a sixth sense which aroused my professional envy, promptly went into reverse until we were facing each other again. It was as if he had been drawn towards me by a powerful magnet, and I began to realize that here was a man who was capable of selling his own grandmother. Indeed, from his earlier conversation, it was possible that he had already disposed of the old lady, venerable accoutrements and all. Making a mental note to be careful in my dealings with Mario, I asked him if he could remember a Trevor J. Colvin staying at the hotel in April.

"I remember him." Mario nodded, but I could tell he was puzzled and slightly disappointed, which meant he had no idea of the money potentials involved. I decided to keep it that way.

"Why do you remember Mr. Colvin in particular? Had you any ... ah ... business dealings with him?"

"No - he didn't want a woman, either. All I did was introduce him to Crazy Julio from Paesinoperduto, my home village."

"Why was that?"

Mario shrugged. "Signor Colvin is an art dealer. Crazy Julio, who hasn't two lira to rub together, came to me with some ridiculous story about an old painting he had found on his farm. He wanted to show it to an art dealer, preferably one from another country. I knew it was a waste of time, but I'm a businessman and if Crazy Julio was prepared to pay for my services ..."

Wondering how much he knew of what had transpired, I said, "Did you perhaps translate for them?"

"No. Julio has English. Not very good English, though - he is too crazy for that."

"You didn't believe he had a painting which might be worth money?"

"Crazy Julio?" Mario sniggered into his hand. "His farm is just a patch of rock and his only crop is empty Pepsi bottles."

'I see. Can you take me to him?"

Mario stopped sniggering on the instant, all his predatory instincts aroused. "Why do you want to see Crazy Julio?"

"The arrangement we have," I reminded him, "is that you answer my questions. Can you take me to him?"

Mario stuck out his hand. "A hundred dollars," he said peremptorily.

I touched his hand, trying to esp enough information to be able to proceed without him. All I could pick up was a blur of anonymous grey-green hillside strewn with boulders. The information I already had was enough to let me find Julio by working through a local inquiry agent, but that would use up extra time as well as money.

"Here's fifty on account," I said to Mario, slapping five bills into his palm. "When can we go?"

"Tomorrow morning I will borrow my mother's car and drive you to Paesinoperduto myself. How's that?"

"It suits me."

Mario gave a dry cough. "There will be a small extra charge for the use of the car. My mother is a widow, you understand, and hiring out the car my father left her is the only way she can afford a few little luxuries."

"That's all right." Wondering if I had been too harsh in my assessment of Mario's character, I arranged to meet him outside the hotel early the following day. I went back to the table and gave a glowing progress report to Carole. She was pleased enough to let us get on to first-name terms, but any hopes I had of further developments in the relationship were dashed when she insisted on our going to bed early, and separately, so that we would be fresh in the morning.

My room was cold and I slept rather badly, troubled by ominous dreams about a dark place and a strange wheel-like machine.

In the morning we waited outside the hotel for about ten minutes before Mario arrived to pick us up in a mud-spattered Fiat. It was my first time in Italy and, under the impression that Mediterranean countries were warm even in the winter, I had brought only a light showerproof. I was shivering violently in the raw wind while, in contrast, Carole looked rose-pink and competent in tweeds and fur. When Mario saw her the whites of his eyes flickered like the tallies of a cash register.

"*Three* thousand," he whispered to me as she got into the car. "That's the top rate around here."

I bundled him into the driver's seat and put my mouth close to his ear. "Keep quiet, you little toad. We Americans don't sell our women - besides, she doesn't belong to me."

Mario glanced again at Carole and then eyed me with surprise and contempt. "You are a great fool, *signor*. A woman like that cries out for love."

"You'll be the one who cries out if you don't shut up and start driving." I slammed the door on Mario, but he rolled down the window and held out his hand.

"Two hundred kilometres at twenty-five cents a kilometre makes fifty dollars," he said. "Payable in advance."

Seething with hatred, but trapped, I paid him the money and

got in the back seat beside Carole. As the car moved off with a loud churning of dry gears, she drew her coat closer around her and gave me a cool stare.

"You're very generous with my money," she said. "I could have *bought* this heap for fifty dollars."

"Very funny." I huddled up in the opposite corner, numb with the cold, and brooded on the unfairness of life. Mario was a character straight out of a blue movie, but I had an uneasy feeling he might be right about Carole. Perhaps, in accordance with the whole blue movie ethos, she was sitting there, ice cold on the outside and burning hot within - a human antithesis to a Baked Alaska - just waiting for me to produce my dessert spoon and gobble her up. Perhaps, incredible as it seemed, she was a girl who longed to be dominated and ravished. I allowed myself a lingering glance at Carole's slim-sculpted legs and waited for her response.

"Keep your eyes on the scenery, junior," she snapped.

"That's what I was doing," I said weakly. Mario's shoulders twitched a little and I guessed he was sniggering again. I began staring out of the window, but the scenery was little consolation because we travelled only two blocks, went round a corner and halted in the dimness of a shabby garage.

"Just a short delay, folks - I'll be with you in a minute," Mario called out. He leaped from the car, disappeared underneath it and a few seconds later we heard a querulous whine, like that of a dentist's drill, coming up through the floor. I bore it for as long as I could, then got out and looked under the vehicle at Mario. He had disconnected its speedometer cable and was turning it with a power drill.

"Mario!" I bellowed. "What in hell do you think you're doing?"

"Just covering my expenses, *signor.*"

"What do you mean?"

"I swore to my mother, on my honour, that we were only going twenty kilometres today, but I saw her taking a speedometer reading anyway." He began to sound aggrieved. "The old bitch doesn't even trust her own son! How do you like that? Every time I use her car I have to turn the speedo back or she would rob me blind."

I gave a strangled cry of fury, grabbed Mario by the ankles and dragged him out from under the vehicle. "This is your last chance," I told him in a shaking voice. "Drive us to Paesino-whateveryoucallit right now, or the deal is off."

"All right. There's no need to get tough." Mario looked furtively around the garage. "By the way, now that you're at my depot - are you interested in drugs? Pot, hash, speed, snow. You name it, I've got it."

"Have you a telephone? I want to call the police."

The effect on Mario was gratifying and immediate. He pushed me back into the car and we drove off without even waiting to disconnect the power drill from the speedometer cable. It thumped on the bottom of the car a few times before falling behind us. Carole gave me a puzzled look, but I shook my head, warning her not to ask any questions. All I knew for sure was that, if Mario got the slightest inkling of our business with Crazy Julio, he would move in like a hungry shark let loose in a paddling pool.

The drive westwards into the first slopes of the Graian Alps was far from pleasant. There appeared to be no heater in the car and, for some reason known only to themselves, my nipples reacted to the cold by becoming unbearably painful. They were so hard they almost tore my shirt each time we lurched into a pothole. Carole was remote, wrapped in her plumage like a haughty bird. Even Mario had nothing to say, no criminal propositions to make. He drove with broody concentration, swerving every now and then in attempts to run over stray dogs. When we reached

Paesinoperduto two hours after setting out, I felt like a very old man.

"Here we are," Mario announced, suddenly regaining his voice.

"And I have a good idea."

"Yes?" I said warily.

"Crazy Julio's farm is two kilometres north of here, and the road gets even worse. You and the *signora* will stay here and have some coffee and I will bring Julio to meet you."

I shook my head. "Nothing doing, Mario. *You* are going to stay here while Miss Colvin and I drive to the farm by ourselves."

"That is impossible, *signor*. The car insurance would not cover you to drive it."

"The car hasn't even got insurance," I challenged.

"Also, you don't know the way."

"I can psi myself straight to it at this range."

"But, do you think I could permit a stranger to drive off in my mother's car?"

"Let's see." I glanced around the deserted market square in which we had stopped. "I bet I can even psi the local police station from here."

"Be careful with the brakes," Mario said resignedly, getting out of the driver's seat and holding the door while I got in. "They pull to the right."

"Thanks." I let but the clutch pedal and steered the car towards the square's only northern exit.

"That was quite an exhibition," Carole said as we left the shabby cluster of dwellings behind. "Did you have to be so tough with that poor boy?"

"If that poor boy isn't in the Mafia," I assured her, "it's because they gave him a dishonourable discharge."

We drove along a deteriorating road which took us up into the sunlit boulder-strewn hillsides I had psi-glimpsed on the previous evening. At one point - as if entering a baronial estate - the road crossed the remains of what had been a massive stone wall some centuries earlier. Faintly surprised at the idea of any medieval nobleman spending money on such unpromising land, I skried all around with a mounting sense of anticipation. There was a definite impression of richly apparelled horsemen coming and going. When a track branched off to the right towards an isolated farmhouse clinging to the mountain, I knew at once that we had reached our destination. The car rocked violently on the stony ground, but I was too excited even to wince at the sawing of my nipples on the inside of my shirt.

"Is this it?" Carole's voice was full of doubt. "It doesn't look to me like a place where you'd pick up an original da Vinci."

"Me neither - but I can tell you something big was going on here a few hundred years back." I stopped the car as it became in danger of being shaken to pieces. "Da Vinci spent a lot of his life in Milan, and it would have been quite easy for him to come up here in person any time he wanted."

"To that hovel?" Carole said scornfully, looking at the farm house ahead of us.

"It doesn't seem old enough. No, there's a cavern of some sorts around here, and that's probably where Julio found your painting." My heart speeded up as, once again, I glimpsed the circular wooden machine. This time I discerned something extra - there seemed to be a whole series of canvases arranged in a curving row. "I've a feeling there could be a lot more paintings in it."

Carole's gloved hand touched my shoulder. "You mean there's an underground storehouse?"

"I don't think that's the ..." I stopped speaking as the figure of an elderly man emerged from the farmhouse and approached us. He was dressed in a pricy-looking chalk-striped grey suit, but the effect was spoiled by his frayed, collarless shirt and filthy ten-

Bob Shaw

nis shoes. The double-barrelled shotgun on his arm confirmed my opinion that he had a very poor taste in separates.

I rolled down my window, projecting friendliness, and shouted, "Hi, Julio! How are you? How's it going?"

"What you want?" he demanded. "Go away."

"I'd like to talk to you."

Julio raised the shotgun. "I no want to talk, to you."

"It's just for a few minutes, Julio."

"Listen, mister - I shoot you as soon as look at you." He scowled in the window at me. "In your case, sooner."

Stung by the insult, I decided on a more forceful approach. "It's about the Mona Lisa you sold to Signor Colvin, Julio. I want to know where you got it, and you'd better tell me."

"I tell you nothing."

"Come on, Julio." I got out of the car and loomed over him.

"Where is the cave?"

Julio's jaw sagged. "How you know about the cave?"

"I have ways of knowing things." I used quite a lot of echo chamber in the voice, aware that peasants tend to be afraid of espers.

Julio looked up at me with worried eyes. "I get it," he said in a low voice. "You are pissy."

"P-S-I is pronounced like sigh," I gritted. "Try to remember that, will you? Now, where's that cave?"

"You make trouble for me?"

"There'll be no trouble as long as you're a good boy, and there might even be some money for you. The cave is this way, isn't it?" Following a powerful instinct, I began striding up the hillside towards a stand of dark-green trees. Julio jogged along at my side and Carole, who for once had nothing to say, left the car and came after us.

"I find it three-four year ago, but for long time I no touch," Julio said, panting a little as he struggled to keep abreast. "I no tell anybody because I want no fuss. Then I think, why should I not have smart city clothes? Why should Crafty Mario be the only one to have smart city clothes? But I take only one picture to sell. Just one."

"How many paintings are in the cave?"

"Fifty. Maybe sixty."

I gave a short laugh. "Then it was pretty dumb of you to pick one as well known as the Mona Lisa."

Julio stopped jogging. "But, *signor*," he said, spreading his hands, "they are all Mona Lisas."

It was my turn to stop in my tracks. "*What*?"

"They are all Mona Lisas."

"You mean there are fifty or sixty paintings in there, and they're all the same?"

Julio shifted his feet uneasily. "They are not all same."

"This doesn't make sense." I glanced at Carole and saw she was equally baffled. "Come on - we've got to see this for ourselves."

By that time we had reached and entered the cluster of trees. Julio set his shotgun down, darted ahead of us and dragged some pieces of rusty corrugated iron out of the way. Beneath them was an irregular opening and the beginning of a flight of stone steps which led downwards into blackness. Julio went down them, nimble in his tennis shoes, while Carole and I followed uncertainly. I felt her hand slip into mine and I gave it a reassuring squeeze as we reached the bottom step and began moving along what seemed to be a subterranean corridor. The daylight from the entrance rapidly faded.

I tapped Julio's shoulder. "How are we going to see? Have you got a flashlight?"

"Flashlight no good. I buy one with money Signor Colvin give me, but the crooks no tell me I have to keep on buying batteries. This is better." Julio struck a match and used it to light a storm lantern which had been sitting on the stone floor. As the oil flame brightened I saw that the tunnel ended at a massive wooden door. Julio rumbled at the lock and pushed the door. In spite of its weight and great age, it swung open easily, with uncanny silence, and there was spacious darkness beyond. Carole moved closer to me. I put my arm around her, but at that moment I was too pre-occupied to derive any enjoyment from the embrace - the myste-rious chamber, at whose entrance we stood, contained the answers to all the questions which were pounding in my head. I could almost feel those cloaked figures from half-a-millennium in the past brushing by me, I could almost hear the master himself as he went secretly about his work, I could almost see the strange machine. The greatest genius of all time had left his imprint here, and his lingering presence was so overwhelming that ordinary mortals felt humbled and unwilling to intrude.

"What you wait for?" Julio snapped, marching into the cham-ber with the lantern held high.

I followed him and, in the shifting light, discerned the out-lines of a circular framework which resembled a wheel lying on its side. It was large - perhaps twenty paces in diameter - and at its rim was as tall as a man. Beneath the spokes of the wheel was a dimly seen system of gears with a long crankshaft running out to a position near where we stood. The whole thing reminded me of an early type of funfair merry-go-round, except that in place of the carved horses - and difficult to see properly because of the inter-vening frames - there was a series of paintings. All of them were attached to the inside of the rim, facing the centre. At the closest point on the machine's circumference there was a structure like an elaborately ornamented sentry box, on the rear wall of which were two small holes at eye level.

I gaped at the wheel for a moment while a fantastic concept struggled to be born in my mind. The device did look like a roundabout, yet it had more in common with a Victorian cartoon animation machine. Realization exploded behind my eyes like a grenade.

Leonardo da Vinci - possessor of one of the most fertile minds in human history, creator of technologies that were far ahead of their times - had also invented moving pictures!

This machine, hidden for centuries in a cavern on a poor farmer's land, had to be the richest treasure ever to come out of antiquity. Beside it the tomb of Tutankhamun was a trifle, the Elgin marbles were reduced to insignificance - because the device itself was only one part of the incredible find. Where a lesser man would have experimented with the animation of simple drawings or silhouettes, Leonardo's towering vision and ambition had prompted him to aim for perfection, to base his work on his most acclaimed painting.

If my surmise was correct, the Mona Lisa was merely one frame in the world's first movie!

Hardly daring to breathe, I stepped into the viewing box and peered through the two holes. I had been right. Lenses concealed within the woodwork brought my gaze to a focus on yet another painting of the beautiful Florentine lady. She looked startlingly real in the uncertain light, and in this picture her hands were in a much higher position, as if she was raising them to her throat. The famous smile seemed a little more pronounced, too. I had to step back to give myself time to assimilate what I had seen, and I noticed that Julio had hung his lantern on a hook projecting from the wall. He scuttled about, lighting other lanterns, then took hold of the long crankshaft in preparation for turning it.

"Does the mechanism still work?" I asked him.

Julio nodded. "I grease it and made it work." He wound the iron handle and the framework began to turn. It moved very slowly at first, then settled into a smooth noiseless rotation which indicated perfection of balance. Julio gestured with his free hand, inviting me to look through the eyepiece again. He was grinning with proprietary glee.

I swallowed painfully as I stepped into the ornate box. Wonder was piling on wonder in a way that was almost too much to bear. On top of everything else that had transpired, I was about to have the privilege of actually viewing Leonardo's supreme masterpiece brought to magical life, to commune with his mind in a manner which nobody would have thought possible, to see his sublime artistry translated into movement. Perhaps I was even to learn the secret of the Giaconda smile.

Filled with reverence, I put my eye to the viewing holes and saw the Mona Lisa miraculously moving, miraculously alive.

She raised her hands to the neckline of her dress and pulled it down to expose her ample left breast. She gave her shoulder a twitch and the breast performed the classiest circular swing I had seen since the last night I witnessed Fabulous Fifi Lafleur windmilling her tassels in Schwartz's burlesque hall. She then drew her dress back up to its former position of modesty and demurely crossed one hand over the other, smiling a little.

"Oh, God," I whispered. "Oh, God, God, God, *God*!"

Julio kept cranking the machine and I watched the show over and over again, unable to take my eyes away. It was a marvellous simulation of reality, marred only by one slight jerk near the beginning of the sequence - obviously where Julio had abstracted a painting to sell.

"Let me see it," Carole said, tugging at my sleeve. "I want to see it, too."

I stood back and let her look through' the eyepiece. Julio twirled the crankshaft happily, jumping up and down in his tennis shoes like a demented dwarf. Carole viewed in silence for a full minute, then turned to me with wide eyes.

"It doesn't seem possible," she said faintly.

"Of course it's possible," I replied. "With a bit of practice some girls can do fantastic things with their accoutrements. Why, I remember when Fabulous Fifi Lafleur used to ..."

"I'm talking about da Vinci," Carole snapped. "I don't know much about art, but I didn't think he would go in for that sort of thing."

"All artists are the same - they do whatever the paying customer wants them to do." I was speaking with new-found cynicism. "It's known that da Vinci was commissioned to design entertainments for various nobles, and some of the high-born were pretty low-minded."

"But all that work ..."

"He probably had the assistance of a whole school of artists. Beside, a project this size accounts for the long periods of apparent unproductivity in da Vinci's career. When he should have been working on the Sforza statue he was down here working on Lisa's left ..."

"Don't be vulgar," Carole put in. She turned back to the still rotating machine. "How much do you think it's worth?"

"Who knows? Say there are sixty paintings involved. If they were smuggled out and away from the Italian Government they could fetch a million dollars each. Perhaps ten million each. Perhaps a billion - specially that one where she ..."

"I *knew* this was going to be a lucky day," a familiar voice said from behind me.

I spun and saw Crafty Mario standing at the entrance to the chamber. He was holding the shotgun which Crazy Julio had dropped outside, and its barrels were pointing at my stomach.

"What do you want?" I demanded, and then - realizing just how rhetorical the question was in Mario's case - I added another. "Why are you pointing that gun at me?"

"Why did you steal my mother's car?" Mario gave one of his most unpleasant sniggers. "And why did you threaten me with the police?"

"You mustn't pay too much attention to the things I say."

"But I can't help it, *signor* - especially when I hear you saying things like sixty million dollars."

"Now see here!" I started forward, but Mario stopped me by raising the shotgun.

"Yes?"

"We're being silly, with so much loot to go around. I mean, out of sixty million you can have fifteen."

"I prefer to have sixty."

"But you wouldn't take a human life for an extra forty-five million, would you?" I looked into the polished pebbles that Mario used in place of eyes, and my spirits sank.

"Back against the wall, the three of you," Mario ordered.

Carole clung to me as we moved to the wall. Crazy Julio tried clinging to me as well, but I fended him off - with perhaps only a minute to live I was entitled to be choosy.

"That's much better," Mario said. "Now, I will inspect the merchandise for myself."

He went towards the machine which was still spinning on its well-greased bearings. Covering us with the gun, he stepped into the viewing box and peered into the two holes. I saw him stiffen with shock. He kept glancing back at us and then into the eye-piece again, fascinated. When he finally emerged from the box his face was almost luminescent with pallor. He walked towards us, his mouth working silently, and I held Carole close against me as we waited for the explosion of pain.

Mario appeared not to see us. He took the storm lantern down from its hook on the wall, and with a stiff-armed movement flung it into the centre of the machine. There was a sound of breaking glass, then flames began to lick up around the dry timber structure.

"You fool!" I howled. "What are you doing?"

"You will see what I'm doing." Holding me in check with the gun, Mario collected the other lanterns and hurled them against the machine as well. The wooden rim of the wheel began to burn fiercely and I knew that the paintings, my sixty Mona Lisas, were igniting, crumpling, turning to worthless ash.

"You're mad," I shouted above the crackling of the flames. "You don't know what you've done."

"I know very well what I have done, *signor*," Mario said calmly. "I have destroyed a piece of pornographic filth."

"*You!*" I cackled like a madman. "But you're the most evil person I've ever known. You've robbed me since the minute we met, you rob your poor old mother, you tried to sell me a woman, you tried to buy Carole for the white slave trade, you're a drug pusher, and you were prepared to murder us a minute ago. You can't even drive a car without trying to run over cats and dogs."

"These things you say may be true, *signor*," Mario said with an odd kind of dignity, "but they do not prevent me from being a patriot. They do not prevent me from loving my glorious Italia."

"Huh? What the hell has patriotism got to do with it?"

"The great Leonardo was the finest artist who ever lived. He is the pride of my country - but tell me, *signor*, what would the rest of the world think of Italy if it was learned that the immortal Leonardo had prostituted himself in this way? What would they say about a nation whose noblest artist had wasted his divine gifts on … ' Mario's voice quavered with anguish, " … on medieval skin flicks?"

I shook my head, blinking back tears as the machine collapsed inwards on itself in showers of topaz sparks. The chamber filled with smoke as the last fragments of the oil paintings were consumed.

Mario pointed to the exit. "All right - we can leave now."

"Aren't you going to shoot us?"

"It isn't necessary. Even if you were mad enough to talk about this, nobody would believe you."

"I think you're right." I gave Mario a curious stare. "Tell me, doesn't it bother you that you've just lost sixty million dollars?"

Mario shrugged. "Some days you win, some days you lose. By the way, because of all the trouble I've had, if you want to travel back to Milan in my mother's car there will be a small extra charge …"

Carole stared at me thoughtfully as we sipped our after-dinner liqueurs. "You were very brave once or twice today - even with a gun pointed at you."

"It wasn't much. For all we know, Crazy Julio had no shells in it." I smiled at Carole across the candle flames. "I mean, he wouldn't even buy flashlight batteries."

"No, you were brave. I was quite impressed." Carole lapsed into another silence.

She had been like that all through the meal, even when I had pointed out that the painting she still had back in Los Angeles would make her a very rich woman. I guessed that the events of the day had been quite a strain on her, and that she was suffering from a reaction.

"It hardly seems possible," she said in a small voice.

I squeezed her hand. "Try to forget it. The main thing is that we got out of the cave in one …"

"I'm talking about the Mona Lisa," she interrupted. "That trick she did with her … um … accoutrement. Do you think I could do it?"

I drained my brandy in one gulp. "I'm sure you could."

"Are you an expert on these things?"

"Well, I've seen Fabulous Fifi Lafleur a few times, and if she can do it you probably could."

"Lets go up to my room and find out," Carole said in a low husky voice.

I tried to gulp more brandy from the empty glass and almost shattered it against my teeth. "You're kidding," I said, not very brilliantly.

"Do you think so?"

I looked at Carole, and something in her eyes told me she wasn't kidding. I'm too much of a gentleman to say anything about how the rest of that night worked out, but I'll tell you this much.

Every time I look at a copy of the Mona Lisa, especially when I notice that famous smile, I can't help smiling back.

Seán Mac Roibin was born in 1969 and lives in Tallaght, Dublin. Much of his writing is characterized by a stark sense of humour, and he once described himself as liking 'work not in the least ... socially retarded (and drifting) through life in that daze one emerges startled from aged sixty.' He has published his own very personal style of fiction in magazines such as *Albedo One*, both as short stories, graphic stories and comics, with his work being thought of highly in Ireland and the UK. A sample can be found at www.geocities.com/rhubarb108 and is well worth a look. Seán has also worked with a number of US comics publishers, including Dark Horse and Caliber Press, creating cartoons and comic strips. He also works freelance for the Irish newspaper, *The Echo*, and contributes reviews to Bugpowder.com, the website of the UK small press comics community. The following story well sums up Seán's off-beat and tilted view of the world, emphasizing the humour in even the darker aspects of life.

Something Occurred;
Bennie on the Loose

Seán Mac Roibin

Met Jayo on the 77. He was going to town himself. I slipped down beside him without a word, smiling all the while. Saw him trying to catch a side-ways peek at me; see who I was.

"Story Jay?"

"Johnner, ye fuckin' shite for brains! Where ye headin'?"

"Ah, thought I'd catch a flick."

"In town? What's wrong with The Square?"

"Nothing; I just -"

"Ah yeah, ye fuckin' sleeveen! Your sister works in that newsagents, doesn't she?!"

He smells of shampoo. Just been to the hairdressers, so he

says - got a "one". He's poking his left hand up the back of his clothing most of the time; fucking hairs.

"The bird in the place; Jesus!" he's saying to me, and I'm listening to his bullshit all the way. I know her: red hair, big smile, moves about you real awkward like.

"Swear to God," he says, "tits in my face the whole time; or brushing my shoulder. Crotch nudging me knee too."

"Yeah?"

"Like a fuckin' wet dream."

Bullshit!

The awl one in the next seat was starting to blow her nose. Sounded like a long skid on a wet tyre. She kept blowing even when there was nothing there, and made this hollowed out dry noise. Jay and me just looked at each other and laughed.

"She'll be spurting blood out her ears if she's not careful," I whispered.

"Fuckin' sure!"

Then she was up off her seat wiping condensation from the windows; with the bloody tissue she'd been poking her nose with no less. Mad as a fucking hatter. When I got off the bus I think she moved into my seat, because I went to wave at Jay and she was leaning over him mopping his window. He looked sort of frightened, and feebly waved at me with a finger.

I don't go straight to the pictures; never do. There's this routine I'd stick to: Penney's for a bottle of Coke, then up to Cinelli's, get myself a sausage and chips special. It's special 'cause it's only a quid for two bangers and a single; but you get less chips than in a normal single, and they always seem to be re-heats - as if they put some chips aside just so they can cool off and be used in the specials; just 'cause you deserve no more for your pound.

The spotty girl behind the counter wasn't much older than me; probably just done her junior cert. The other guy behind there with her, this hairy Italian bloke, probably Cinelli himself, kept calling her "Double".

"S-salt and v-v-vin-v-vinegar?" she asked.

"Just salt, thanks," I said. Bastard.

I slinked up to the Garden of Remembrance then, just half way up that road at the top of O'Connell Street where the pigeons hang out. It smells of bus diesel, the road, and there's those distorted rainbow patches slithering across it every few paces.

It being autumn there was a nip in the air, so there was only a splattering of people in the garden. And the birds. Like, no problem finding a free bench. So I sat meself down and started into the soggy chips. Sure I'm not half-way through my third chip when some awl-fella in a leather jacket tells me that it's a nice day; like I hadn't fucking noticed.

"Nice day," he said.

The pigeons scarpered; I looked up from my single.

"Uh, yeah; I guess."

"I've seen you here before, haven't I?"

I'm back in my bag then; like, preoccupied beyond conversation.

"Yeah, I'm often here."

"It's a nice spot all right," he grinned, "if the birds'd leave you alone."

"Ah, they're sound," I muttered. "Sure we have one at home - a budgie. The thing's older than me!"

"Really?"

"Yeah, must be near enough sixteen now. He's on his last legs though."

"Sad," he sighs, then meandered off.

Fucking cheek; talking to me!

He's at it again a few minutes later; like, on his way out. I hadn't even finished my chips.

"Live round here?" he says, and stands right in front of me, hands firmly hidden in his jacket pockets. I can smell his beer breath he's so close.

"Nah; I'm from Tallaght."

"Oh, Tallaght." (Like it means something to him!) "I suppose you're still with your parents, huh?"

"Yeah," I smiled, "sure they've been like a mother and father to me!"

The mouldy cunt looked puzzled.

"Ah, no," I said. "I don't think I'll be stuck with them much longer."

"Oh?"

His right foot starts tapping the ground; slow at first, then like ninety.

"Soon as I get my exams from school," I shrugged, "I'll get meself a job; then I'm out of there. Well hard I am!"

"I see," he laughed. "I guess it must be difficult bringing the girlfriend home, huh?"

"Nah, don't have one."

"Too right," he nodded, his hands flying out of his pockets into folded arms pose. "Women are just trouble; they're all money. You're better off without."

I sort of grunted approval and guiltily shoved the last few chips into my mouth. Fuck, I hate eating in company.

"That said," he continued, like I was interested or something, "it gets lonely. I live alone myself, and you need a bit of company sometimes. Ye know?"

Again that noise; caught somewhere between a grunt and a hum. It doesn't stop the awl-fella rabbiting on...

"That's why I'm just out for a ramble; maybe just drop into a pub. Do you drink, yourself?"

"Me? No," I spluttered. "Well, sometimes; Coke anyway." I pointed towards the bottle at my feet, by way of sample beverage.

"Ah, sure you're better off without," he frowned. "You're too young yet."

He touched me with his left hand on the side of my head then, like some fatherly figurey type thing, and buggered off.

"Better make a move for that pub," he says. "Fill in the day."

Thanks be to fucking Jesus, I'm thinking; I hadn't even touched me Coke. I usually drink to the top of the label on the bottle; leave the rest for the cinema. Still, the popcorn does be salty enough; like, there was no problem there.

And I'm down in the jacks in the middle of O'Connell Street a little later, like always, making sure I take a leak before the film. The four cubicles are occupied and I'm standing there reading the 'no loitering' sign. I've been in this place loads of times, but I'm really uncomfortable then, all of a sudden. One of the blokes at the urinal kept turning his head slightly, as if he thought I was looking at him or something. I was! He had his legs spread a good bit, like he was making some sort of kick-ass statement, but he wasn't pissing. There was no piss, to my mind.

Anyway, the fucking cubicle door opened then and some baldy fella came out sheepishly. (It's gas; when someone's waiting, guilt and toilet emergence seem to go hand-in-hand.) I went in and turned to shut the door behind me. I glimpsed the kick-ass bloke: he was looking straight at me, and seemed to be, like, legging it in my direction. I sort of stalled a second. I don't know, I suppose I was kind of shitting it. For no reason really; he was probably just heading for the sinks...though like, I shut that fucking door quick anyway!

Someone had omitted the first 's' from "fascist" in the graffiti on the inside of the cubicle door. It's difficult then to take seriously "British Facist Army Out", I think. I didn't even have a ballpoint pen on me.

'Course, the kick-ass scumbag's gone when I come out. Still, I didn't wash me hands.

Met Jayo on the 77 again the following Saturday. He's sniffing the air the minute I sat in beside him.

"That you?" he says. "Smells like expensive shit."

"Must be me ma's washing powder," I laughed.

I didn't know if I should mention the awl-fella in the Garden of Remembrance. Don't know why; it's not as if anything happened.

"The guy's a fuckin' faggot," Jay yelped. "I'll go with ye today, and if he's there we'll kick the crap out of him!"

"Nah," I smiled, "sure maybe it's all innocent. I mean, your da' touches ye on the side of yer head and you think nothing of it..."

"Not my fuckin' da', he doesn't; not if he knows what's good for him!"

Bullshit!

Just then a 'B' flies past us, and Skinner Reagan's mouthing something at us from one of the windows. Jayo gives a surprised wave, then shifted uncomfortably in his seat.

"Ha; Skinner Reagan," he mumbles, "fuckin' header!"

We passed the bus a few minutes later, and this time Jay's ready: he stands up at one of those sliding window things above the main window and cocks his middle finger...

"Swivel on it, Skinner ye bollox!" he shouts out, laughing all the while.

Some woman behind us tuts, but Jayo doesn't give a fuck; he poked most of his arm out the window and followed the bus with his digit as it slipped behind us. Some buzz!

"Like a bucket," he bellows at me next while looking round with gleeful smirk at the tutting woman. "Like a fuckin' bucket!"

I'm at the garden a little earlier than usual. There's two geriatric awl-biddies there saying the rosary, or novena of grace or something. They were muttering incoherently anyway, so it must have been some sort of religious thing. Not that there's much wrong with that: I'm pro-God, meself. Like, I believe there should be one. Definitely!

I sat down on my usual bench. I guess I was sort of praying, myself, glancing around every few minutes, for no reason. Just didn't want conversation is all. Then I'm into me sausage and chips, and all of a sudden the fucker's right there in front of me.

Shite.

"Ah, you're back I see," he said.

"Sure am."

"Ah sure I might as well sit down a minute, myself."

He's down beside me then, just bent forward, leaning on his knees with his elbows. That beer breath again; and Jesus H: Old Spice!

"So," he sighs, "how's the sex life?"

"Oh I wish!" I mumbled. "I don't get out much. Haven't even put meself on the market yet."

"Ha; into boys are you?!" he laughed, his head flung back slightly, his right hand lifting from his knee, then landing on my thigh. (His hand on my thigh!) He shakes the thigh a little, before snapping his hand back in to a clammy clap.

"Nah, not at all," I'm saying, scratching my nose furiously and gawking at those grannies in the next bench; obvious like.

"What's that," he went, "prayers?"

"Nah," I said, "they were shooting-up just before you came."

He grinned; and still looking at the awl-ones, mentions he's never even seen drugs; actually. (I am the manipulator of conversation, I am!)

"Sure there's not much to see," I assured him. "Most of them are just like tablets; though ye get some and they're just these little bits of paper dipped in acid or something."

"Oh," he began to smile, "do they make you feel sexy?"

Like, I really don't want to be there then. (Leave it out ye awl-bollox!) He gives this stupid laughy-cough thing, and his hand

102

settles on my thigh again. It's warm, and he pretty much has my leg in his big hand. He gives a squeeze.

"Large thighs," he grimaced expertly with nodded head, squeezing once more, then releasing his grip.

"Oh eh, yeah," I spluttered, calmly covering my thigh with my non-chips holding hand, "I cycle a lot; I guess."

He's in like a shot:

"And do you wear those shorts things?"

"Sometimes."

I'm scratching my nose furiously then. Fuck the thigh; like, I have to get in a bit of nervous panic while he wipes the drool from his chin.

"Big muscley thigh," he confirmed, his hand suddenly resting on my vacant thigh for the third time; and I feel sort of detached from my leg. This time his hand stays there. He doesn't bother removing it; and like, he's not even looking at me.

"I better make a move," I muttered, not moving. (Damn legs not responding!) "Don't wanna miss the start of the film..."

The fucker's hand still grasped my leg.

"Y'know, get in before the lights go down..."

"Oh," he says, all of a sudden wide-eyed and looking right at me, "how dark does the cinema be?"

Bollox, I'm thinking. I pushed myself to the edge of the bench; knees still bent as if I'm carefully cradling some poxy cat or something. And I'm ready to scarper, big time; but yer man's hand doesn't budge. There's a sort of strength in it now; like urging me not to go.

Me bum's practically off the edge of the seat before he releases his hold. I'm standing then, turned toward him, stepping backwards a little. He winces.

"What you going to see anyway," he asks.

"Dunno," I said. "Probably an action film; if I can get in!"

"Might see you again next week then," he smiled lamely as I edged away.

I met his glance a second; he looked lost or something.

"Maybe," I said softly, and legged it; adrenalin pumping; bag of chips still in my right hand; Coke forgotten.

Maybe fuck!

Just missed the 77 the next week. Got the 'B' though; it was right behind. Skinner hopped on the next stop. He was sitting a few seats back from me most of the way. Suited me. Then he spots me: "Johnner! Didn't see your fat head there," he says and pushes in beside me. "What happened the Pool during the week; fuckin' lucky, weren't they?"

"Me bollox!" says me. "The chances we had!"

"Don't gimme that!" he barked. "When I think of the goals United just couldn't put away!"

"How can you say that?! The Pool could of easily had six more than United if only we'd finished well."

"Just don't give me that," he shrugged real aggressive like, throwing his right hand at the air. "The Pool didn't not score more goals than United; there's no way!"

We both went sort of quiet then a second, though the conversation resumed soon after. At one stage I heard myself boasting the fact that the Pool had the Mersey, and United had fuck-all. Skinner mumbled something about some trickling puddle or other.

We parted company at the terminus in town. Gobshite! The 77 I'd missed was already there. Its driver was putting 'garage' on the front of the bus instead of its usual destination; musta been having problems.

The bus limped past me a couple of minutes later on the way. Don't know why, but I glanced up at the top deck - there, a few seats from the back, I could see Jayo. And someone else. Like, what the fuck??

Jay's head and left shoulder were sort of pressed up against the window, and this other person, some man, was lying against him or something; I think he was asleep. Poor Jayo, ha! He looked like he was shittin' bricks. Fuckin' eejit!

Didn't know whether to head up to the garden or not - looked like it was going to piss down from the heavens. And anyway, didn't really want to bump into that dirty fuck again. So like, I get me Coke and pound special, and I'm wandering around trying to eat it, but it's no use: you can't enjoy the fucking thing. Really, you have to be sitting down.

The garden's empty; not a soul. And like, I'm nearly not going in, but I'm thinking: fuck it - I been coming here yonks!

I don't sit on my usual bench though; I headed to the ones furthest on, just at the foot of the steps to the Children of Lir statue - give me time to make a move if I see him coming. Like, just on the way out kind of thing.

I'm pretty jumpy, scoffing my chips and sausage as quick as I can; guzzling my Coke too; always glancing back towards the gates at the entrance, just in case. Christ, even up the other way towards the statue, and sure that's a dead-end.

I'm looking at the statue then: the transformation of four children into swans, from Irish history, or mythology, or somethin'. Sounds nice, but I think the kids are stuck that way for nine hundred years before the change back into humans. 'Course, they're ancient and decrepit then, and like snuff it pretty much immediately; or something to that effect anyway. Typical!

And I'm staring at my Coke bottle then: there was fuck-all left.

"Shite!" I'm saying to myself. "I'll have to fork out for another."

I'm not listening of course; too busy lifting the bottle up close to my face, forcing my vision through the label, just to see exactly what damage there was. When I look round again it's too late.

"Ah, back again, I see."

He had this broad smile on his face, a plastic bag in his hand, and sat down beside me like it was an inevitable progression of his step. Myself, I couldn't seem to move.

"So, anyone on the mat yet," he asked.

"No mat!" I shrugged.

"Never mind," he said, handing me the bag. "Got you something..."

"A plastic bag," I smiled sourly, "very nice! Now I've something to put things in."

"No," he laughed, and shifted uneasily on the bench, "in the bag..."

It was a video; previously viewed; ex-rental.

"Uh, thanks very much," I said. "What's this for?"

"Ah, nothing really. I know you like action movies..."

He's leaning forward on his knees then, rubbing his hands together like he's cold or something. His foot's goin' ninety at the ground again, this constant twitching tap - like a blinking eye, except in his foot.

"Never seen this one," I nodded, scanning the details on the back of the video box. "Any good?"

"Oh yeah; just as good as the first," he says.

"Now there was a film," says me.

"Oh, you liked the first? Must keep an eye out for that one for you."

"Really?" I says. "Janey, that'd be great!"

A silence descended, and the awl-fella just sat there fidgeting; rubbing his hands together in slippery prayer. I wanted to go, but I just didn't seem to know how to make the break.

"Do you ever play with yourself," he suddenly asked. (He was staring at the palm of his left hand with this mad preoccupied glare, and I deduced that the question was in fact meant for me.) "What?" I feebly laughed.

"Does it ever go hard?" he whispered, his desperate eyes fleetingly turned towards me. "Your penis."

"Uh, yeah; sometimes," I gulped.

"Ah, I'd say you do! With thighs like that sure you'd have to, wouldn't you?"

And his hand was on my left thigh, just stationary at first, then slipping down my inside-leg in circular motion. His little finger kept jutting out, and nudging my balls. I could feel it through my jeans.

"Looks like rain," I says.

I gaped at the sky a moment, concentrating on the wide expanse that I might somehow lose myself in it; like, oblivion would be nice. Oblivion and collapse upwards.

And his hand was at my groin: he was squeezing the fold in my jeans that buckled every time I sat down. He had it between fingers and thumb, and glanced at me each time he gave a little pinch. I don't know; he must have thought he had something else. It didn't matter: I felt myself grow hard.

"Looks like rain," I repeated, again diverting my gaze elsewhere.

I heard my fly gradually pulled down; it sounded like a stifled fart grudgingly released. I almost laugh at the thought. But his hand is in my underpants then, his arm reaching in like a soft JCB. He cups my balls first, squashing my cock against them, then slowly dragged his hand back out. My cock comes with it. The cold air is almost soothing.

I'm well hard then, and the awl-fella grasps my erection; lightly at first, then with a stronger grip as he begins his sweaty tugs. They're slow to start, then settle to a firm pumping rhythm. The rub of the zip is sharp against me, but it's sort of nice. I'm startled though by the sight of my prick a second. I almost pull back in horror - my knob for the first time slightly protruding. It's like an open wound, something internal. Had he hurt me? No, everything was fine: I was a good boy.

"That's a good boy," he says, smiling at me.

I met his gaze an instant: he looked kind of sad. And I don't want to think about him. I seemed to be frozen in a moment or something, shoving my mind elsewhere. Thinking anything but him. Thinking, I don't know: my life. All this stuff that happens, for the best. Like getting up, or putting down the budgie. Twelve gauge; one shot. Burial just seems silly then. All the best, Joe. The best.

And there's this feeling of acceleration then; a rush of warm glow. And for a split second I know what's happening: a bone grinding over a cog of soap, or sliding against it; frothed suds. And there's something wet and hot slipping down my penis, over yer man's hand.

"Cum," I muttered wide-eyed. "It's mine."

He gently wiped me off with a tissue; tucked me in.

"There," he said, "all set now. All set for the cinema."

I briefly rubbed my nose, and scratched the side of my head. The fucker just sat there and watched me a while. Don't know what the hell he was up to, but when I met his gaze again, it seemed like I just had to cry. I didn't.

"I've to bring back my bum," he said softly. "It's got a crack in it."

Things were silent then. I could almost hear the flap of stone wings. He chuckled nervously a time, rocking back and forth a bit, his hands slipping up and down his own thighs for a change.

"So, what you going to see," he asked. "Another action film?"

"Dunno," I hummed.

He touched the side of my head. I pulled away and quickly converted a sob to a sniffle; it sounded like a collision of bubbles in my nose.

"Well, I'll work on that video for you; probably have it next week if I see you."

"Yeah," I mumbled.

He's gone ten minutes and it lashes down. I could still smell the beer and the old-spice; and the scented page I had ripped from one of the glossy magazines from which my sister had torn the covers and sneaked home. It was down my vest - a sample advertisement for Fahrenheit. I felt sick. Wet too, soaked to the skin. And I was thinking about Jay then, with that sleeping man on the bus; suddenly hoping he was all right. Jay, not the man. And it was pissing down like mad. Unfamiliar clouds so massive it was impossible to see the floated blue.

David Murphy lives in North County Dublin and has two grown-up children. He finally gave up the day job in 2003 and has been writing full-time ever since. The novel *Longevity City*, due this summer from Five Star, is the second of his science fiction novel to be published in America. The first, *Arkon Chronicles*, appeared in 2003. Some of his best short stories to date were gathered in an Irish collection, *Lost Notes* (Aeon Press 2004).

This story deals with one of the author's favourite themes: the consequences of living in a society where to be fashionable is deemed more important than other, more profound, values.

Everyone This, Nobody That

David Murphy

At first, I found Monica's fetish for hankering attractive. It was an interest she shared with her closest colleague, Trish, at the fashion house where they both worked. In the first weeks I knew her, she and Trish attended two hankerings, both minor. When she asked me to hanker with her - at the mother of them all, an event she had already attended once - I was flabbergasted. More than that, I wondered how I could afford it.

She volunteered to pay. Her career in the fashion business (behind the catwalk, though I believe she had the face and body for a career on it) had little to do with earning money. An old friend of mine, George, once famously called her a Sloan Ranger. I chided him for his outdated terminology, putting his opinion of Monica down to jealousy. So it was that I, a grafter in a retail park computer company, a once proud socialist, found myself sitting in the back seat of a limo, a beautiful woman by my side. In the distance, the theatre beckoned like an iridescent fishing lure spinning ever closer.

"I haven't eaten all day," she said as our car pulled in.

Something in my eyes prompted her to add, "Don't worry, Cal. Nobody eats on Oscar Day. Everyone indulges at the parties afterwards."

Monica did not notice my annoyance. Everyone this, nobody that: that sort of talk gets my hackles up. She failed to notice because she was checking her shoulders for dandruff. Not that she needed to check. She looked stunning. I hoped the pins and boob-tape would hold her in her dress as crosswinds pummeled us on our way out of the car. She waved royally, walking along the red carpet past wedges of fans, wannabees and photographers. None of them paid me any attention, just as well considering how self-conscious I felt. Something my mother used to say floated into my mind; about it being far from this I was reared. She would have made a fuss had she lived long enough to see her son in a monkey suit. I took Monica's hand and led her into the foyer. Security men, recognising who she was coming as, stepped aside to let her past. One of them leaned forward to check the discreet badge in my lapel with a tiny hand-held scanner. I had opted to go as a member of the audience. Us Ordinary Joes had been known to fake our ID.

Once inside, it was all I had expected, and more.

"Can't you feel the speculation?" Monica was breathless. "It's so rife! There are many potential upsets, especially in the four major categories."

I had trouble recalling what exactly the four majors were - a difficulty alien to most attendees, to judge by their relaxed demeanour. I had three categories worked out when Monica nudged my elbow, pointing with her eyes to a suave-looking man walking through the door.

"Know who he is?"

The likeness was remarkable, the pencil-thin moustache a giveaway.

"Frankly, my dear," I guided Monica to a wine waiter, "I don't give a damn."

One of the few movie quotes I know brought a smile to her face as we sipped two flutes of bubbly. The smile stayed with her, not because of Clark Gable, but because we stood awhile drinking in the atmosphere. She was with the beautiful people, in their most perfect habitat on her night of nights, and she was the most beautiful of all. For a moment I was happy, glad to be part of the latest craze.

"You should have hankered fully, Cal, rather than being just an invited guest."

"Thought I'd dip my toes before jumping in."

"To hanker properly you have to be someone else, not a member of the audience. You should have come as your favourite actor. I would have paid for it."

I grunted and counted the bubbles in my glass.

"Nobody's wearing anything outrageous this year. Thank goodness for that."

"Restraint must be this year's theme," I said.

She gave me that funny look. But she was right. Nothing was over the top. If anything, hers was the most revealing dress. It stopped just short of being gauche, and was attracting some attention, especially from a few older men standing nearby.

"Barbra!"

"Juliette. Darling!"

I turned. Trish came swanning across the floor, larger than life. From her beehive hairstyle it was obvious which Barbra she had opted for, but Monica?

"Juliette?" I ventured. "You mean Julia Rob-"

"Oh my God!" Trish gasped as she caught Monica by the hand, nearly spilling her champagne.

"I can't take him anywhere," hissed Monica. "He didn't want me to tell. He wanted to guess."

Now that I'd made an ass of myself, I decided to ham it up. "You mean you're not here as Julia Roberts?"

"Oh my God!"

Trish's repetition was becoming tiresome. Monica leaned toward me and explained, "Juliette Binoche, winner of best supporting actress for The English Patient. Nominated, but did not win, for Chocolat."

I hid behind my champage glass again and let them chat. Thankfully, it was time to take our seats. "Juliette?" I offered her an arm to link with. That brought her smile back, though not as effusively as before.

We had barely warmed our seats when she said, "We're in the right part of the auditorium, not up there with the cheapo's."

I craned my neck. With an orbital sweep my eyes took in the balcony and the high, imposing ceiling. "Impressive," I said, finding myself spellbound by the ultimate theatre of dreams.

"Recognise anyone?"

I looked around. On the other side of the central aisle, not far from Barbra Streisand, an unmistakable Marilyn Monroe.

"Lookalikes are obvious, Cal. They go as the same person each time. Others are more difficult. There, third row back, five seats in from the left. Who's that man?"

Also audience gazing, he had turned in our direction. I studied him hard but his face was a mystery to me.

"It's not fair to ask who he is when you haven't heard his voice. I heard him speak last time. Very posh."

My face remained blank as an Oscar statuette.

"Richard Burton, stupid. Nominated seven times, never successful. That's the most ever nominations without a win, a record he shares with Peter O Toole."

Monica's encyclopedic knowledge did not faze me, though the presence of a seven-times nominee worried me in a different way. "How long will this go on for... Juliette?"

"Three hours - half an hour less than the historic Academy Awards. There are fewer technical gongs, apart from costume design, and none of the nerdy stuff like Best Sound Editing or Best Live Action Short. Has to be like that, with so many multiple nominees."

Absence of technical awards cheered me, though the prospect of each nominee having all nominations listed did not. Juliette's category, Best Supporting Actress, contained thirteen nominations - her two plus eleven between the three other nominees. This meant her odds of winning were 13/2, longer than at the traditional Oscars. Experience, in the form of her chagrin, had taught me never to refer to the traditional Oscars as real, but to always use a euphemism such as her own personal favourite: historic.

Juliette was not successful this time. She took it well, having told me beforehand that the selection committee was notoriously biased toward big names. When a multiple winner like Katherine Hepburn turns up in your category, chances are she'll win again. Though it didn't always happen like that. This was the excitement of it, she said, not knowing whose turn it might be. That and the thrill of seeing your face burned in on the nomination clips on the big screen.

The evening went well. Steve Martin played a host of devastating wit. Instead of tacky dance routines, we were treated to a number of tight, tasteful songs by impersonators of the highest calibre. The speeches, which I had been dreading, were remarkably restrained. Nobody threw a Paltrow or a Berry. Winners untimely enough to stray beyond their allotted thirty seconds were drowned out by the orchestra. The half minute rule did have one entertaining side-effect: everyone spoke very fast.

The mechanics of the ceremony seemed clear when Monica explained them to me. The nominee's age was irrelevant. Portray them in their twenties, or depending on your years, impersonate them at the end of their careers. At an interlude Monica showed me a photo of Binoche. She resembled her in many ways and was the correct age, yet it was uncanny how many of the non-looka-like nominees adopted the mannerisms and persona of their subjects. Take Judy Garland. I recognised her through a combination of garish make-up and a bottle protruding from her handbag. Her companion, young enough to be a daughter, had short black hair. Their relationship seemed rather tetchy if their demeanour at our après-ceremony table was anything to go by.

"Don't worry," Juliette reassured me with a whisper. "Those two are always like that. Judy had to be content with an honorary Oscar. She's never forgiven her daughter for winning the real thing."

A rare silence fell on Judy Garland, Barbra Streisand, Juliette, and the four others sharing our table. I chose that moment to lead the conversation. "I must say, Lisa, that was one great performance in Cabaret. Did you win an Oscar for that role?"

Her doe-like eyes expanded like gas balloons. Her ruby lips pursed. She looked away. So did everyone else at our table, except Garland, who slugged back her gin and banged her glass on the table. With an overdone glint in her eye, she laughed: "Guess you're not well up in the knowledge department, honey. Cabaret got eight Awards. Of course Little Missy here walked away with a gong."

"It's okay for not knowing," her daughter glared at me. "Not everyone is an expert."

"At least nobody did a Brando tonight," Juliette said, quickly. I thought better of digging more holes and let them chatter on without me. Juliette seemed ashamed to look my way, preferring the animated conversation of Barbra Streisand's companion, a man by the name of Jeff. Probably Goldblum, one of the few celluloid faces I could put a name to, though something about this Jeff did not seem right. Between the champagne and the whisky I was getting beyond caring. I let my attention wander to the exotic people at other tables, lit up as they were in the stark spotlight of this crazy, twisted reality.

My eyes did my thinking. The men looked like they had been cast in bronze. It was a wonder they were not hunched over by the weight of their jewellery and their puffed-up wallets. Some were unspeakably wealthy, so many Tom Hanks's and John Fords shelling out small fortunes to have a better chance of winning. The current rate ranged from two grand to be in the audience up to fifty for impersonating Walt Disney - or Bob Hope, who had presented the historic Oscars thirteen times (hosting was allocated not by the committee, but by lottery).

I wondered how many hundred speeches would go unheard.

These were not my kind of people, these hankerers. To them it scarcely mattered that their Oscars did not have eight hundred million viewers, nor that this was not the real theatre, but a phony one, dressed, like them, to kill. What counted was the peer kudos of being there. It must have cost Monica twenty grand for both of us. She still chatted to Jeff, and looked very happy. It wasn't her beauty that drew my eyes. An aura surrounded her, a radiance from somewhere - possibly just from being here. Other women had it, too. Their beauty stopped my breath. Indigo was obviously the new black, if their dresses were anything to go by. As for the flesh, I had never seen such tanning, styling, dieting, buffing, preening, plucking... So much effort to look so fabulous. A lady at the next table drew my gaze, so attractive was she in an effortless kind of way. I heard her name and turned to Juliette, hoping to drag her attention away from Goldblum.

"Look. That's Lauren Bacall at that other table."

"I know." Juliette shrugged. "I spoke to her last time. She's a loser, famous for being the hottest favourite never to have won an Oscar. Some people like being losers. Sad, really."

Her dismissive tone fazed me. I turned to look at Bacall again. Juliette's voice whispered in my ear: "The Mirror Has Two Faces was the Academy's last chance to honour her after her long career. Biggest shock in Hollywood history when the envelope for Best Supporting Actress was opened and they chose not to award it. Gave it to me instead," she grinned.

I knew nothing about The Mirror Has Two Faces. What I did know was that I was staring at the Bacall of To Have And Have Not. I watched her shake her wavy blonde mane and stub out a cigarette. I read her sultry lips as she asked those at her table, "Anybody got a match?" A man of middling age handed her a book of matches. I wondered if there was a huskiness to her voice and tried to make sense of what Juliette had said about losers. Something in Bacall's character, that strange fusion of hard sex and open vulnerability, made me think that the only people here that I could get on with were losers... Seemed ironic to me that Bacall had been pipped by my girlfriend. It started me thinking that perhaps there was a lesson in this somewhere.

I knew I was getting maudlin. I turned my shoulder on Lauren Bacall and tried to mingle at my own table. I tapped Juliette's arm to get her attention, so engrossed was she in what-ever Jeff Goldblum was saying.

"Darling," she said, "Jeff's been telling the funniest jokes!"

She asked him to repeat them. I listened. Whatever humour the man had was lost on me, but in his telling I noticed familiar-ities, like the set of his jaw, a certain jerkiness to his head move-ments. Then I realised who the joke-teller was. It was not Goldblum at all.

Starman had come back down to Earth and was telling a Polish joke.

We finally jettisoned Jeff Bridges at four in the morning at a taxi rank. Monica seemed reluctant to let him go. She was not talkative in the cab except to remind me: "Don't call me that. Say Juliette."

I did, especially in bed, hoping it might arouse her. She flicked my hand away with a sullen, "You nearly ruined the whole night. We were with stars from every era and you fucked everything up."

"I'm sorry," I muttered, moving over to the cold part of the sheet.

Next day Monica looked me bitterly in the eye. "Time we stopped playing games, Cal. You and I are growing apart. You better go. We both need the distance."

Who was I to argue? The sleepless space of the previous night had brought it home to me that we were not suited. She had obviously been thinking the same thing.

"Goodbye... Juliette." I stood beside my car and it crammed with all my belongings.

Wordlessly, she stepped back and closed the door of her townhouse behind her.

My good friend George and his wife Rhia took me in for a few days to tide me over until I could find a place of my own. During my first night there, after too many malts, I confided to George that he been right to call Monica a Sloan Ranger, though I still berated him for his out-dated terminology. On my second night, after an unsuccessful day spent flat-hunting, I glimpsed several issues of Hankerer, Inc in their magazine rack. When I scoffed at hankering - typical me, I couldn't keep it in - they seemed preoccupied for the rest of the evening. George wouldn't even come to the pub that night, very unusual for him. "Go out yourself," he said, and I did.

Next day I found a comfortable flat not far from work. I moved in the same evening, conscious that I had overstayed my welcome with George and Rhia. That night, sorting through my stuff, I found three of Monica's CD's in among box-loads of my own. Next morning I put them in the glove compartment, making a mental note to drop them at her place whenever I might pass by.

Hankering was gaining a hold on my colleagues at the computer company, too. They could talk of little else. It scared me the way it was becoming very incorrect to question it. It seemed like a grip, a noose, was tightening, encompassing everyone. Scepticism like mine was increasingly no longer an option.

One week after moving into my flat, a business call brought me within sight of Monica's road. Rush-hour traffic was painful so I pulled in to a convenient parking spot. I thought about dropping the discs through her letterbox but changed my mind and rang the doorbell. At five in the afternoon I figured she'd be in.

"Cal!"

"Hello, Monnie."

For a moment she looked startled. Other than that she seemed okay. Her hair was the way I remembered it from the Oscars. Though her dress was different, it exuded the same sense of glamour as the creation she had worn on our last night. Strange clothing to wear, I thought, at this time of the day. In the doorstep exchange that followed, the obligatory How-have-you-been-keeping? leading to the compulsory Fine, I began to sense something from her, an air that was not real, not right. Ignoring it, I waved the CD's under her nose. "Thought you might want these."

"Y-yes. Actually, I found something belonging to you. Your box of brushes and paints."

I hadn't dabbled in watercolour for months, and only then recalled putting the painting set behind her piano.

"Wait here." She half closed the door on me, forgetting the discs.

I forgot about them too, until I saw them in my hand and decided to follow her in. Old longings haunted me down her hallway, as far as the sitting room. The longing stopped when she heard me walking in. She turned from the piano, a panicky look rooting across her face.

"Hello Cal."

One glance at the hard set of the jaw, the jerky flick of the head, and I knew who it was.

"Em, do you remember Jeff?"

Of course I remembered him.

"Juliette's been telling me about you."

He was walking toward me, hand outstretched. Greetings, Earthling.

"Juliette? You mean Monica. You're not still playing that game, are you, Monnie?"

In the periphery of my eye, the coffee table was strewn with celebrity mags, fashion glossies, and the latest hankering guides. More of them than when I'd lived here. I noticed one of the celebrity-surgery supplements that came with the latest issues.

"Cal, everyone's doing it. Nobody sees any harm in it."

There she went again. Everyone this, nobody that. Something snapped.

"What are you up for now?" My voice was harsh, loud, almost a shout. "A Bafta? A Brit?"

"Cal. You don't understand-"

"-A Tony? A Grammy?"

"It's all the rage, Cal. Everyone's doing it. It's uncool not to."

"That's all you care about, isn't it? Image. Surface. Gloss. Nothing else matters. This is pathetic!" A sweep of my hand took in all of her magazines and guides.

"I think you'd better go." Starman stepped closer, finger-pointing at me, then at the door.

"Jeff, don't." With one hand she held him back and with the other shoved the art box at my chest.

"He's not Jeff Bridges, and you're not Juliette Binoche!"

"Just go." She rammed the art box further into my chest.

I took it in my hands and turned on my heels. As a parting shot I couldn't resist, "And the Oscar goes to... Jeff Bridges, the fastest mover in all of Tinseltown."

I heard her hold him back again, her voice rattling down the hallway. "Get out!" she shrieked. "Get out!"

Work kept me sane for more than a fortnight. Even in the busiest periods Monica was never far from my thoughts. Night after night I sat in my lonely flat, head and heart bursting with empty feelings. I felt like a religious nut losing his faith. It was for the best that we had split yet it pained me to think her mind was blotted out by this caricature of a lifestyle - a dreamy, insubstantial lifestyle fostered by dozens of hanker guides and agencies springing up like jungle shoots. The growing popularity of hanker-surgery was something I could not tolerate. The experience I had gone through with Monnie and her phony celebrity-identity left me with no desire to meet other people. Hankering was happening all over town. I sought escape in music and the occasional documentary.

There were nights when the sun slipped too quickly below the city skyline, when there was nothing on the channels and I had no ears for music. I would go to bed early, waiting for darkness to come, to release me from the zillion what-ifs flitting in my head. I convinced myself that I was working so hard I needed extra sleep. One of those nights someone rang my flat-bell. I scrambled out of bed and hobbled downstairs. No silhouette in the porch. Cautiously, I opened the door and looked out. No one. A shiver came from somewhere, resonating through me in the mild autumn night. A cat screamed in the distance. Something moved behind me. I swivelled. She was standing right behind me.

"Time to get blanked, Cal."

Her face, the dead set of her eyes, broke on me the coldest sweat.

"People everywhere are getting blanked."

I almost fell backwards down the steps to the pavement. Instinctively I grasped the garden railing to stay upright.

"I know who you can be, Cal."

She was gliding across the porch toward me.

"It won't hurt."

She floated after me as I bolted down the steps. I ran into the street, a fugitive from my own doorstep. City lights towered overhead, bending their arcs to illuminate me, chasing me until I ran so far the city faded with every stride. Cover of darkness was no use. She still followed, a ghost gliding on tarmac. Brambles ripped my face as I blundered off the road. I hid out in the woods. Wolves howled, rain pelted me. My throat ached, so ragged was my breath. Terror stalked the trees, my legs hurt from wild running. Everywhere I looked she was there, circling, watching, waiting. Police lights and helicopters lit up the woods. In the distance I heard the howls of sniffer dogs.

I swam against the tide of a mighty river and nearly drowned. I hauled myself up the far side, heart jumping like a bullfrog, clambered across a ridge and saw a row of houses. I was back where I had started, at the fraying edge of the city. Sprinting again, I hoped to lose her in suburbia. Pains battered my chest but fear kept me going. I turned a corner and ran into a pile of dustbins on the pavement. I tried to hurdle them but the clatter of metal on concrete proved my undoing. The deadly sound of converging sirens had me sprinting again. I tilted full pelt into an alleyway, only just stopping myself from scudding into a brick wall.

I had run into a dead end.

Harsh, gritty breath tore my throat like strips of gravel. My heart wrenched loose from my ribs with every pounding beat. Bent over, unable to stand, legs quivering like tree stumps in an earthquake, I lifted my gaze.

"It's no use, Cal."

She stood at the head of the alley. Her head creaked unnaturally to her left. A man stepped from the shadows.

"Looks like you've captured him at last, Officer," I heard her say.

Sweat dripped from my forehead into my eyes. The gloom of the alley nearly blinded me. I was nearly collapsing from the chase. Through salty blinks I saw enough to recognise the man standing beside her. There was no mistaking that grin. Self-satisfied, in an understated way.

My favourite actor, Mr Tommy Lee Jones, took a scissors from his pocket and pointed it at me. The scissors forked, silver blades lurching forward, growing large in a cartoonish way. The huge scissors reached across the alley and had me in an instant, pinching my arm tight, pinning it against a brick wall. The blades had expanded so much that Binoche and Jones were each able to take a handle in both their hands. Then I understood. If Tommy Lee Jones was Officer Gerárd, I was the One-Armed Man.

Suddenly sleeveless, I watched the skin on my arm bulge. It turned purple as the icy blades pressed into my naked, tender flesh. I could do nothing but stare at my own amputation. Veins stood like ridges. My bones compacted as silver metal pinched tighter, constricting me in a sharp, steely grip, crushing me like a sausage in a vice. Still my skin held out, though my arm looked like twin balls of blood in balloons of pale, skein-like flesh. I glanced pleadingly at Binoche and Jones. They shoved the handles closer together, gorging on me with their eyes, a crazed look on their faces. I felt then the give of soft flesh. The skin on my arm exploded in a slow-motion way. In my throat I felt a rising scream. My eyes could not leave my arm, so drawn were they to the cutting… Binoche and Jones heard my silent scream. I know they heard it. As blood spurted, my open mouth vented its silence with a shriek so blood-curdling it blew darkness from the alley, illuminating me in a light that was shrill and white, the light of purest pain.

As the scream came I pitched sideways, sweating and shivering in the creamy light of dawn that streamed in through the window of my flat. I sat up in bed, breathing hard. I felt my arm hanging from me, unsevered. I stayed upright like a terrified child, my heart not slowing for minutes. My head tried to come to terms with the worst nightmare I had ever had. I glanced at my bedside clock. It was 5.28am.

I turned up for work early, freshly showered, looking almost as if I'd had a good night's rest. Our receptionist, Nikki, had gone for the full surgery makeover. There was no mistaking her coy look as she welcomed me from behind her desk. I noticed my colleagues waxing on about hankering even more than usual. At coffee break I saw the poster on the wall and realised why they were excited. It was not because our receptionist had changed into Lady Di, but because a staff hankering party was to be held that night. Everyone would be expected to attend. At lunch time the boss put his hand on my shoulder. "Who are you coming as, Cal? Star of music, stage or TV? Some other kind of celebrity? Do you want to win an Award?"

"I-I'm not sure yet."

"Have a look at these." He handed me a bundle of the latest guides. "Don't be out in the cold. Everybody wants to be there. Nobody wants to be left out."

During a lull in the office I sifted through the hanker guides, opened one and slipped it into the hard-drive. I flipped through the files until I came to a star with a mischievous twinkle in his eye. For one night only, it said. I put my elbows on the desk and cupped my chin in my hands. One night only. My own reflection peered out from behind the portrait on the screen, eerily matching it like a dissolve between two criminal faces in one of those documentaries about forensics. One night. If I didn't make my move now somebody else might reserve it. There would be no availability then until the next day. Maybe just this once. What harm could there be in just one night? This was the only star for me. My finger hovered for less than a second before pressing the button with a tremulous 'yes'.

It took me a while to download all the tips on favourite sayings, postures, mannerisms, facial expressions. I thought I knew most of them but it's amazing how much homework needs to be done for correct hankering. Surgical makeover was not an option, given the shortage of time, not that I wanted that for a single night. My hair was similar to his both in colour and style. Though my nose was not prominent enough, it was of a size to let me get away with it.

Now that I'd decided to commit, my excitement grew. At lunchtime I phoned a theatrical shop to reserve what I needed. They had it all and were remaining open until six. I wouldn't even have to hurry after work to get there. As afternoon turned to evening I found myself getting on better with my colleagues than I had in months. They seemed friendlier, as if I had suddenly become a team player. I felt happier than I had been in weeks.

There seemed a certain karma about the way the day was

shaping up, a coming together of things to convince me that my decision to hanker was the right thing to do. The party would be for me a trial run. As the day wore on I even contemplated undergoing surgery if things worked out well that night. Who knows, I might re-introduce myself to Juliette and Jeff... well, Juliette anyway.

At twenty to six I picked up the suit. It fitted perfectly. The glasses were exact replicas. The moustache looked real enough to shave. I spent a few hours learning off my homework before taking a cab to the office party.

I made a grand entrance, brandishing my cigar with an appropriate flourish. Everyone turned to look. The party music faded in one of those heart-stopping cinematic moments. My heart stopped too. What if I had it wrong? Would my own nose look ridiculous? I knew I had got it right when I saw the smile on the boss's face as he stepped toward me. Everyone else smiled too when they saw him lead the way. He spread his arms to welcome me with a bear-like embrace. He took my hand and shook it warmly. "So glad you could make it," he said. "Now, the drinks are on me, Groucho."

William Trevor was born in 1928 in County Cork, to Protestant parents. Because he belonged to a minority religious group, Trevor says he developed a sense of being on the 'outside looking in.' His fiction articulates the tensions between Irish Protestant landowners and Catholic tenants. He is the author of several collections and novels, among which Whitbread Novel Award winners *The Children of Dynmouth* (1976) and *Fools of Fortune* (1983). *Felicia's Journey* (1994), about an Irish girl who becomes the victim of a sociopath, won both the Whitbread Book of the Year and the Sunday Express Book of the Year awards.

His early story 'Miss Smith' is a chilling reminder how ordinary evil can be.

Miss Smith

William Trevor

One day Miss Smith asked James what a baby horse was called and James couldn't remember. He blinked and shook his head. He knew, he explained, but he just couldn't remember. Miss Smith said:

"Well, well, James Machen doesn't know what a baby horse is called."

She said it loudly so that everyone in the classroom heard. James became very confused. He blinked and said: "Pony, Miss Smith?"

"Pony! James Machen says a baby horse is a pony! Hands up everyone who knows what a baby horse is."

All the right arms in the room, except James's and Miss Smith's shot upwards. Miss Smith smiled at James.

"Everyone knows," she said. "Everyone knows what a baby horse is called except James."

James thought: I'll run away. I'll join the tinkers and live in a tent.

"What's a baby horse called?" Miss Smith asked the class and the class shouted:

"Foal, Miss Smith."

"A foal, James," Miss Smith repeated. "A baby horse is a foal, James dear."

"I knew Miss Smith. I knew but-"

Miss Smith laughed and the class laughed, and afterwards nobody would play with James because he was so silly to think that a baby horse was a pony.

James was an optimist about Miss Smith. He thought it might be different when the class went on the summer picnic or sat tightly together at the Christmas party, eating cakes and biscuits and having their mugs filled from big enamel jugs. But it never was different. James got left behind when everyone was racing across the fields at the picnic and Miss Smith had to wait impatiently, telling the class that James would have to have his legs stretched. And at the party she heaped his plate with seedcake because she imagined, so she said, that he was the kind of child who enjoyed such fare.

Once James found himself alone with Miss Smith in the classroom. She was sitting at her desk correcting some homework. James was staring in front of him, admiring a fountain pen that the day before his mother had bought for him. It was a small fountain pen, coloured purple and black and white. James believed it to be elegant.

It was very quiet in the classroom. Soundlessly Miss Smith's red pencil ticked and crossed and underlined. Without looking up, she said, "Why don't you go out and play?"

"Yes, Miss Smith," said James. He walked to the door, clipping his pen into his pocket. As he turned the handle he heard Miss

Smith utter a sound of irritation. He turned and saw that the point of her pencil had broken. "Miss Smith, you may borrow my pen. You can fill it with red ink. It's quite a good pen."

James crossed the room and held out his pen. Miss Smith unscrewed the cap and prodded at the paper with the nib. "What a funny pen, James!" she said. "Look it can't write."

"There's no ink in it," James explained. "You've got to fill it with red ink, Miss Smith."

But Miss Smith smiled and handed the pen back. "What a silly boy you are to waste your money on such a poor pen!"

"But I didn't-"

"Come along now, James, aren't you going to lend me your pencil sharpener?"

"I haven't got a pencil sharpener, Miss Smith."

"No pencil sharpener? Oh James, James, you haven't got anything, have you?"

When Miss Smith married she stopped teaching, and James imagined he had escaped her forever. But the town they lived in was a small one and they often met in the street or in a shop. And Miss Smith, who at first found marriage rather boring, visited the school quite regularly. "How's James?" she would say, smiling alarmingly at him. How's my droopy, old James?"

When Miss Smith had been married for about a year she gave birth to a son, which occupied her a bit. He was a fine child, eight pounds six ounces, with a good long head and blue eyes. Miss Smith was delighted with him, and her husband, a solicitor, complimented her sweetly and bought cigars and drinks for all his friends. In time, mother and son were seen daily taking the air: Miss Smith on her trim little legs and the baby in his frilly pram. James, meeting the two, said: "Miss Smith, may I see the baby?" But Miss Smith laughed and said that she was not Miss Smith any more. She wheeled the pram rapidly away, as though the child within it might be affected by the proximity of the other.

"What a dreadful little boy that James Machen is," Miss Smith reported to her husband. "I feel so sorry for the parents."

"Do I know him? What does the child look like?"

"Small, dear, like a weasel wearing glasses. He quite gives me the creeps."

Almost without knowing it, James developed a compulsion about Miss Smith. At first it was quite a simple compulsion: just that James had to talk to God about Miss Smith every night before he went to sleep, and try to find out from God what it was about him that Miss Smith so despised. Every night he lay in bed and had his conversation, and if once he forgot it James knew that the next time he met Miss Smith she would probably say something that might make him drop down dead.

After about a month of conversation with God James discovered he had found the solution. It was so simple that he marvelled he had never thought of it before. He began to get up very early in the morning and pick bunches of flowers. He would carry them down the street to Miss Smith's house and place them on a windowsill. He was careful not to be seen, by Miss Smith or by anyone else. He knew that if anyone saw him the plan couldn't work. When he had picked all the flowers in his own garden he started to pick them from other people's gardens. He became rather clever at moving silently through the gardens, picking flowers for Miss Smith.

Unfortunately, though, on the day that James carried his thirty-first bunch of blooms to the house of Miss Smith he was observed. He saw the curtains move as he reached up to lay the flowers on the windowsill. A moment later Miss Smith, in her dressing gown, had caught him by the shoulder and pulled him into the house.

"James Machen! It would be James Machen, wouldn't it? Flowers from the creature, if you please! What are you up to, you dozy James?"

James said nothing. He looked at Miss Smith's dressing gown and thought it was particularly pretty: blue and woolly, with an edging of silk.

"You've been trying to get us into trouble," cried Miss Smith. "You've been stealing flowers all over the town and putting them at our house. You're an underhand child, James."

James stared at her and then ran away.

After that, James thought of Miss Smith almost all the time. He thought of her face when she had caught him with the flowers, and how she had afterwards told his father and nearly everyone else in town. He thought of how his father had had to say he was sorry to Miss Smith, and how his mother and father had quarrelled about the affair. He counted up all the things Miss Smith had ever said to him, and all the things she had ever done to him, like giving him seedcake at the Christmas party. He hadn't meant to harm Miss Smith as she said he had. Giving people flowers wasn't unkind: it was to show them you liked them and wanted them to like you.

"When somebody hurts you," James said to the man who came to cut the grass, "what do you do about it?"

"Well," said the man, "I suppose you hurt them back."

"Supposing you can't," James argued.

"Oh, but you always can. It's easy to hurt people."

"It's not, really," James said.

"Look," said the man, "all I've got to do is reach out and give you a clip on the ear. That'd hurt you."

"But I couldn't do that to you because you're so big. How d'you hurt someone who's bigger than you?"

"It's easier to hurt people who are weaker. People who are weaker are always the ones who get hurt."

"Can't you hurt someone who is stronger?"

The grass-cutter thought for a time. "You have to be cunning to do that. You've got to find the weak spot. Everyone has a weak spot."

"Have you got a weak spot?"

"I suppose so."

"Could I hurt you on your weak spot?"

"You don't want to hurt me, James."

"No, but just could I?"

"Yes, I suppose you could."

"Well then?"

"My little daughter's smaller than me. If you hurt her, you see, you'd be hurting me. It'd be the same, you see."

"I see," said James.

All was not well with Miss Smith. Life, which had been so happy when her baby was born, seemed now to be directed against her. Perhaps it was that the child was becoming difficult, going through a teething phase that was pleasant for no one; or perhaps it was that Miss Smith recognised in him some trait she disliked and knew that she would be obliged to watch it develop, powerless to intervene. Whatever the reason, she felt depressed. She often thought of her teaching days, of the big square schoolroom with the children's models on the shelves and the pictures of kings on the walls. Nostalgically, she recalled the feel of frosty air on her face as she rode her bicycle through the town, her mind already practising the first lesson of the day. She had loved those winter days: the children stamping their feet in the playground, the stove groaning and crackling, so red and so fierce that it had to be penned off for safety sake. It had been good to feel tired, good to bicycle home, shopping a bit on the way, home to tea and the wireless and an evening of reading by the fire. It wasn't that she regretted anything; it was just that now and again, for a day or two, she felt she would like to return to the past.

"My dear," Miss Smith's husband said, "you really will have to be more careful."

"But I am. Truly I am. I'm just as careful as anyone can be."

"Of course you are. But it's a difficult age. Perhaps, you know, you need a holiday."

"But I've had difficult ages to deal with for years-"

"Now now, my dear, it's not quite the same, teaching a class of kids."

"But it shouldn't be as difficult. I don't know-"

"You're tired. Tied to a child all day long, every day of the week, it's no joke. We'll take an early holiday."

Miss Smith did feel tired, but she knew that it wasn't tiredness that was really the trouble. Her baby was almost three, and for two years she knew she had been making mistakes with him. Yet somehow she felt that they weren't her mistakes: it was as though some other person occasionally possessed her; a negligent, worthless kind of person who was cruel, almost criminal, in her carelessness. Once she had discovered the child crawling on the pavement beside his pram: she had forgotten apparently to attach his harness to the pram hooks. Once there had been beads in his pram, hundreds of them, small and red and made of glass. A woman had drawn her attention to the danger, regarding curiously the supplier of so unsuitable a plaything. 'In his nose he was putting one, dear. And may have swallowed a dozen already. It could kill a mite, you know.' The beads were hers, but how the child had got them she could not fathom. Earlier, when he had been only a couple of months, she had come into his nursery to find an excited cat scratching at the clothes of his cot; and on another occasion she had found him eating a turnip. She wondered if she might be suffering from some kind of serious absent-mindedness, or blackouts. Her doctor told her, uncomfortably, that she was a little run down.

"I'm a bad mother," said Miss Smith to herself; and she cried as she looked at her child, warm and pretty in his sleep.

But her carelessness continued and people remarked that it was funny in a teacher. Her husband was upset and unhappy, and finally suggested that they should employ someone to look after the child. "Someone else?" said Miss Smith. "Someone else? Am I then incapable? Am I so wretched and stupid that I cannot look after my own child? You speak to me as though I were half crazy." She felt confused and sick and miserable. The marriage teetered beneath the tension, and there was no question of further children.

Then there were two months without incident. Miss Smith began to feel better; she was getting the hang of things; once again she was in control of her daily life. Her child grew and flourished. He trotted nimbly beside her, he spoke his own language, he was wayward and irresponsible, and to Miss Smith and her husband he was intelligent and full of charm. Every day Miss Smith saved up the sayings and doings of this child and duly reported them to her husband. "He is quite intrepid," Miss Smith said, and she told her husband how the child would tumble about the room, trying to stand on his head. "He has an aptitude for athletics," her husband remarked. They laughed that they, so un-athletic in their ways, should have produced so physically lively an offspring.

"And how has our little monster been today?" Miss Smith's husband asked, entering the house one evening at his usual time.

Miss Smith smiled, happy after a good, quiet day. "Like gold," she said.

Her husband smiled too, glad that the child had not been a nuisance to her and glad that his son, for his own sake, was capable of adequate behaviour. "I'll just take a peep at him," he announced, and he ambled off to the nursery.

He sighed with relief as he climbed the stairs, thankful that all was once again well in the house. He was still sighing when he opened the nursery door and smelt gas. It hissed insidiously from the unlit fire. The room was sweet with it. The child, sleeping, sucked it into his lungs.

The child's face was blue. They carried him from the room, both of them helpless and inadequate in the situation. And then they waited, without speaking, while his life was recovered, until the moment when the doctor, white-coated and stern, explained that it had been a nearer thing than he would wish again to handle.

"This is too serious," Miss Smith's husband said. "We cannot continue like this. Something must be done."

"I cannot understand-"

"It happens too often. The strain is too much for me, dear."

"I cannot understand it."

Every precaution had been taken with the gas-fire in the nursery. The knob that controlled the gas pressure was a key and the key was removable. Certainly, the control point was within the child's reach but one turned it on or off, slipped the key out of its socket and placed it on the mantelpiece. That was the simple rule.

"You forgot to take out the key," Miss Smith's husband said. In his mind an idea took on a shape that frightened him. He shied away, watching it advance, knowing that he possessed neither the emotional nor mental equipment to fight it.

"No, no, no," Miss Smith said. "I never forget it. I turned the fire off and put the key on the mantelpiece. I remember distinctly."

He stared at her, drilling his eyes into hers, hopelessly seeking the truth. When he spoke his voice was dry and weary.

"The facts speak for themselves. You cannot suggest there's another solution?"

"But it's absurd. It means he got out of his cot, turned the key, returned to bed and went to sleep."

"Or that you turned off the fire and idly turned it on again."

"I couldn't have; how could I?"

Miss Smith's husband didn't know. His imagination, like a pair of calipers, grasped the ugly thought and held it before him. The facts were on his side, he could not ignore them: his wife was deranged in her mind. Consciously or otherwise she was trying to kill their child.

"The window," Miss Smith said. "It was open when I left it. It always is, for air. Yet you found it closed."

"The child certainly could not have done that. I cannot see what you are suggesting."

"I don't know. I don't know what I am suggesting. Except that I don't understand."

"He is too much for you, dear, and that's all there is to it. You must have help."

"We can't afford it."

"Be that as it may, we must. We have the child to think of, if not ourselves."

"But one child! One child cannot be too much for anyone. Look, I'll be extra careful in future. After all, it is the first thing like this that has happened for ages."

"I'm sorry, dear. We must advertise for a woman."

"Please-"

"Darling, I'm sorry. It's no use talking. We have talked enough and it has got us nowhere. This is something to be sensible about."

"Please let's try again."

"And in the meanwhile? In the meanwhile our child's life must be casually risked day in, day out?"

"No, no."

Miss Smith pleaded, but her husband said nothing further. He pulled hard on his pipe, biting it between his jaws, unhappy and confused in his mind.

Miss Smith's husband did indeed advertise for a woman to see to the needs of their child, but it was, in fact, unnecessary in the long run to employ her. Because on his third birthday, late in the afternoon, the child disappeared. Miss Smith had put him in the garden. It was a perfectly safe garden: he played there often. Yet when she called him for his tea he did not come; and when she looked for the reason she found that he was not there. The small gate that led to the fields at the back of the house was open. She had not opened it; she rarely used it. Distractedly, she thought he must have managed to release the catch himself. "That is quite impossible," her husband said. "It's too high and too stiff." He looked at her oddly, confirmed in his mind that she wished to be rid of her child. Together they tramped the fields with the police, but although they covered a great area and were out for most of the night they were unsuccessful.

When the search continued in the light of the morning it was a search without hope, and the hopelessness in time turned into the fear of what discovery would reveal. "We must accept the facts," Miss Smith's husband said, but she alone continued to hope. She dragged her legs over the wide countryside, seeking a miracle but finding neither trace nor word of her child's wanderings.

A small boy, so quiet she scarcely noticed him, stopped her once by a sawmill. He spoke some shy salutation, and when she blinked her eyes at his face she saw that he was James Machen. She passed him by, thinking only that she envied him his life, that for him to live and her child to die was proof indeed of a mocking Providence. She prayed to this Providence, promising a score of resolutions if only all would be well.

But nothing was well, and Miss Smith brooded on the thought that her husband had not voiced. I released the gate myself. For some reason I have not wanted this child. God knows I loved him, and surely it wasn't too weak a love? Is it that I've loved so many other children that I have none left that is real enough for my own? Pathetic, baseless, theories flooded into Miss Smith's mind. Her thoughts floundered and collapsed into wretched chaos.

"Miss Smith," James said, "would you like to see your baby?"

He stood at her kitchen door, and Miss Smith, hearing the words, was incapable immediately of grasping their meaning. The sun, reflected in the kitchen, was mirrored again in the child's glasses. He smiled at her, more confidently than she remembered, revealing a silvery wire stretched across his teeth.

"What did you say?" Miss Smith asked.

"I said, would you like to see your baby?"

Miss Smith had not slept for a long time. She was afraid to sleep because of the nightmares. Her hair hung lank about her shoulders, her eyes were dead and seemed to have fallen back deeper into her skull. She stood listening to this child, nodding her head up and down, very slowly, in a mechanical way. Her left hand moved gently back and forth on the smooth surface of her kitchen table.

"My baby?" Miss Smith said. "My baby?"

"You have lost your baby," James reminded her.

Miss Smith nodded a little faster.

"I will show you," James said.

He caught her hand and led her from the house, through the garden and through the gate into the fields. Hand in hand they walked through the grass, over the canal bridge and across the warm, ripe meadows.

"I will pick you flowers," James said and he ran to gather poppies and cowparsley and blue, beautiful cornflowers.

"You give people flowers," James said, "because you like them and you want them to like you."

She carried the flowers and James skipped and danced beside her, hurrying her along. She heard him laughing, she looked at him and saw his small weasel face twisted into a merriment that frightened her.

The sun was fierce on Miss Smith's neck and shoulders. Sweat gathered on her forehead and ran down her cheeks. She felt it on her body, tightening her clothes to her back and thighs. Only the child's hand was cool, and beneath her fingers she assessed its strength, wondering about its history. Again the child laughed.

On the heavy air his laughter rose and fell; it quivered through his body and twitched lightly in his hand. It came as a giggle, then a breathless spasm; it rose like a storm from him; it rippled to gentleness; and it pounded again like the firing of guns in her ear. It would not stop. She knew it would not stop. As they walked together on this summer's day the laughter would continue until they arrived at the horror, until the horror was complete.

Michael Carroll was born in 1966 in Dublin. He is the author of the SF novel *The Throwback* (2001), and ten other novels, mostly young adult SF & F and women's romantic fiction under the pseudonym Jaye Carroll.

'In Dublin's Veracity', published in *Albedo One*, was shortlisted for the Aisling Gheal Award. The author says it took him two days to get his brain back in order after writing the story.

In Dublin's Veracity

Michael Carroll

I spent all day Thursday crossing back and forth on Nassau street, about a hundred yards up from the entrance to Trinity College. I wanted to improve my spatial awareness, and become one with the traffic.

A man who works in Judge Roy Bean's phoned the police. They didn't arrest me, though. When I saw the Gardaí approaching I stood still on the pavement and pretended to be looking at the clouds. Out of the corner of my eye I could see the man from Judge Roy Bean's talking to the Gardaí. One of them was looking in my direction and taking notes. I couldn't see what the notes were because he was quite a bit away and he was only using a pencil. I think he was writing a poem about the number seven bus stop.

I don't know why I think that. It just seems like it might be true. I have never written a poem about a bus stop myself, but if I were to, it would probably be about the number seven. Of course, the number eight bus also stops there, so I might be wrong.

When the Garda with the notebook came over to me and asked if I was all right, I said that I'd dropped my gold pelican pin on the street earlier that day, and that I was looking for it. I've never given blood even once, so I hoped he wouldn't ask me to hold out my arm to show him the needle marks, because I didn't have any. The Garda seemed to believe me, because he put away his poem and asked mc to be careful. Then he said that I should use a pelican crossing, and he laughed the way policemen do when they're trying to catch you out.

I said I would be careful. I walked home but nothing happened on the way. Then I went in and lay on the floor to sleep. I would have slept in the bed, but I couldn't remember where it was.

That night I dreamed that I walked barefoot across an endless black marble floor. Behind me I could see where my damp footprints had marked a rough dotted line stretching to the horizon. Before me, there was nothing. I considered changing direction, but as I paused I noticed that the light was growing brighter. The air became dry and the marble warmed. Behind me, my footprints faded into mist. Above me, the sun was coming closer; it almost filled the entire sky. I reached up, and placed my palms against the surface of the sun. And I stood there for the longest time, convinced that I was the only thing that kept the light and dark apart. When I woke up the next morning I changed my jacket - which is something I do every Friday as I am a creature of habits - and went out again. The very first thing I did when I got to Rathmines was buy a pair of good strong gloves. The young girl in Dunnes who looks like Sandra Nolan from school wasn't sure at what temperature the gloves would burn, but she did assure me that they were made in Ireland.

I didn't bother with road-crossing that day, as I felt that my spatial awareness was probably at its optimum and wouldn't need to be topped up for a couple of weeks.

Instead, I walked into town and spent some time at the Garden of Remembrance. While I was there I noticed that they had installed a pool. I was surprised at that, but then remembered that they'd had a pool there last time too, so this was very likely the same one.

I was pleased to discover that the garden had lived up to its name, so I tried to remember where my bed was. Quick as a flash it came to me. In my bedroom, of course! Such connections are always obvious with hindsight.

It then occurred to me that perhaps Dublin's other parks are blessed with such powers. I called upon the Garden to give me the names of the other parks (for I could not remember any unaided) and it did so. Saint Stephen' s Green was the first. But the name didn't mean anything to me; it didn't seem to have any special powers attached to it.

Next I thought of the Phoenix Park. This is a huge park to the west of the city. West is the one on your left hand when looking at a map, provided that you have North at the top. That makes it easier to remember.

I guessed that the Phoenix Park probably had special powers. I remembered my Grandfather - the romantic fool that he was - telling me that wild deer were said to roam the park at night. Of course, in this age of reason no-one believes a word of it, but times were simpler then. The computer age has brought rationality and reality to an irrational and superstitious world.

My grandfather was killed in France during the Second World War. People are of course still getting killed in France, but it's been almost fifty years since anyone was killed in the Second World War, so I guess that's progress of a sort.

I took out my black biro and wrote "Phoenix Park" on the bench so that I would remember it. Next I wrote "Saint Stephen's Green", which I underlined and followed with a question mark, so I'd remember that I wasn't sure about it.

I decided then that the Phoenix Park was the place to start, so left the Garden and walked around Parnell Square to the number ten bus stop. The number ten is a bus that goes out to University College Dublin sometimes, and to the Phoenix Park other times. I was lucky this time, as the bus went straight to the park.

When the bus came to the stop I stood at the sign that said "Exit Only", but the driver didn't open the door so I had to go out through the entrance, I'm sure that the people getting on were secretly laughing at the sight of someone exiting by the entrance.

I wasn't sure where in the park to go for inspiration, so I just kept walking in the hope that I would spot something. Eventually I saw the place where the Pope had been when he came in 1979 to tell the young people of Ireland that he loved them, so I walked over there and stood beneath the huge white cross. Nothing happened so I concluded that I was in the wrong place, and went sort of northwards, towards the main road where the lunchtime traffic was zooming by pretending not to see the "50km" signs.

As luck (or was it providence?) would have it, I found myself coming to a small roundabout, in the very centre of which was a statue of a Phoenix. The tarmac on the side road where I walked had been freshly laid, and when I looked back I could see small fading patches of steam rising from where my grass-soaked shoes had walked. This reminded me of my dream, so I put on my made-in-Ireland gloves just in case.

The traffic was very heavy at the roundabout, and I had to use my heightened spatial awareness to cross the road. I was very nearly knocked down as I crossed - I heard a beep from an approaching car and stopped to see if it was anyone that I knew.

It wasn't but I waved anyway. Then I decided that I 'd better get out of the way, so I kept walking. The car beeped again as it passed, this time more fiercely, so I suppose that the driver had probably been trying to warn me. I still think that it would have been just as easy for him to slow down.

The roundabout didn't have any grass the way most of them do; it was cobbled, the stones rising towards the centre to make a sort of little hill, on the crest of which was the statue. The base of the statue was stepped, like an Inca pyramid, and supported a huge pillar, which in turn supported the phoenix.

I stood at the base of the statue for a while, pretending to read so that I'd just look like any normal person standing by a statue. I didn't actually have anything to read, so I pretended I did. My double-bluff must have worked, because nobody said anything.

After a while the traffic died down, and as soon as the roads were clear and there was no one in sight, I climbed up onto the base of the statue, then tried to climb the pillar. This wasn't as easy to do as you might think. Statue-climbing has never been recognised as a national sport, and no wonder. The thing was dirty and covered in bird-droppings.

I clearly remember thinking how lucky I was that I'd brought my new gloves.

After a couple of tries I gave up, and decided to sit on the top step of the base. I took off my gloves and put them down to sit on, After all, they were already smeared with bird-droppings and there was no sense in getting the backside of my pants dirty. I'd planned to go home on the bus and if it was full I'd have to stand and then everyone would see.

As soon as I sat down, something happened. I felt the blood pumping through me, and I could hear my heart beating and I was aware of every breath that I took. I was even conscious of every time I blinked. Pretty soon those feelings faded, and as they did so I noticed that there was a heavy fog developing. Even now I'm not sure if it was really a fog or if I was experiencing some form of ethereal awareness.

I don't believe in God or fairies or UFOs, but something did happen to me there on that statue. It was as though I was being consumed by the very fires from which the phoenix itself is said to have risen. I felt every cell in my body change into something better. My mind expanded to take in the park, the whole country, finally the entire universe.

I felt that every atom of every star was changing its orientation. Everything turned and pointed back to me. The cosmos was telling me in the most unequivocal manner that I was the one.

When I spoke the planets paused to listen.

When I conjectured, the galaxies nodded in compliance. When I smiled, the universe breathed a sigh of relief.

I found myself on the cobbles, standing at the base of the statue looking up. I couldn't remember climbing down, but I was wearing my gloves so I must have. If I'd fallen my gloves would have been where I'd left them.

I wiped off as much of the bird-droppings as I could, then I turned my gloves inside out so they wouldn't soil my jacket when I put them back in the pocket.

Then I walked back to the number ten bus stop, got on the bus and went back to the city. As luck would have it the bus stopped almost exactly across the road from the Garden of Remembrance, so I got off - again via the entrance, though this time there was a woman with a tweed coat getting off as well so I didn't feel quite so embarrassed - and went over to the Garden.

There was an old man sitting on the bench where I'd made the note earlier. I told him what had happened in the park, and as he got up and began to walk away he told me I was either hallucinating or on drugs. I tried to reach into his mind and use my full powers to give him a vision of what had happened to me, but it didn't work.

My note was still there on the bench. I took out my black biro and put a tick beside "Phoenix Park". The next one was "Saint Stephen' s Green", which was still underlined and followed by a question mark. I decided that it would be my next port of call.

I left the Garden and walked down O'Connell Street keeping my fingers in my ears as I passed the Savoy in case anyone leaving the cinema should - while discussing it with a friend - accidentally reveal the ending of a film I hadn't yet seen.

When I reached Trinity I remembered the man from Judge Roy Bean' s who had called the police the previous day. I decided to go in and use my powers to give him a headache. I don't normally commit acts of revenge, so I decided that it would only be a small headache.

There was a different man in Judge Roy Bean's, and he wouldn't let me in.

He told me to get lost or he would call the police. I laughed at the irony of this and decided that it would be best to leave. So I walked down Nassau Street towards Dawson Street, which was where I intended to turn towards Saint Stephen's Green.

As I neared the corner I noticed something bright lying on the road. I waited until the traffic cleared, then walked over and picked it up.

It was a small gold lapel pin in the shape of a pelican.

Laughing to myself, I walked home and climbed into my bed, which was in my bedroom.

No overview of fantastic literature in Ireland would be complete without Anne McCaffrey. Her fourteen Pern novels rank among the most popular series in either fantasy or science fiction. Born in 1926 in Cambridge Massachusets, she moved to Ireland in 1970, where she now lives in a house of her own design in Wicklow County. She has written some ninety books, countless short stories, and was named a SFWA Grand Master in February 2005.

'Velvet Fields' is a haunting science fiction story about colonists finding a place that is just too good to be true and we feel that it beautifully reflects the influence of the lush pastures of her adopted homeland on her writing.

Velvet Fields

Anne McCaffrey

Of course we moved into the cities of the planet we now know we must call Zobranoirundisi when Worlds Federated finally permitted a colony there. Although Survey had kept a watch on the planet for more than thirty years standard and the cities were obviously on a standby directive, the owners remained conspicuous by their absence. Since Resources and Supplies had agitated in council for another breadbasket planet in that sector of the galaxy and Zobranoirundisi was unoccupied, we were sent in, chartered to be self-sufficient in one sidereal year and to produce a surplus in two.

It would, therefore, have been a great misdirection of effort not to have inhabited the cities - we only moved into four - so patently suitable for humanoid life-forms. The murals that decorated a conspicuous wall in every dwelling unit gave only a vague idea of the physiology of our landlords, always depicted in an attitude of reverent obeisance toward a dominating Tree symbol so that only the backs, the rounded fuzz-covered craniums, and the suggestions of arms extended in front of the bodies were visible.

I suppose if we had not been so concerned with establishing the herds, generally breaking our necks to meet the colony charter requirements, we might have discovered sooner that there had been a gross error. The clues were there. For example, although we inhabited the cities, they could not be made fully 'operational' despite all the efforts of Dunlapil, the metropolitan engineer. Then, too, we could find no single example of the Tree, anywhere on the lush planet. But, with R&S on our backs to produce, produce, produce, we didn't take time to delve into the perplexing anomalies.

Dunlapil, with his usual urbane contempt for the botanical, quipped to Martin Chavez, our ecologist, that the Tree was the Tree of Life and therefore mythical.

"Carry the analogy further," he would tease Martin, "and it explains why the Tree worshipers" - that's what. we called them before we *knew* - "aren't around anymore. Some dissident plucked the Apple and got 'em all kicked out of the Garden of Eden."

Eden might well have been modeled on this planet, with its velvet fields, parklike forests, and rolling plains. Amid these sat lovely little cities constructed of pressed fibrous blocks tinted in pleasant colors during a manufacturing process whose nature frustrated Dunlapil as much as the absence of Trees perplexed Chavez.

So, suppressing our pervasive sense of trespassing, we moved into the abandoned dwellings, careful not to make any irreparable changes to accommodate our equipment. In fact, the only sophisticated nonindigenous equipment that I, as colony commissioner, permitted within any city was the plastisteel Comtower. I ordered the spaceport constructed beyond a low range of foothills on the rather scrubby plain at some distance from my headquarters city. An old riverbed proved an acceptable road for moving cargo to and from the port, and no one really objected to the distance. It would be far better not offend our landlords with the dirt and chaos of outer space commerce close to their pretty city.

We pastured the cattle in neatly separated velvet fields. Martin Chavez worried when close inspection disclosed that each velvet field was underpinned by its own ten-meter-thick foundation of ancient, rock-hard clay. Those same foundations housed what seemed to be a deep irrigation system.

I did ask Martin Chavez to investigate the curious absence of herbivores from a planet so perfectly suited to them. He had cat-alogued several types of omnivores, a wide variety of fowl, and a plethora of fishes. He did discover some fossil remains of herbi-vores, but nothing more recent than traces comparable to those of our Pleistocene epoch.

He therefore was forced to conclude - and submitted in a voluminous report with numerous comparisons to nearby galac-tic examples - that some catastrophes, perhaps the same that had wiped out the humanoids, had eliminated herbivores at an earlier stage.

Whatever the disaster had been - bacterial, viral, or something more esoteric - it did not recur to plague us. We thrived on the planet. The first children, conceived under the bluish alien sun, were born just after we had shipped our first year's surplus off-world. Life settled into a pleasant seasonal routine: the beef, sheep, horses, kine, even the windoers of Grace's World import-ed on an experimental basis, multiplied on the velvet fields. The centenarian crops from half a dozen worlds gave us abundant yields. We had some failures, of course, with inedible or grotesque ergotic mutations, but not enough to be worth more than a minor Chavezian thesis in the record and the shrug of the pioneering farmer. If a colonist is eating well, living comfortably, with leisure time for his kids and time off with his wife on the languid southern seas, he puts up with minor failures and irritations. Even with the omnipresent guilt of trespassing.

I was not the only one who never felt entirely easy in the pretty cities. But, as I rationalized the intermittent twinges of conscience, it would have been ridiculous to build facilities when empty accommodations were already available, despite their obstinate refusal to work no matter how Dunlapil tried to energize them. Still, we managed fine and gradually came to ignore the anomalies we had never fully explored, settling down to make our gardens and our families grow.

The tenth year was just beginning, with surprising warmth, when Martin Chavez called a meeting with me and Dunlapil. Chavez had even convened it on a Restday, which was annoying as well as unusual.

"Just in case we have to call a meeting of the colony," he told me when I protested. That statement, on top of his insistence on a meeting, was enough to make me feel apprehensive. Although Martin was a worrier he was no fool; he did not force his problems on anyone unnecessarily, nor was he one for calling useless meetings.

"I've an unusual report to make on a new plant growth discernible on the velvet fields, Commissioner, Sarubbi," he announced, addressing me formally. "Such a manifestation is not generally associated with simple, monocotyledonous plants. I've cross-checked both used and unused pastures, and the distortions of the growth in the used fields are distressing."

"You mean, we've imported a virus that's mutating the indigenous grasses?" I asked. "Or has the old virus that killed off the herbivorous life revived?"

"Nothing like this mutation has ever been classified and no, I don't think it's a return of a previous calamity." Chavez frowned with worry.

"Ah, champion, martyr," Dunlapil said with some disgust. "Don't go calling for a planetary quarantine just when we're showing a nice credit balance."

Chavez drew himself up indignantly.

"He hasn't suggested anything of the sort, Dun," I said, wondering if the urban engineer was annoyed because Chavez might be closer to solving the enigma of the Tree than Dunlapil was the mechanics of the cities. "Please explain, Specialist Chavez."

"I've just recently become aware of a weird evolution from the family Graminaceae, which these plants have resembled until now." He snapped on the handviewer and projected a slide onto the only wall in my office bare of the ubiquitous murals. "The nodular extrusions now developing in the velvet fields show none of the characteristics of herbaceous plants. No joined stems or slender sheathing leaves." He looked around to see if we had seen enough before he flashed on a slide of magnified cellular material. "This cross section suggests genus *Helianthus*, an improbable mutation." Chavez shrugged his helplessness in presenting such contradictory material. "However, something new is under every sun and we have not yet determined how the usual blue light of this primary will affect growth after prolonged exposure. We might get a Bragae Two effect."

"The next thing you'll be telling us, Martin," Dunlapil said as if to forestall a discourse on galactic comparisons, "is that these plants are the aliens who built these cities." He shot me a grin.

"That ought to be obvious," Chavez said with such a lack of rancor that the disbelief I had been entertaining disappeared. "Commissioner" - Chavez's grave eyes met mine - "can you give me another reason why every city has similarly fenced lots, all placed to catch full daily sun? Why the velvet fields with that central dominant Tree symbol appear to be the reverent focus of the aliens - excuse me - the indigenous species?"

"But they're humanoid," Dunlapil said in protest.

"Their culture is agrarian. *And* there are no grazers. Nor a single example of that blasted Tree anywhere on the planet - yet!"

That was when I truly began to be afraid.

"There are no grazing beasts," Chavez went on inexorably, "because they have been eliminated to protect the velvet fields and whatever is growing in them now."

"You mean, when those fields bloom with whatever it is they bloom with, the aliens will return?" Dunlapil asked.

Chavez nodded. "If we haven't irreparably altered the growth cycle."

"But that's fantastic! An entire civilization can't be dependent on a crazy who-knows-how-long cycle of plant life!" Dunlapil was sputtering with indignation.

"Nothing is impossible," replied Chavez at his most didactic.

"Your research has been sufficiently comprehensive?" I asked him, although I was sick with the sense of impending disaster.

"As comprehensive as my limited equipment and xenobotanical experience allow. I would welcome a chance to submit my findings to a board of specialists with greater experience in esoteric plant-life forms. And I respectfully request that you have Colonial Central send us a team at once. I'm afraid that we've already done incalculable damage to the-" He paused and, with a grim smile corrected himself "-*indigenous* organism seeded in those fields."

The semantic nicety jarred me. If Chavez was even remotely correct, we would require not only xenobotanists and xenobiologists but an entire investigation team from Worlds Federated to examine our intrusion into domain that had not, after all, been abandoned by its occupants like a *Marie Celeste* but had simply been lying fallow - with the *indigenous* natives quiescently in residence.

As Chavez, Dunlapil, and I walked from my office, toward the Com tower, I remember now that I felt a little foolish and very scared, like a child reluctant to report an accident to his parents but dutifully conscientious about admitting his misdemeanor. The plastisteel tower had never looked so out of place, so alien, so sacrilegious as it did now.

"Hey, wait a minute, you two," Dunlapil protested. "You know what an investigation team means ..."

"Anything and everything must be done to mitigate our offense as soon as possible," Chavez; said, interrupting nervously.

"Dammit!" Dunlapil stopped in his tracks. "We've done nothing wrong."

"Indeed we have! We may have crippled an entire generation." Chavez spoke with an expression of ineffable sorrow.

"There are plenty of fields we never touched. The aliens - natives - can use them for food ..."

Chavez's sad smile deepened and he gently removed Dunlapil's hand from his arm. "'From dust ye came, to dust ye shall return, and from dust shall ye spring again.'" It was then that Dunlapil understood the enormity of our crime.

"You mean, the plants are the *people*?"

"What else have I been saying? They are born from the Trees."

We did what we could even as we waited for the specialists and investigation team to arrive.

First we cleared the animals and crops from every one of the velvet fields. We removed every sign of our colonial occupation from the cities. The team, composed of five nonhuman and three humanoid species, arrived with menacing expedition well before the initial flood of xenospecialists. The team members did not comment on our preliminary efforts to repair our error, nor did they protest their quarters in the hastily erected dwellings on the bare, dusty plain and the subsequent roaring activity of the space-port close by. All they did was observe with portentous intensity.

Of course, except for vacating the cities - and occupying them was apparently the least of our cumulative crimes - everything we did to remedy our trespass proved horribly inept in the final analysis. We would have been less destructive had we kept the cattle on the velvet fields and not slaughtered them for food. We ought to have let the crops ripen, die, and return to the special soils that had nourished them. For the fields we stripped produced the worst horrors. But how were we to know?

Now, of course, we know all too fully. We are burdened to this very day with guilt and remorse for the wholesale dismemberment and dispersal of those irretrievable beings: eaten, digested, defecated upon by grazers. And again, eaten, digested, and eliminated by those who partook of the grazers' flesh. Of the countless disintegrated natives removed from their home soil by unwitting carriers, none can bear fruit on foreign soil. And on their own soil, to repeat, the fields we had stripped produced the worst horrors ...

I remember when the last report had been turned in to the eight judges composing the investigation team. Its members wasted no further time in formulating their decree. I was called to their conference room to hear the verdict. As I entered, I saw the judges seated on a raised platform, several feet above my head. That in itself was warning that we had lost all status in Worlds Federated. A flick of the wrist attracted my attention to one of three humans on the team. Humbly I craned my head back, but he refused to glance down at me.

"The investigation is complete," he said in an emotionless tone. "You have committed the worst act of genocide yet to be recorded in all galactic history."

"Sir ..." My protest was cut off by a second, peremptory gesture.

"Xenobiologists report that the growths in the velvet fields have reached the third stage in their evolution. The parallel between this life-form in its second stage and that of the cellulose fauna of Brandon Two is inescapable." Chavez had already told me of that parallel. "Now the plants resemble the exorhizomorphs of Planariae Five and it is inevitable that this third stage will give way to the sentient life pictured in the murals of their cities.

"You came here as agrarians and agrarians you shall be, in the fields of those you have mutilated. What final reparations will be levied against you, one and all, cannot be known until the victims of your crimes pronounce the penance whereby you may redeem your species in the eyes of the Worlds Federated."

He stopped speaking and-waved me away. I withdrew to announce the verdict to my dazed fellow colonists. I would far rather that we had been summarily executed then and there, instead of being worn and torn apart by bits and pieces. But that was not the way of judgment for those who trespass in modern enlightened times.

We could not even make an appeal on the grounds that the planet had been released to us, for the colony in its charter took on all responsibility for its subsequent actions, having reaped benefits now so dearly to be paid for.

So we worked from that day until Budding Time late that heinous fall. We watched anxiously as the seedling exorhizomorphs grew at a phenomenal rate until they were ten, then twenty, finally twenty-five feet high, thick-trunked, branching out, lush with green triangular foliage. By midsummer we knew why it was that during our time on the planet we had never been able to find any examples of the Tree: such Trees grew once every hundred years. For they were the Trees of Life and bore the Fruit of Zobranoirundisi in the cellular wombs, two to a branch, three to eleven branches per Tree. In the good fields - that is, the unviolated fields.

In the others. . .

The galaxy knows we tried to atone for our crime. Every man, woman, and child was devoted to tending the twisted, stunted, deformed, half-branched Trees that grew so piteously in those desecrated fields. Everyone of us watched with growing apprehension and horror as each new day showed further evidence of the extent of. our sacrilege. Oh, the hideous difference between those straight, tall, fine Zobranoirundisi and - the Others. We were ready for any sacrifice as penance.

Then, the morning after the first good frost, when the cold had shriveled the stems, the first Zobranoirundisi tore through his vegetable placenta. He shook his tall willowy body, turned and made obeisance to his natal Tree of Life, ate of the soil at its roots, of its triangular foliage. . . and knew!

I can never retell the agony of that day, when all those Zobranoirundisi faced us, their maimers, and announced the form our expiation would take. We bowed our heads to the inevitable, for we knew the sentence to be just and of Hammurabian simplicity.

We had to give back to the soil what we had taken from it. The handless Zobranoirundisi, recognizing his missing member from the cells now incorporated into the fingers of a young colony child nurtured on milk from cattle fed in the velvet fields, had every right to reclaim what was undeniably his own flesh. The legless Zobranoirundisi could not be condemned to a crippled existence when the Terran child had used the same cells to run freely for seven years on land where previously only Zobranoirundisi had trod.

We rendered, all of us, unto the Zobranoirundisi that which was truly theirs - seed and soil of the velvet fields, part and particle of the originally fertilizing dust that would have been reconstituted during the cycle we had so impiously interrupted.

Nor were we permitted to evade the least segment of required reparation, for the galaxy watched. I will say this of us proudly, though I no longer have a tongue: Mankind will be able to live with its conscience. Not one of us, when required, failed to give his flesh to the Zobranoirundisi in atonement!

Dermot Ryan was born in Dublin in 1971 and studied Natural Science at Trinity College Dublin, before working for a time as a scientific researcher, examining the influences of atmospheric methane on climate. He's been a well-known contributor of fiction to *Albedo One*, with stories featuring in issues 13, 16 and 21, as well as in other publications in Ireland. His short story, 'The Last Laugh' was published in the anthology *Phoenix Irish Short Stories 1997*, edited by David Marcus and his collected short fiction was published in *This Way Up* from Aeon Press (2002), alongside the work of Nigel Quinlan. Dermot's work is characterized by the intersections of real characters dealing with improbable situations and perplexing philosophical issues. His stories are often difficult to forget, and the one below is no exception. It was winner of the 'Best in Issue' prize as voted upon by the readers of *Albedo One* for issue 13.

The Burnished Egg

Dermot Ryan

It is not all books that are as dull as their readers. There are probably words addressed to our condition exactly, which, if we could really hear and understand, would be more salutary than the morning or the spring to our lives, and possibly put a new aspect on the face of things for us. How many a man has dated a new era in his life from the reading of a book!

Henry David Thoreau, Walden

All my family were good readers, but my brother, Liam McHugh, knocked the rest of us into a cocked hat. That is not to say that he was a very rapid reader, because he was not - he was never hasty, he always fully deliberated the book before him - but where words were concerned, he was intense and appreciative to an unusual extent. When he read a book, he did not devour it whole, as some do; he broke a morsel off, chewed it with great deliberation, and let it dawdle on his tongue and surrender all its juices. Perhaps unusually, he also read dictionaries with great relish; he craved to know every nuance, every nicety of every word he encountered, and so he diligently checked the several meanings of any word that was new or not entirely familiar to him. I never knew anyone for whom language was such a three-dimensional, sensual experience. A particularly pregnant word could leave him staring into empty space, rapt. You could almost hear the brisk electric crackling and sparking inside his head as his thoughts ramified.

My father's brother, Hugo, and his wife, Fiona, were frankly amazed by Liam's absorption in the world of letters - or perhaps aghast is a better word, for they remained resolutely unimpressed. They had no books in their house, because they would make it look untidy and gather too much dust. Like many semiliterate people, they saw themselves as exemplary pragmatists. I still remember the day they saw Liam reading Around the World in Eighty Days, surrounded by encyclopaedias and atlases, into which he delved at least as often as the novel itself. They helped him better to visualise the locations in the book, he said.

"It's not healthy, all this reading. He'll ruin his eyes!" was Aunt Fiona's opinion.

"He's a lazy hound. You should discourage him, Frank!" said Uncle Hugo to my father. "He's idling away his life!"

"What do you get out of it, Liam?" Uncle Hugo once asked.

"Nothing, as far as I can see!"

Liam responded calmly with a shrug. He was so convinced of the superiority of the written word that he never bothered to defend it.

"It'll injure him in the long term!" said Aunt Fiona.

"He'll never make a penny from all that reading!" said practical Uncle Hugo.

Well, on those last two points she was right and he was wrong.

The whole unfortunate train was set in motion by me, I'm ashamed to admit. Liam had just gone upstairs to his bedroom to study for his school exams, and I was downstairs preparing the dinner with my mother. Liam had brought Dickens' *Great Expectations* up with him, since that was a text set for his English exams. He was enjoying it, even though he was forced to follow and analyse to death all of Pip's movements and motivations.

All of a sudden, my mother and I stopped what we were doing and stared at each other. There was an uproarious sound blaring down from upstairs. It sounded as if there were a pony and trap in Liam's room, and sixty spectators walking about in ponderous boots.

"Liam must have the radio on," said my mother. "Tell him to turn it down, love, would you?"

"I doubt that he's got the radio on, Ma. He's *reading*."

She nodded. She knew that he would never allow any distractions come between him and his appreciation of a text. Besides, he found radio and television broadcasts uninspiring. He scorned them.

"Whatever it is then; go and find out what it is." She waved her hands at me.

So I ran up the stairs and down the landing to Liam's door. I threw it open to ask just what he thought he was doing, but I found myself unable to speak. Liam was not making any noise; he was just sitting down reading. But above his studious head, in a luminous volume of air the shape of an egg and the size of a bed, there was what I can only describe as a *vision*. Inside that golden egg, whiskered gentlemen walked cobbled streets, wearing ulsters and frockcoats. Ladies, arms linked to the gentlemen, wore poke bonnets and bodiced petticoats, and carried prim, unopened umbrellas in the crook of their free arm. Hansom wheels and horse hooves clattered over the cobblestones, as urchins ran hither and thither. Everything was drifting from the centre to the margins of the vision in a most kinetic manner, as if the eye that viewed them was in a moving coach.

Pip had got as far as London.

Of course, right then, watching the vision with my jaw hanging down, I was ignorant of its meaning.

"Liam!" I managed to gasp.

The vision (and the noise) switched off with the immediacy of a light bulb.

"What's up, Joe?" he said evenly.

"Your head! Above your head -"

He looked up. "Where?"

"It's gone now!"

"Oh, very funny. Haw-haw." He returned to his book.

And before my disbelieving eyes, streams of light transuded through his skull, rose to a point three quarters of a metre above his head, and re-knit themselves into the vision once more. The din began anew.

I screamed faintly. "Liam!"

"What!" He snapped the book shut indignantly. The vision blinked off again; the sound halted as abruptly.

"What do you want!"

"An egg!" I blurted. "An egg above your head! But it's gone now!"

"Oh, cop on, will you!" He was about to begin reading again, when I remembered the book in his hand and I was fired with sudden inspiration.

"Liam, what are you reading?"

He held up the book so I could see the title.

"Yes, yes! I know that! But what's happening in the book? Right now, in the section you're reading!"

"Pip's on his way to-"

"Somewhere in a carriage!"

"Yes-"

"In London!"

"Yes-"

"I don't believe it!" I ran out the door. Minutes later, with the noise once again blasting from Liam's room, Ma was following me up the stairs, wiping her hands on her apron and panting slightly. I opened Liam's door slowly.

"Look in," I whispered. "Not a squeak out of you, though."

She stepped in front of me, and peeped around the corner. She screamed: "Oh God protect us! What is that?" She ran behind me. The noise and, I presume, the vision faded.

Liam came round the corner, his finger inserted into the book to keep his place. "Have you all gone mad? What for the love of God is wrong with you all?"

"You're dabbling in the occult, aren't you? I'll tan your hide!" said Ma.

"What? What have I done? I'm just sitting quietly in my room reading -"

"That's just it, Ma," I told her. "It only happens when he's reading. I think I know what's happening, though I can't believe it. Liam," I put my hand on his shoulder, "you are reading vividly. Yes, I think I am safe in saying that. Vivid Reading. You're not aware of it, but you are seeing everything in your head in such copiously realistic detail that you are projecting it into the outside world. Onlookers can see what is passing through your mind as you read. Your appreciation of literature has moved onto a new plane!"

His blank gaze damped my enthusiasm.

"Joe, just feck off, will you?"

He went back in and closed the door. My mother and I exchanged anxious looks. The noise resumed.

Later, my father came home with Uncle Hugo. He dropped his bag on the floor, patted the dog, and pecked my mother on the cheek. Uncle Hugo had already sat down in the other room, and was looking for the remote control for the television.

"Why all the long faces?" my father said.

"It's a long story," I said dryly.

He stopped and cocked an ear. There were plummy English voices coming down from upstairs. There was an urbane conversation proceeding in *Great Expectations.*

"Does Liam have the radio on?" he said in a voice hushed with wonder.

"No. That's the long story."

We told him all that happened earlier that day. Our sincerity was evident, or at least he wasn't that hard to convince. I suppose the story was only slightly more fantastic than the idea of Liam voluntarily listening to the radio. Da thought for a moment and then went upstairs.

He returned minutes later, looking pale.

"Well?" Ma and I chorused.

"Pip is talking to Herbert Pocket."

"Then you believe us?"

"I don't have any choice." He rubbed his head in an agitated fashion. "This is a very queer thing."

"What's a queer thing?" said Uncle Hugo, entering from the sitting room. "Hello Sara, hello Joe. Frank, I can't find the remote control."

"It's probably gone down the edge of the couch, Hugo. I bet you'll find it there!" my mother said, all too hastily.

"Why, what's wrong, Sara? Is something wrong?" He stopped and cocked an ear in an inquisitive manner so like my father, that for once you'd believe they were brothers.

"Is Liam listening to the radio?" he asked incredulously. "This I have to see!"

"Stop him, Frank!"

Too late; already he was up the stairs. The next thing, we heard Liam's door fly open, and the heavy thump of Uncle Hugo hitting the floor in a dead faint. When we got upstairs, Liam was standing over Hugo, an expression of acute disbelief on his face.

"Mad. You've all gone mad today," he said firmly.

"Liam," my mother said, "go downstairs to the kitchen. We have to talk. Joe, put your Uncle Hugo on the bed. We'll deal with him when he comes round."

Liam didn't believe us. Of course, he hadn't seen the vision floating above his head, so why should he believe us?

"Look, please, this is a waste of time. Let me get back to studying. I have exams coming up."

"Liam, this isn't a prank. Why would we all lie to you? Why did Ma scream? Why did Uncle Hugo faint? Something uncanny has happened to you. You must believe us!"

He hesitated. "But what has happened to me? What?"

"How do we know? But just because we don't know the cause, it doesn't mean the effect isn't real! Look, ask your Uncle Hugo-"

"Yes, where is he?"

"Upstairs, on the bed -"

But he wasn't. Four footsteps, nimble as a hare's, brought the eavesdropping uncle from the kitchen door to the front door. Four more and he was off in his car.

"What's up with him?"

"Oh Lord, I hope he keeps this to himself," sighed my mother.

"Now, listen to me everyone," barked Uncle Hugo. "This is too good a thing to keep to ourselves!"

"We're not going on the news!" interrupted my mother, scandalised.

"Too right we're not! We're going to give public readings!" said my Uncle Hugo. "The demand for this is going to be huge!"

"No, no, Hugo! Think of the boy - he's only sixteen!"

"I don't mind-" said Liam.

"Keep out of this, Liam," warned Da.

"- as long as I get to choose the book."

"Good boy, Liam!" trumpeted Uncle Hugo. "I have the Apollo auditorium booked for next week. Leave it all to me. What are you going to read anyway?"

After hiring the Apollo auditorium for six nights, he did not have much money left for publicity, but Hugo was not deterred. He spent the last of his free cash on one large poster in the centre of town.

Not to be Repeated!
Not to be Missed!
The **Pan-sensual** Experience of a **Lifetime!**

A Public 'Vivid Reading'

of

Treasure Island

Thursday Night
The Apollo Auditorium
Admission £4
Doors Open: 7 pm

And we had a half-full auditorium on the strength of that one, cryptic advertisement. I had never fully appreciated the talents of Uncle Hugo. He understood quite intimately the easy purchase of curiosity. He had even persuaded a local-radio reporter to attend. And it was he - level headed pragmatist that he was - who had convinced Liam of the veracity of my theory of vivid reading (though, as it turned out, we wished in the end that he hadn't).

When the crowd had seated itself but was still conducting whisper-debates about what form this mysterious reading would take, Uncle Hugo took to the stage to quell their talk and announce Liam's entrance.

"Ladies and Gentlemen, I thank you for coming here. I promise you that you will not disappointed. No words can do justice to what you are about to witness -" From where I was sitting I could see Liam cringe in the wings. I know him well; I know what he was thinking: that words well-chosen can do justice to anything. "- so without further pomp, I give you: Liam McHugh!"

There was a smattering of polite and bemused applause, but not much more - except of course for our family; we were pounding our hands together and cheering him on. Liam walked to the centre of the stage, where a simple chair and the book awaited him. He sat down without looking up at the audience. I could tell he was nervous. He began to read, not aloud, but to himself. Expectant silence gripped the spectators.

For one long minute, nothing happened. Liam's eye kept leaving the page, as he cast sidelong, apprehensive looks at the large auditorium. He couldn't concentrate. It seemed that our venture would founder just as it was beginning. Some members of the audience began to suspect a hoax, and indignant chatter began to manifest itself sporadically. That all stopped instantly though, as Liam's concentration slipped into gear, and the splendid vision, the burnished egg, began to form above his head. The crowd gasped, and little children hid their heads. It was far better than the cinema - Liam would despise the comparison even - because it was of a far higher visual quality and resolution, and because it was in three dimensions, rather than two. Coupled with the extraordinary richness of the sound, and the fact that never in their entire lives had the spectators come upon a like phenomenon, it was enough to hush the usual coughs, splutterings and munchings at any public event. An awe-struck silence held sway.

Inside the bright vision, the captain was making his way up to the door of the 'Admiral Benbow' inn, his sea-chest following behind him in a hand-barrow. We could see the proud flesh around his livid, dirty-looking scar. We could see the tiny motes of wood-dust fly up as his stick rapped against the door, and when the proprietor appeared, and the Captain bawled for a glass of rum, we could hear the years of sea-air in his voice. The vision was convincing beyond measure. We were enthralled.

And at the end of the reading - this reading of Part I of *Treasure Island*, wherein we had seen miserable Black Dog, and evil Blind Pew, and the death of the captain, and the death of Blind Pew beneath the hooves of the rescuers' horses (how we cheered to see his body trampled, and the blood!), and with the map of the island discovered and the plans made for Jim and Squire Trelawney and Dr. Livesey to seek the island and its hidden treasure - Liam snapped the book shut, and the vision shimmered away. Liam stood up, gave a low bow and left the stage without a word. For an overwhelmed half-minute, the audience did not move; then it rose to its feet in frenzied applause.

Liam was on the news that night.

Radio, international television, print media - all beat a path to the door of the Apollo auditorium. For the next five readings, every square foot of the auditorium, whether or not it contained a seat or indeed a flat surface, was full. The back wall of the auditorium bristled with lenses and mikes. We followed the fortunes of Jim and the Squire and Dr. Livesey as they searched for the treasure, and we abhorred the treachery of Silver and his crew. We followed it every night, we took it all in avidly: the Man of the Island, the abandonment of the ship, the battle in the stockade, the nerve-racking fight between Jim and Israel Hands - we followed everything. Even those unable to get into the Apollo were following it - imagine this! - by actually reading the book! *Treasure Island* became a bestseller all over again. The publicity mounted with every reading, and every night brought a fresh round of newscasters to the doors of the Apollo. Poor Liam didn't enjoy being so much in the public eye - and all this in less than a week!

I was more worried however - and I don't know how I came by this premonition of the misfortune that was to be Liam's next reading - by a curious development that I had only noticed during Liam's reading of Part V. The visions had become more realistic over the week - not only grander in scale, but more *substantial* almost. The earlier apparitions in Liam's bedroom were small; this was large, its breadth the equal of the auditorium, and very intricately detailed. But what truly made me realise how much the apparitions had changed was that now I could smell the salty sea air and the musket shot; before I could smell nothing but buttered popcorn. In fact - and I was by no means certain of this at the time - a thin, moist aerosol seemed to settle on us when the great sail bellied in a sudden gust. The phenomenon was extending to take in every sense. The more Liam read, the more vivid became his vision. Somehow, this made me uncomfortable.

Finally, Part VI was read to its conclusion. Jim had returned from sea safe with the treasure, as a ruby sun blushed over the calm home straits. The audience applauded rapturously, and Liam went home too. There were camera crews there from all around the world as he left the theatre. A forest of microphones sprang up before him; an ordnance of lenses was trained on him. Just then, he really wanted to get away from the publicity that had risen up around him. We were keen for this to be an end to the whole venture too. It was straining the poor lad. We told Uncle Hugo that Liam was retiring.

Uncle Hugo looked up from his calculations.

"Well, we have made a killing. Well done, Liam."

He put the lid back on his pen, and switched off his calculator, and set them neatly side by side on his desk. He took out a handkerchief and rubbed his nose in an embarrassed fashion, as if he was about to broach a subject of great delicacy.

"I have been offered the use of the town park for another reading. The rate of hire is very reasonable, and the capacity is far greater than that of the Apollo."

"What!" exclaimed my father. "Hugo, you promised that this reading would be enough! The boy has exams to study for, he has to plan a career for himself!"

"This will be the last," said Uncle Hugo steadfastly.

"You'll turn him into a circus freak!"

"Never!" affirmed Uncle Hugo. "This is the very last venture I propose."

"You are not Colonel Parker, Hugo, and this boy is not Elvis Presley!"

Liam interposed here. "I don't mind doing one more -"

"Good boy!" chuckled Uncle Hugo. "And this is what you will be reading." He pulled a novel out of his pocket. It was some sensationalist piece of trash about dinosaurs taking over the planet.

"Hugo, no! That rubbish!"

Looking offended, Uncle Hugo defended his choice. "It's a number one best-seller! The crowds will turn up in droves! Besides," he shrugged, "I've already printed the posters up."

"I won't read that," said Liam quietly.

"Now, see here, Liam-"

"You didn't let me finish what I was going to say originally. I don't mind doing another reading, as long as I get the choice of what I read. I won't read that book though."

"Quite right, Liam." said my mother.

"Why don't you read *The Children of Lir*, Liam?" I suggested.

"Yes, or *The Cattle Raid of Cooley*!"

"No. Those are good suggestions, but I have a book in mind, a work of rare genius and accomplishment, of great imaginative power and artistry that is hardly ever read. It is a book that deserves a wider reading. Even if the shagger who wrote it did support Cromwell."

"Really, what is it?" I asked.

"I don't really think that the public will go for a book of rare genie -" began Uncle Hugo.

"It's *Paradise Lost*. Don't even try to dissuade me. I've made up my mind. You might as well go and change the posters, Uncle Hugo."

"What's *Paradise Lost*?" whispered Hugo to my father when Liam had left the room.

"Poetry," said my father quietly.

Uncle Hugo gasped for air.

So, in spite of all our misgivings, the reading in the park went ahead. It must have been the most well-attended and unusual poetry reading ever. Usually at a poetry reading you'd expect some titivated fop, announcing:

Of Man's fahst disobehdience and the Frrruit
Of the Fohhhbidden Trrree ...

But Paradise Lost as read by Liam McHugh was a far different thing. For a start, it was going to net us a fortune.

The crowd assembled in the park at seven o'clock as advertised. The fact that it was a poetry reading did not seem to damp the enthusiasm of the masses for the unprecedented novelty that was *Vivid Reading*. The audience was of frightening size. It spread before the stage that had been specially built for the occasion, it moved out over the swards, and spilled out onto the playing fields. Some younger spectators had scaled lamp posts with the alacrity of Polynesians climbing palm trees. I hoped that everyone would be able to see and hear.

I was worried for another reason. We lost some money that day, I know, because I could see kids clambering over the park walls, so avoiding the turnstiles. I shouldn't have been greedy though. It was infectious.

Liam's choice of *Paradise Lost* was not motivated by any base or commercial instinct, of that I was sure. He thought it was a work that should be more popular, and if he could help, all well and good. Nevertheless, it is a particularly visual piece of writing, with many lively and apt descriptions of battles, heroism, good and evil. In particular, I was looking forward to the reading of Book VI, in which Raphael relates to Adam in panoramic detail the bitter and long battle fought between the forces of Satan and God by the crystal walls of Heaven. There are some powerful scenes in it. But, now I think of it, considering what happened during the reading of Book I, it is perhaps as well that Liam didn't get that far. He'd have trashed Dublin, at the very least.

The sea of human beings rippled randomly, as people sat down and rose up from the grass, trying to get comfortable. The square, temporary dwellings of outside-broadcast units littered the park grounds. A T.V. helicopter glittered in the evening sun, like a delicate fly. The gathering was a little impatient, but they had to wait until we had everyone in. Finally, Uncle Hugo took the stage, a megaphone in his hand, looking for all the world like a P.T. Barnum.

"Ladies and Gentlemen, thank you for your patience," he announced with expansive gestures, "I apologise for the delay in starting. But now relax, and prepare yourself for the experience of a lifetime. None of us will ever forget this day!"

Uncle Hugo left the stage, and Liam took it. He carried the complete *Paradise Lost* and a wooden chair. These apart, he had no props. He moved to the very centre of the stage, bowed gravely, and sat down. He did not begin to read at first, but instead sat breathing calmly and slowly, his eyes closed, the book resting in his lap. Nobody said a word. All we could hear was the quiet thrum of traffic somewhere in the town and the distant whirr of the helicopter.

Then Liam lifted the book, turned past the scholarly introduction to the opening words of the poem. The golden streams
oozed out into the space above the dais where Liam sat, and there
they reconstituted the brilliant egg of light, but on a scale that we
had never seen before. Its greater diameter was at least equal to
the length of a Zeppelin, its lesser diameter about half that. It was
stupendous. There were gasps of awe breaking out all around us.
It glowed warmly. We were bathed in oracular light.

A peruked man robed in seventeenth-century English style
appeared in the vision, reading from a great scroll. His voice was
deep and authoritative. It delivered the opening invocation of the
Heavenly Muse with such timbre and feeling that, although I
think that the sense of it was lost to some of the audience, the very
music of it won them over. I settled back into my seat.

As the invocation ended and the true narrative portion of the
poem began, the egg began to contract and the voice of the narrator grow fainter. Above, another, larger golden ovoid formed, in
which Satan's drama unfolded. As that drama progressed, the
lower ovoid continued to contract and the new one expanded. I
presumed at the time that it was Liam forgetting about the presence of the narrator - him literally slipping to the back of Liam's
mind. By the end, we could no longer even see the first egg.

The spectacle - a word I do not use lightly - began with the
rebel Satan's long precipitous descent into Hell, hurled from the
walls of Heaven after his defeat at the hands of God, the air groaning and ripping before him. With a terrible crunch and a resound-
ing boom that had the audience wincing in sympathy, Satan's fall
ended in Hell. It was the most impressive thing I had ever seen.
Dark flames vaulted into the air and the park shook upon impact.
Satan writhed agonisedly in the burning lake. You had to feel
some pity for him, scorched in that twilit fury. And the look on
his face would either break your heart, or set it crossways in you:
such stern, dignified nobility, and yet how underscored by vanity

and ruined pride. Liam looked minuscule beneath him, and you felt that if Satan fell out of the egg he would crush Liam into oblivion.

Eventually, after a despairing interval, Satan saw a companion, transfixed by the same pain, rooted to the same fiery spot. He addressed him - it was Beëlzebub - and in an exhortation of great persuasiveness and mellifluence, during which the pursuing armies of God returned to heaven with a final retributive hail of sulphur, he coaxed Beëlzebub to join him, to lift himself above this miserable place, and go to a more solid part of hell that was visible from where they lay.

When Satan rose with difficulty to reach that less incandescent plain, we all gasped at this daring and courage, but also at Satan's staggering size. The ovoid had swelled again, but it did not encompass his entire length, as he rose above the flames and extended his long, powerful body into the dreepy air.

Forthwith upright he rears from off the Pool
His mighty Stature; on each hand the flames
Driv'n backward slope their pointing spires, and roll'd
In billows, leave i' th'midst a horrid Vale.

Then he extended his wings - which spread from the blunt end to the sharp end of the ever-growing egg, and flew to his destination. And after him struggled Beëlzebub. Curiously, as Satan looked around at the endless sweep of hell, and lamented the loss of heaven:

Farewell happy Fields
Where Joy for ever dwells: Hail horrors, hail
Infernal world, and thou profoundest Hell
Receive thy new Possessor

I could have sworn that the audience were sympathetic to his grief, some of them even sighing regretfully. I have to concede that there was a forlorn quality in his voice.

But he was huge; even now the egg, expanding, could not

take him all in - his spear disappeared out the top, his huge shield only just fitted inside. Now he raised his bellowing voice to exhort his troops to awake, arise or be forever fallen! His voice thundered through the park and out into the empty city sky.

The stricken droves of fiends then forsook their remorse and forgot their agony, and shook their wings until they rose up in their countless multitudes - Moloch, smeared with blood, Baal, Ashtaroth and thousands or millions of others unnamed, all the lewd, treasonous and perverted faded angels, beating their dark wings above Liam's head. It was a discomforting sight. Satan's ensign streamed in the breezes of hell and shone in the darkness like a limelight, and the demons rallying before him raised their flaming swords from their scabbards and beat their sounding shields until our ears hurt, and the children, silently terrified until now, began to bawl. The egg was full of furious activity: the banners, the swords, the thick flocks of winged infantry. A reek of pitch and sulphur was making us gag.

The vision was now directly over the crowd. Its area in cross-section was probably greater than that of the park. It had descended a little from its original altitude. Its realism was now hair-raising. I could feel the blood draining from my face. It was disturbingly vivid, far more so than at the beginning of the reading. Trumpets and brass and flutes joined the noise, and thousands more banners rose in the air, as the demons marched in perfect formation towards their leader, who towered above them like a colossus. All those faces twisted with demented glee made me fell faint. The park was dusky by now, and the shadows cast by the cheerless flames of hell were as dark as blood in the first chamber of the heart.

Their accursed chief began to comfort them, telling them that they could yet fight Good with Guile, and that they would not always reside in Hell - and here I flinched, because he actually looked out of the egg towards us - that there were other worlds where they might make their home. As he looked out through the surface of the egg, he said wistfully:

Thither, if but to pry, shall be perhaps
Our first eruption

The brutes then beat their sounding shields again, even more thunderously than before, so that our ears began to ring. The brass and flutes rebegan the cacophony. Within minutes, they had contaminated and blackened the air of Hell once more with their airborne presence, and flown off in a huge, brooding cloud. With a deafening roar and the shrill whine of drills and the flat smack of hammers, they tore up the ground of Hell, extracted metallic ore, and built a startling edifice of gold and battered metal before our startled eyes, so rapidly that they were just a blur, and on such a huge scale that the egg expanded to a point where I was sure it would break asunder. They flew inside without hesitation to debate their escape from hell, and their campaign beyond. The Council Chamber was like a gilded cavern, lit by blazing torches. At the far end, on a throne taller and blacker than a Gothic spire, sat the King of the fiends. Everything we had seen before was as nothing to this. The egg was so many times its original size. I have never seen anything so terrifying as that sea, wave after wave, of expectant brutish faces and glinting weapons, congregated beneath the frowning vaults of Pandemonium.

And there, just as the diabolical meeting, the Great Consult, was beginning, Liam snapped the book shut. That was the end of Book I. He rose, bowed and tried to leave the stage, but somehow he could only stagger a few steps, and then he stumbled to his knees. The first hearty rounds of applause pattered away into silence. The intricate, glistering, staggering, fabulous, towering vision had not disappeared.

The audience did not move or make any sound. The demons did not move. The only motion was the flickering of the thousands of torches that hung from the roof of the vast council chamber. We stared at each other across the polished surface of the egg. That surface was all that separated us.

Uncle Hugo was on stage announcing that Book II would be read next week, at this same venue. He stopped when he saw that the vision was still there, and that the innumerable and unbearable troops of fiends were looking out of the egg at us. A hungry, knowing, patient smile disgraced every one of their faces. That smile was self-satisfied, as if they had fooled us into doing something we had not wanted to. We faced them for a long time; they looked out from their world, and we looked in. Every one of us was hoping with all our hope that this was a delay, that it would be only a matter of a few minutes more and then the vision would blink off as it had always done before.

Eventually we left the park in sober silence. It had not disappeared. We brought Liam home and sent for the doctor.

The recital of Book II was scratched, the park was sealed off, and no-one was allowed to re-enter it. However, the vision was enormous. You could see it from any point in the city, and the sight of it ruined every day for us.

The whole miserable incident incapacitated Liam. He wasn't physically crippled, but the poor scrap was never the same again. It is hard to recover from the things that had passed through his young mind. He barely spoke; he spent days on his own in his darkened room, head to the wall, shivering under the blankets. Sometimes he would cry out in the night like an animal, panic-stricken. He became gaunt, his eyes got dull and glassy, and cysts and boils formed on his legs, back and neck. The doctor said that he was suffering from shock and anxiety. The shock and anxiety seemed to go on without end. He remained a pale shadow. We never forgave Uncle Hugo for pushing him into it, or ourselves for letting him do it.

And ever since, the vision has remained there, motionless but for the dancing of the torch flames, static above our unhappy town, like a grim weather balloon. Satan and his cohorts never change expression. Occasionally they blink; perpetually they show their patient smile, as if all they need to do is wait. And so it has remained. We live in fear. Nobody can say what will happen. Will the burnished egg vanish? Will it break and release its contents?

Liam's vision hovers above us; it casts a terrible shadow over all we do.

James Lecky was born and lives in Northern Ireland. He has tried his hand at writing, editing and more recently acting, describing himself as being widely regarded as Ireland's 327th greatest Shakespearean actor. James was also editor of the well-respected magazines *Dark Eyes* and *Odyssey*, which had a name so popular, other magazines occasionally 'borrowed' it. Both publications are unfortunately no longer in production, as is so often the fate of even the best genre magazines. In terms of fiction, James has had his work published widely in the small presses in UK and elsewhere, in venues such as *Zest*, *Tales of the Grotesque & Arabesque* and *Threads*. It is often said that art imitates life and vice versa, but in the story that follows (praised as one of the best stories of 1998 by Tangent Online) that may hold truer than we imagine.

Skin-Tight

James Lecky

It had been a long time since I was last in Istanbul, but nothing had changed. The streets were still the same ad hoc mixture of ultra-modern and fading Imperial - like a three-d polaroid superimposed on a sepia photograph. There were neon Coca-Cola signs on the entrance to the Topkapi Palace and fat American tourists dragged their blowzy wives and screaming brats through the hallowed halls of the Hagia Sophia. Under any other circumstances I would have found the whole thing funny. But not today.

I felt like the city, basking in my former glory but unwilling, or unable, to relinquish it and take a step forward. It wasn't anything as grand as artistic block; the truth was I was bored, both with myself and my so-called art; Bio Noveau as LifeNet had dubbed it, Neural sculpture to the uninitiated.

I had been trying to come to terms with my proposed Paris collection for months but everything I had produced recently was self-derivative shit. There were still those critics who called me a genius with straight-faced sincerity, but I needed to do something, anything, to prove that Angel McKeown still meant something more than a corporate brand name. Perhaps it was the spirit of the garret artist, still resentful of the way I had sold out.

Either way I needed a new muse, or failing that a few blasts of good Turkish hash to forget myself for a while.

I wandered along the Harbour of the Golden Horn, listening to the buzz of voices - a hundred different languages melting into one - and watching the U.N. and Mujaheddin patrols eyeing each other nervously. No one recognised me - just another Arabic woman, insular and anonymous in a black yashmak - and no one looked close enough to see that my eyes were blue.

Twenty minutes later I was in one of the sprawling bazaars that filled every available inch of space in the city. Street vendors dressed in the ubiquitous striped robes and greasy fez hawked everything from mangoes to leather bound copies of the Koran and further back, hidden in the shadows of smoky cafés, European drug pedlars sipped scalding coffee and stared at the world with dead but predatory eyes; their trade was legal here but the habits of a lifetime died hard and they still preferred the shadows to the light.

I wandered through the ramshackle stalls, finding nothing except the usual junk, and then finally made my way across an empty square to one of the cafés.

There was a young man, or at least a man who looked young, sitting at one of the street-side tables. It was easy to tell his occupation; pushers always look the same, world-weariness combined with a disdainful superiority. He had short-cropped blonde hair, bleached from too long in the sun, and wore a crumpled white suit that was the unofficial uniform of the European male in Istanbul.

He paid no attention to me until I sat opposite him and even then there was only a slight look of astonishment in his grey eyes.

"I want some hash," I said in English, pitching my voice low in deference to the customs of drug trafficking.

He nodded slightly, "How much?"

"About three kilos."

If he was surprised then he hid it well. He made a quick mental calculation, then added his commission on top of that.

"Eight thousand," he said at last.

"Pounds or Euros?"

He grinned, showing a gold incisor, "Dollars", he said, "US dollars. In cash, if you please. "

I shrugged and produced a roll of bills from inside my robe, holding it discreetly but making sure he got a good look before putting it away again. His eyes lit up and his grin broadened, a gold tooth glinting in the sun.

"Wait here," he said, then slipped away into the gloomy interior of the cafe.

I ordered a coffee and sat sipping gingerly at it while I waited. I have never really developed a taste for Arab coffee: too strong, too thick and too sweet. A Pepsi or a Coke would have suited me better but in Istanbul such luxuries are only bought by tourists desperate for a taste of home, and paid for through the nose.

I sat and watched the world go by, content for the moment to have nothing better to do, and tried not to think about my upcoming Paris show.

The whole thing had been Warbeck's idea; my sculptures had been selling well in New York, London and Tokyo but for some reason had never really caught on in Europe. Perhaps it was something to do with the fact that they were "alive" - in a limited sense - more suited to cultures fascinated by the moving image than by those preoccupied by the concept of "real" art. Whatever the reason Warbeck was determined to crack the French market and, according to him, a big Paris collection, complete with all the New World hype that was Warbeck's stock in trade, would be the breakthrough that I so desperately needed. Or to be more accurate, the breakthrough that Damien Warbeck so desperately needed.

I had been working with Warbeck for nearly five years, ever since he had discovered my work in a tiny Dublin gallery. He was a self-avowed cynic when it came to art but shrewd enough to know what people would buy, especially if backed up by the right sort of publicity. He had taken a grubby, down at heel sculptress and turned her into an overnight sensation moulded in the image of what he saw as the perfect media-friendly artist - a little unconventional, good looking in an odd sort of way and prepared to defend her work to the hilt against hostile critics, even to the extent of the much publicised brawl in a popular New York nightclub. I wasn't the only neural sculptor in the world, I wasn't even the best, but thanks to Warbeck I was easily the most famous. My sullen, gene-modified face graced a million posters in a million student bedrooms and barely a week went by that someone somewhere was debating the merits of my work on an arty television show.

My self-pitying meditations were interrupted by the return of the Dope pedlar.

"Three kilos," he said and pushed the package towards me, "The best shit you can get anywhere."

I grunted in reply and tore a comer from the brown paper, checking my purchase before I handed over any money.

"Don't you trust me?" he said, mock irony heavy in his voice.

"Not much," I replied. Then, satisfied that I wasn't buying three kilos of tea, I handed him the money.

He grinned and pushed the cash into his pocket without counting it, as if to say 'At least I trust you'.

Then, without warning, his face disappeared in a shower of bone and blood, spraying me with red-grey brain matter. A nanosecond later I heard the sharp sound of a spit-gun from across the square. For long, long moments I was frozen with shock, my mind screaming in panic but my body refusing to listen.

Another snap and the table beside me shattered, and it was this, rather than the dead drug dealer, that finally snapped me out of my trance. I dived for cover, cursing the fact that I was weaponless and helpless.

Behind me a small group of men had emerged from the café, armed with a motley collection of spit-guns and machine pistols - old fashioned but deadly for all that.

I kept my head down while the brief, but bloody battle was fought out, silently muttering a prayer to whichever god keeps hack artists from harm and hoping that it would be heard.

When the rattle of gunfire had stopped at last I stood up, knees shaking and expensive bio-forge heart beating in my chest. I've seen death before - a year in the virtual war zone of New York exposed me to every kind of violent death imaginable - but I have never gotten used to the sights and sounds and even the smells of it.

Three men lay in pools of rapidly cooling blood, their faces already taking on the waxy cast of corpses, and across the square two more, barely recognisable as human beings, their bodies stitched with dozens of impact holes, blood bright red against the white material of their suits.

It may sound cold - it is cold - but standing there surrounded by dead men, my nostrils filled with the stink of cordite and voided bowels, I was suddenly glad I had come to Istanbul.

I knew what my next collection was going to be.

"You're crazy!" Hito said.

"That's what they said about Victor Frankenstein," I told him. It took a second or two, via the intercession of the Global Communications Network, for my words to reach him. When they did he grimaced slightly.

"Of course Mister Warbeck will love it."

"As long as he's prepared to put up the extra money I don't care what Warbeck thinks."

"I'll talk to him." Hito was Warbeck's flunky, self-important in the way that only rich orientals can be.

"No," I said firmly, "I'll tell him about this personally - put me through to his office."

"Mister Warbeck is a very busy man, I'm not sure that I can distur -" Hito began.

I cut him off in mid sentence, "Just do it, Hito."

Hito gave an exasperated shrug, as if to disassociate himself from me and my warped ideas about art.

"Have it your own way, Angel."

The screen went blank for a moment, Hito's face replaced with a hissing wall of white noise. When it came back on-line the dog-food features of Damien Warbeck stared out at me.

"Angel McKeown," he said, "What a pleasant surprise. How's the exhibition coming along?"

"I drowned them in acid this morning."

Warbeck looked shocked, but not half as shocked as the tiny faces in the neural-sculptures had been when I plunged them into the tank.

"I suppose there was a reason for that, or were you just feeling pre-menstrual?"

I smiled icily in response, "It was all crap anyway, the French would have hated it."

"And I suppose an empty gallery will appeal more to their sense of the avant-garde." The way he said it made it sound like a question and a statement at the same time.

I smiled again and said, "Perhaps it would at that. But what I have in mind will definitely rock them off their Gallic asses."

He returned my smile. The sight of those perfect white teeth against his deformed face made me shudder. In an age of designer, made to measure perfection and beauty, Warbeck revelled in his natural deformity. "And what is it that you have in mind, exactly?" he asked.

I told him. And by the time I was finished Damien Warbeck's mouth was gaping in disbelief. He may have been totally disinterested in neural-sculpture but he knew a money-spinning scheme when he saw it. Or when someone told him about it.

"What do you need from me?" he asked at last, when the concept had finally sunk in.

"A quarter of a million to buy supplies - I'll have to use the black market, naturally. No reputable company would have anything to do with this."

"I'll wire the money to you tonight." He gave me a last gleaming smile then broke the connection.

Not many people understand neuro-sculpture. I'm not sure I fully understand it myself - it's linked to telekenesis, precognition and all those other things that we didn't understand until about fifty years ago. Put simply it is the mental manipulation of matter - the creation of life from amino acids and single cells, a building up of complex structures that has come to be regarded as an art form rather than a science for the simple matter that it has no other practical application.

Little lives, like those in the bio-domes, can last indefinitely - a good investment for art dealers - but large-scale lifeforms have a strictly limited existence, measured in days rather than years. Even heavy investment by some of the major corporations, trying to find ways to exploit the art form commercially, resulted in nothing more than an awful lot of money down the drain.

But that didn't matter too much at the moment, I wasn't thinking in terms of long lasting art, more the impact that the collection would cause.

I had put Warbeck's quarter of a million to good use and my studio looked like an abattoir at closing time. Illegally purchased limbs were stacked in neat piles all over the floor and my work table was littered with rapidly thawing hearts, livers and spleens. It would have been better, less of an artistic compromise, to have built each and every one of them up from nothing, but I had neither the time or the inclination to do so. The end result, rather than the method, was much more important.

I slipped off my robe and stood naked in the middle of the room, shivering slightly in the frigid air. For the past three days I had eaten nothing and drank only sterilised water in an attempt to 'clean my spirit'. An unnecessary act perhaps - a large number of artists actively dismiss the whole spiritual aspect of neural-sculpture - but important enough to my own methods of working. I took a deep breath and folded myself into the lotus position, then began to chant mantras to focus my mind.

The name of the collection is Skin-Tight Nightmares," I said again, speaking slowly and clearly in French.

The reporter from Paris Match raised one eyebrow. "An unusual name for a collection, Mademoiselle McKeown, even given the ..." he coughed slightly, "... somewhat controversial nature of your previous work."

I took an angry step towards him and felt Warbeck's restraining hand on my shoulder. "If you please, Monsieur, this is a press conference not an excuse to air your own opinions about art."

A ripple of laughter went around the cramped room. "And do you think, Miss McKeown," an American voice from the back of the room said, "that this exhibition will finally win you acclaim in Europe?"

"It may create waves."

During the last few weeks in my Shetland studio, isolated and alone, working feverishly on the Skin-Tight collection, I had developed a curious empathy towards my art. But it was not the usual emotion that an artist feels for a work in progress. Normally there is a fascination with the subject as it grows and mutates and, hopefully, takes on dimensions other than those originally conceived.

This time I was totally in charge, moulding the black-market limbs and organs into a semblance of human life, hideous and deformed life to be sure, but life for all that. When I was finished - satisfied - I placed each one of the dozen neural sculptures into crude cryo-pods; enough to preserve their fragile lives until the Paris exhibition.

There are those who speak of giving birth to their art, of shaping and adoring until every detail is as perfect as it can be. I had felt like that, once, and now, for the first time in literally years, I experienced the emotion again.

I muddled through the rest of the conference, allowing Warbeck to answer most of the questions on my behalf and smiling stoically for the cameras. I felt drained, physically and mentally. The last month had cost me fifteen pounds of weight and added at least ten years to my appearance. Nothing that good surgery couldn't fix though.

When the conference was finally over Warbeck led me through the self-consciously rococo corridors of the gallery into the main exhibition area where the Skin-Tight Nightmares collection had been set up.

Released from the cryo-pods most of the pieces were simply shambling around the stark white room, barely aware of each other's presence. Their minds, functional at best, were still fogged from the time spent in the pods and I was certain that most of them had no idea where they were or even that they were. At least not yet.

Hito was waiting for us, standing under a low archway and casually smoking a cigarette. He was doing his best to be indifferent to the sculptures but, by the way his gaze constantly returned to the grotesque pieces as they shuffled and stumbled, I could tell that he was impressed despite himself.

"Nice work, Angel," he said as Warbeck and I approached, "A hint of Dali in there unless I miss my guess."

I ignored his compliment. "Did you bring the stuff I asked for?"

He reached down and patted a black vinyl hold-all by his feet. "It's all here."

"Good." I turned to Warbeck, "Give me about an hour to prepare and then you can let the vultures of the press in."

Warbeck nodded. "Good luck," he said. Then he leaned over and kissed me softly on the cheek. I could smell his expensive cologne and see the worry in his eyes. A quarter of a million either way would hardly break the bank but his reputation, as much as mine, was resting on Skin-Tight Nightmares and I knew that he was fervently hoping that everything would go well.

As soon as Warbeck and Hito had left I walked into the centre of the room and assumed the familiar and comfortable lotus position, the hold-hall resting on my knees. I slipped off my jacket. The flesh coloured bodysuit beneath gave the impression of nudity but allowed me to maintain at least a small degree of decorum and dignity. I closed my eyes and for long minutes concentrated on nothing except breathing. Then I began the mantra, focusing myself into the shuffling, indifferent figures that paraded around me.

It began as a tiny flicker, growing in intensity until my aura glowed as brightly as a searchlight, radiating through the white room and touching each one of the sculptures - invading them, breathing life and consciousness into what had been until now nothing more than mobile sacks of meat.

When I opened my eyes they were all standing in front of me, staring back with faces that eerily and intentionally mirrored my own. Their features were dirty and distorted, a less than idealised self-image that grinned and leered at me.

"Hello," I said, my voice echoing from the sterile walls.

One of the exhibits, a monstrosity with its internal organs carefully placed outside its body said: "Angel?"

The word sounded like a curse. It may have been. Each of them was imbued with a tiny fragment of my essence - they were as fully aware as I was of what was about to happen.

Behind me the gallery doors opened and the crowd of journalists, art critics and media whores stepped in, Warbeck at their head and Hito bringing up the rear. When the last of them was inside the gallery Hito discreetly locked the doors.

"Ladies and gentlemen," Warbeck began, "May I present for your intellectual delight and stimulation the world's premiere of Skin-Tight Nightmares." A sly grin played around his malformed mouth and he quickly stepped back into the shelter of a white-washed pillar, dragging Hito with him.

I was barely aware of the gaping, gasping crowd, or of the sudden intense but isolated explosion of a dozen flashbulbs going off at once. I heard someone with a British accent mutter the words outrageous and disgusting. Never in my entire career have I...

I reached down to the hold-all. The material was smooth and cold against my fingertips, forming a distorted seal over the objects inside the bag. I undid the velcro fasteners, the sound disproportionately loud. As per my instructions Hito had filled the bag with an assortment of hand and machine guns. There were even a couple of long bladed knives, which was a nice touch.

One of the sculptures, the one who had spoken my name, grinned - its crooked face making the expression seem more like a hate filled grimace.

Without moving from the lotus position I fired a revolver at it. The sculpture was a soft and fragile thing that burst open as the bullet struck, showering me with tender fragments of bone and flesh.

From behind me I could hear the beginnings of a scream, the first moments of understanding and revelation that would lead inevitably to panic and flight. I picked a machine-gun from the bag - an ascetic weapon, small and compact, totally in keeping with the mood of the piece I was creating - and walked a long, ragged burst across the sculptures, rising to my feet as I did so, keeping my finger on the trigger until the clip was empty. Then, in deference to Hito's more mundane sensibilities, I took both of the knives and walked into the pile of steaming, bloody meat to complete the final delicate touches to my masterpiece.

Those that still lived were in pain; agony-drenched eyes stared up at me from ruined faces - my ruined face - tacitly welcoming the touch of the cold blades.

But if their suffering was great, mine was greater. For the first time ever I understood that to create also meant to destroy and each bullet, each stroke of the knife, cut its way into my own flesh and psyche, wounding and scarring.

When it was over I stood there, surrounded by the ruins of my sculptures, my body covered in gore and stray pieces of meat, panting hard and doing my best not to throw up. I looked around at the shocked and awed faces of the journalists and critics, cringing in the locked doorway. And then, gradually I saw understanding, acceptance of what I had done and what I had created.

"Now," Warbeck said, stepping out from behind the pillar and straightening his tie, "Who'll start the bidding at one million Euros?"

Nigel Quinlan was born in Limerick in 1971, and raised in a tiny but lovable village called Murroe by large and lovable parents. He says he decided to be a writer while sitting in an exam that had something to do with computers and which he knew for a fact he was going to fail. Some of his best short stories to date have been collected with those of Dermot Ryan in the Aeon Press collection *This Way Up* (2001).

'The Invisible Man Game' has been compared by a critic to 'that most chilling section of Joyce's *Portrait of The Artist*.' Curious? Join the game...

The Invisible Man Game

Nigel Quinlan

First day at school Michael had no real comprehension of what was going on. The world was a vague smear of colour, no different from his dreams. The only fixed points were his mother's arms and his mother's voice. For the rest, he was adrift in a great sea of secrets that tried to squeeze in through his eyes and his ears while he retreated, keeping them a safe watery blur or a high distant muttering. If he wanted anything, it was to sit forever on the cool grass under the warm sun beside his mother and watch vast snowy mountains scaling the infinite blue sky.

But his mother went away and he was alone in a bewildering swirl of new colours, new shapes, new sounds, and he could switch none of them off. He was lead up concrete steps and into a high, wide room and put sitting at a desk. The wood was cold against his bare arms and legs. He didn't dare move. There was a chattering, like birds, and a deep rumble that seemed, once, to be addressed at him. He said his name, and the rumble went away. Blinking, he tried to see the shadow that stalked up and down the room between the rows of desks. He wanted to pee but there was nowhere to go. Forcing himself to sit like a statue, he could feel the pressure building painfully in his belly.

There was a yellow door in the corner, and a huge wide window beside him. Sunlight fell on him and he started to feel hot and sweaty. Squirming in the heat and from the pain in his tummy, he heard a bell ringing far away. Then he heard another, louder, running past the yellow door. Everything around him started scraping and moving and he got out of his seat and followed, out of the room and into a long, cool place, then through a pair of doors and out into sunlight. He still needed to go to the toilet badly, hopping up and down, squeezing down on himself.

"What's up with you?"

He squinted and the figure in front of him peered back.

"I said what's up?"

"I have to pee," he said, voice trembling, shamefully, on the verge of tears.

"Me too," said the voice cheerfully. "Come on."

He followed the figure into the sunlight to the corner of a wall.

"What's your name?" asked the figure, fumbling with his pants.

"Michael," he said, hesitating. "Is this okay?"

"It's fine," said the boy, sending a little yellow stream spattering against the wall, "I'm Jimmy."

"Okay," said Michael, mystified, pulling down his fly. The relief was enormous, but for some reason he felt the need to hurry, and it was taking too long. Drops of warm liquid struck his bare legs and the smell was sharp and unpleasant.

The sun went out. He turned to look, but Jimmy was no longer there. Instead a big fat man was looking down at him. Michael blinked, but he couldn't see the fat man's face. Then the bell was ringing again and everything was moving towards the open doors and he joined them, zipping up his fly.

Later, there was a knock on the yellow door. The shadow said something Michael didn't understand and the door opened and somebody came in.

"Michael Riordan."

He looked around. They'd left the door open and a cool breeze was blowing across his sweaty forehead.

"Michael Riordan!"

It was dark out in the corridor and bright where he was sitting. The contrast made coloured cartoon shapes dance in his eyes and he felt ill looking at them.

"Are you deaf, or just stupid? Michael Riordan!"

The shadow was standing over him, shouting at him, and at last he recognised his own name.

"Get up, boy," the shadow roared. "The Master wants you!"

Blinking, suddenly scared, he climbed down from behind the desk. Then he stood, looking up at the shadow. The shadow waved.

"Go on, follow her."

So he followed the girl out through the door and into the long cold place then through another yellow door.

"Whatever he says," the girl hissed at him, "say you didn't do it."

Inside the yellow door was another room, except this one was full of bigger people, and was quieter and darker. There were blinds across the windows. The big fat man walked over to him. He still couldn't see his face. The fat man's voice rumbled.

"Michael Riordan?"

He nodded.

"Say 'yes sir.'"

"Yes sir."

The fat man pointed. Two girls sitting in a desk on the front row were looking solemnly at Michael.

"Is this the one?" the fat man asked.

They both nodded and then said together, "Yes, sir."

"Were you bothering these girls at break?"

Michael didn't understand the question.

The fat man said something else, but Michael didn't know if it was being addressed at him or not, and anyway couldn't make out what was being said. The man kept talking, looking at Michael sometimes and looking at the girls sometimes and looking out at the rest of the room sometimes. The voice was hard and made no sense. Finally, the fat man bent right over and said sharply into his ear: "Well?"

Michael jumped and looked up, shaking his head, his throat sore like he was going to cry.

"Were you at the girls?"

He shook his head.

"'No, sir!'" the voice roared, and Michael felt something soft go sliding past the pain in his throat and tears poured out of his eyes. "Answer me properly!"

"No sir," he croaked.

"Is that true?" said the man. Michael's eyes were all gummed up and blurred and he'd no idea who the man was talking to.

"No, sir," answered the girls' voices. The man went away and then came back again.

"Hold out your hand," he said. Michael did as he was told. Something thin, hard and cold touched his wrist, pushing his arm out and up. A large rough hand caught hold of his own and spread his fingers. Something whipped through the air and he heard a crack. A line of agony was drawn across his palm and a tingling, electric pain shot up his arm. He cried out in shock.

"Other hand," said the man.

His other hand was raised and flattened. There was another whish and crack and he cried out again.

The man said something, and he found himself being led back to his own room, sobbing, holding his hands out and away from his body as they burned and throbbed.

For the rest of his life, school for Michael would be an unreasoning terror.

The bell rang again and he went outside and sat down and cried, hands still flaming. He didn't understand, didn't want to understand.

"What's up?"

Jimmy sat down beside him. Michael couldn't see him very clearly, but the voice was familiar. He didn't answer.

"Did the Master hit you?"

Michael rocked back and forth on the seat, biting his lip.

"Why did he hit you?"

Jimmy's voice swelled with outrage.

"He shouldn't have hit you. You didn't do nothing wrong."

But the lesson Michael had just learned, the only lesson he would learn well for a long time to come, even though he couldn't have put it in words, was that Michael was wrong, and he had been punished for it. And if anything he did could be wrong, and if he could be punished for doing anything and everything, then the Master, and anyone else, could punish him whenever they wanted; and they would, whenever they wanted. Why this should be was beyond his understanding, it always would be. All he could do was try to follow whatever arbitrary rules they laid out for him, without thinking about them or trying to understand them, and do his best to be ignored and overlooked. That was all he could do.

"He shouldn't have done it," said Jimmy, then, "Come on, lets play."

He went home that evening, and didn't tell his mother what happened, afraid she would be angry at him, too.

The shadow was his teacher and the chattering birds were his fellow pupils. He learned where the boy's toilets were and where all the boys in his class went to play at break and lunch. Jimmy was always there with him when they played. In the classroom the teacher talked to them and did things, but Michael couldn't see what he was doing, and what he was saying made no sense. Often, the entire class would speak up together and Michael tried to make the same noises as the rest of them. They had to make marks on paper with pencils and Michael always had to copy J.J., the boy beside him. J.J. was his best friend apart from Jimmy, though J.J. couldn't run very fast and Michael was always going back to help him when there were chases.

Even though he kept quiet and didn't do anything, the teacher always seemed to be mad at him. He didn't know why. Most days, the teacher would stand over him and give out at least once or twice. Once he threatened to send Michael to the Master if he didn't buck himself up, and Michael started crying, and the teacher never said it again.

Though the harshness of his first day faded, a knock on the yellow door during class would always make him tremble, and leave him with a terrible pain in his stomach.

Saturdays and Sundays he could stay at home with his mother, and there was a holiday at Christmas and another at Easter. Everyone said there was a really long one coming for Summer, when you didn't have to go to school for months, which was nearly forever, but he didn't dare believe them. But it was true, the teacher said so, and on the last day he was sitting in the grass with Jimmy, his best friend, some little part of him knowing he was going to miss cops and robbers and tag and chasing and invisible man fights - a game Michael had invented, where you pretend one of you is invisible and he goes round pretending to punch you and you all fall around pretending you've been punched, falling around, yelling out and rolling on the grass - but nearly breathless with the thought that he wouldn't have to wake up any more mornings clenched in terror.

Jimmy, a pale glow in the sunlight, said softly, "He shouldn't have hit you."

Michael looked up and saw the big fat man, the Master walking slowly down the path towards him. He felt cold and started to shake.

"He won't hit you again," said Jimmy, and he made a gun with his fingers and pointed it at the Master.

"P'chow," he whispered, and his hand flew back in recoil, and straightened, "P'chow."

The Master stopped and bent slightly forward, as if checking to see if his shoelaces were untied.

Jimmy made a fist, and punched the air. The Master doubled over. Then Jimmy punched up in an uppercut. The Master's head flew up and he staggered, then toppled backwards and fell back on the path. All the children kept screaming and running and playing, except some who slowly approached the Master's body and asked him if he was alright, and soon a teacher came running across the lawn and Jimmy was gone and Michael was still sitting on the grass, still cold.

He didn't want to go back to school, but he knew he had to, it was the law, it was the rules. He was scared and upset, but he didn't want his mother to know, didn't want her to find out what had happened. He wanted to tell her, what he had done, what the Master had done, what had happened to the Master, but he was afraid she'd get mad at him, and then she'd be just like the teachers and he'd be as scared of home as he was of school, and he couldn't stand the thought of that betrayal.

There was a new Master, a woman, but she was still the Master, still the same person, just looking different. He said so at break.

"But the Master's dead," said J.J.

"Yeah, right over there," said Mark, pointing.

Michael didn't look.

"But she's still the Master," he insisted. "It's the same!"

"There was an old Master," said John, whispering, "years ago, who killed a kid."

Everyone stared, wide-eyed.

"My brother said so," said John. "Back in the old days, teachers could kill kids if they wanted to."

"Can they still?" asked Gerard.

"If the really want to," said John.

Jimmy tugged at Michael's shirt.

"Come on," he said and they ran off. The others followed behind.

A woman came, a Nurse, who did tests on all the kids. They were kind of fun. You put on earphones and listened for noises and you looked at a chart and called out letters. Sitting in the Nurse's tall, soft chair, Michael obstinately bit back tears. Even the biggest, the ones he could see, he didn't know what they were. The Nurse wanted to talk to his mother, and he thought he was going to be found out for something and get in loads of trouble and get hit again. But his mother just hugged him tight, and the Nurse said he was going to be getting a pair of glasses.

It was scary, in a different kind of way. Wearing the glasses, he was seeing a whole world he'd barely suspected even existed. He couldn't believe that everyone saw things like this all the time, that they all had different faces, that colours didn't have to be blurred or smudged, that what the teacher was doing on the board was writing, and that everyone else understood and he didn't, because he hadn't been able to see.

Looking around the classroom, he felt so proud of his glasses and the clarity they brought. He could make out J.J. and John and Mark and Gerard, all jealous because glasses meant he was smart, not stupid like it had seemed all along. But he couldn't see Jimmy at all.

He had to catch up with the others, who could all read and write, but that was okay. Though it was hard, for the first time he almost felt like he knew what he was doing. It didn't last very long, because there was Maths and Irish and Geography and History, all completely alien to him, but reading and writing he knew and at those at least he could be better than anyone.

Jimmy didn't like the glasses.

"They make you look funny," he said. Anyway, Michael wasn't supposed to wear them while playing, so he left them in the classroom at break and at lunch, which satisfied Jimmy.

He was always good in class. Summer to Autumn to Winter to Spring to Summer, when sitting in class he didn't speak, he didn't move if he didn't have to. He ducked his head and wouldn't look the teacher in the eye. And though teachers still gave out to him, because he couldn't pay attention to what they were saying and all their lessons went over his head, he read and he wrote as much as he could, furiously, frantically. He was never told off for misbehaving, never again sent to the Master. He didn't dare. He was afraid of what the Master would do to him, and of what Jimmy would do to the Master.

To Michael, in third class, the lads in fifth and sixth class were huge. They were the big lads; they thundered up and down the soccer field at violent speeds; if they thumped you your arm was numb for the day; when it snowed, their snowballs stung when they hit you and they laughed at jokes you didn't understand. In one corner of the school where a spare hawthorn bush was growing against the wire mesh fence that separated the school grounds from the long smooth roll of fields beyond, the big lads were building a hut. They got long strips of grass and braided them together, weaving them onto a frame of ash limbs.

The younger kids were fascinated. It was one of the coolest things they'd ever seen. The big lads were just doing it because they could, it wasn't for class or anything. There was a worshipful crowd around them while they worked every break and lunchtime and Michael was always at the front. Jimmy didn't like it and tried to get Michael to play games. Or he pointed at the forest fires in the hills, black columns of smoke pouring out of the greenery. Green army fire trucks were going back and forth past the school all the time, and that was cool too. But Michael needed his glasses to see the hut and the fires, so Jimmy tended to skulk by himself just out of Michael's sight.

The big boys told stories to each other, loud enough for the little kids to hear. They said that when the hut was finished they were gong to hunt for little kids to tie up and leave inside the hut to die, just like the Brothers did. The Christian Brothers used to run the school years ago, and according to the big boys it was a reign of terror of horrific proportions. Awful, violent punishments dished out for the smallest of crimes. The Brothers were savage and brutal, and they liked to hit kids. They liked to lock them in the broom cupboard in the dark until they learned their lesson. And one time, this Brother bashed a kids head against a wall and threw him in the cupboard and left him there, and when they came to let the kid out, he'd died.

The crowd of little kids gasped, but Michael looked into the dark shadow of the hut, took off his glasses and went to find Jimmy, to play. The next day, the hut had been torn down by vandals, the lovely grass pig-tails scattered everywhere, the ash frame broken. Everyone was shocked and mad, except Jimmy, who ignored it.

The teacher, Miss Ryan, went round and filled all the books with new sums for them to do. Her writing was big and bold and red, and she showed Michael what to do. He followed her carefully and forced himself to remember every step, and when she moved on to J.J. he did each step with the first sum, slowly, painstakingly, until it seemed right. Miss Ryan glanced over at his page.

"Very good, Michael," she said.

Michael felt a thrill. Then he went to the next sum, and the next, until he'd finished them all and he put down his pencil and lifted the copy and studied each one, then he put the copy down and folded his arms, wondering when Miss Ryan would look at them and if she'd say it again; well done, Michael.

"Finished, Michael?"

He nodded. "Yes, Miss."

"Are you sure?"

"Yes, Miss."

"All of them?"

"Yes, Miss."

"Michael, don't lie to me. Have you finished all the sums?"

He felt cold, and looked at his copy to check.

"Yes, Miss."

"Come here and show me."

He got up with his copy and went to where she was sitting against the windowsill. He gave her the copy, and she looked at it, then handed it back. Then she slapped him across the face.

"That's for being a liar, Michael. Sit down."

Too shocked to cry, cheek stinging like mad, he sat back down. J.J. leaned over and whispered, pointing at the board.

"We're supposed to do those as well. Didn't you see them?"

Michael straightened his glasses. No he hadn't seen the rows of sums written on the blackboard. Miss Ryan must have done them while he was absorbed with the sums in his copy. He sat, stunned, face tingling. He heard a distant bell ringing.

"Ten to eleven," said J.J., proud of his watch, "That's the bell for Mass. You coming trick-or-treating with us?"

Heat raced up and down his back, hot anger and outrage. He took off his glasses.

It was a cold Halloween, but his mother didn't try to stop him, just made sure he was well wrapped up before letting him go out. He had the mask he'd made in class, cut out of a cornflakes box and covered in red and black crayon. Miss Ryan had showed them a trick way of cutting out eyes and a way of cutting and stapling the corners so it would fit your face like a real mask. He had a cape of plastic bin liner, and he wore another underneath with holes for his arms cut out. He wore a sword in a scabbard that hung around his neck and over his shoulder on a piece of string. The scabbard was a cardboard toilet roll middle and the sword was a broken brush handle. He ran out and met J.J. and John and Mark and Gerard and they flew under the streetlights, capes fluttering, giggling and shouting. They melted into the shadows and haunted the street and flitted from tree to bush to wall, a dark, mysterious fellowship bent on dark deeds.

It was hard, wearing the glasses under the mask, but he wouldn't be able to see otherwise. He missed Jimmy. There was a strong, biting wind blowing, and clouds scudded across the sky, but most of the time the half-moon shone down. At the edge of the village, where there were no houses and where the last light glowed like a lonely beacon outside the school, Michael stood and looked down at the road and the ditch and the wall, all swallowed into darkness. Leaves scraped along the road, then vanished. In his mask and cape and with his sword swinging against his legs, he felt brave enough to go down there, face whatever was hidden by the night, never be hit again, never feel so stupid. He looked up, and a cloud shaped like a skull with a dagger through it crawled across the moon.

"Look!" he shouted, "Look!"

On the last day of school that year he was walking through the school gates and waving at J.J. and Mark in the bus pulling out.

"Hey," said Jimmy. Michael looked up. Jimmy was standing on the wall. The sun was behind his head and Michael squinted.

"Hey, Jimmy."

"Vroom," said Jimmy, turning an invisible wheel, changing invisible gears, "Nyerrrnnnn..."

"Stop it, Jimmy," said Michael. But Jimmy made screeching brakes noises and pretended the steering wheel leaped out of his hands and he threw up his arms with a scream and fell back off the wall, laughing; and Michael could hear metal crumpling and tearing and glass breaking. He started to run, Jimmy's laughter following him from behind the wall.

He had a fascination with maps. His room was covered, wall to wall, with everything from hand-drawn plans of the house or the village, to pages cut from magazines, to road maps he'd persuaded his mother to buy for him. He traced the roads and contour lines with his fingers and said the names of the towns aloud to himself, and assured himself that everything was where it was supposed to be. So when the Master pulled down the world map from where it hung at the back of the room, unrolling it so that it covered nearly half the wall and began talking in her dry, clear voice, pointing with the long stick Michael had been eying nervously ever since he came into the room, he forgot the stiff tension that made his shoulders ache, let his stomach unclench slightly and turned in his desk, craning his neck to see.

Fifth and sixth class were the big boy years, though Michael didn't feel very big. He knew he would soon be leaving this school and going to another, where the boys were really big, and where the lessons were harder and the teachers even angrier. Where he would be small all over again.

Meanwhile, he was finally allowed to join in the eternal game of soccer played on the stretch of ground behind the school, below the trees and at the back of the boy's shed. The grass was worn away completely, leaving bare red clay that went dusty in heat and muddy in rain.

Michael liked playing at the back, protecting the goal, and J.J. who was the goalie. It was usually the long, powerful shots from midfield that got past them. If the general melee that surrounded the ball was carried to his end, he dodged through the scuffling crowd, bowling boys on either team aside until his foot came in reach of the darting grey blob, and belted it back toward the other goal.

Jimmy loved the game and charged around the field, kicking and jumping and yelling, not always at the ball. He left boys tumbling in the dust behind him, he sent the ball smashing into boy's sides, and pushed and pulled until they were piled on top of each other in a struggling mass.

No-one ever touched Jimmy, though. No-one could come near him.

At first Michael had shied away from him, too, after coming back to a new teacher, remembering helping form the guard of honour at Miss Ryan's funeral, feeling like a murderer. Jimmy pretended it had never happened and ignored Micheal's attempts to steer clear of him. Wherever he went during break or lunch, Jimmy was there, joining in whether Michael wanted him to or not. So Michael kept quiet in class, and didn't move, and did what he was told, and bit down on the sharp, red thing that squirmed through his insides.

Going into fifth class was like going into the monster's lair. The Master, the new Master, standing behind her desk as they came in, sitting, calling out the roll. His mouth was dry and his leg trembled. J.J. gave him a kick in the ankle and he jumped, but she didn't notice.

A lot of the time she wasn't the Master, she was Miss O'Mahony. A thin woman with grey hair and level green eyes and long slender hands. He watched her when she wasn't looking, and ducked his head when she was. Most of the time she was Miss O'Mahony, like when she asked him to read out of the English book with the strange pictures of men in suits floating in the sky, or when she let them draw in their art copies for an hour, or she got them to press leaves for Nature class, or to sing for Music, or showed them places on the great map of the world that covered nearly half the wall at the back of the classroom.

But she was the Master, too. She sent someone to fetch kids from other classes and while they stood there asked them if they'd been bad, if they'd been spitting or using bad language to a teacher or fighting. Then she took a long, thin bamboo stick and made them hold out their hand, and then she hit them and Michael closed his eyes and heard the whish and crack, and then the cry, and the terrified silence. And sometimes, in class, she got mad. Someone hadn't done their homework again or said something really stupid or the whole class had started yelling and shouting while she'd stepped outside to talk to a teacher. Then her face went pale, looking like a mask, and her eyes blazed and her voice snapped like a whip over their heads and they cringed, and, sometimes, she slapped.

Mostly, though, she was Miss O'Mahony, and she praised Michael for his reading, and for his project at the end of fifth class to make a map of the village which had all the shops and houses and a key and everything. She said he should make loads of them and sell them, they were so good.

When it rained and they weren't playing soccer, mostly the boys would go to their shed and the girls to theirs, though there was some antagonistic mixing. The sheds were long rectangular boxes open on one side except for a line of thick red pillars. They looked out on wide, open concrete courtyards where the water would pool in the middle, and if the rain was really hard the shed would be flooded too, and you had to walk along the wooden bench to stay off the water, which froze in the winter. You could slide across from one end to the other, flakes of ice flying, turning to sludge as the sun rose higher.

Michael and Jimmy sat in the boys' shed watching the rain pool and spread, watching the grey haze sweep between them and the hills like curtains waving in the wind. They weren't really talking about anything when Jimmy turned to him.

"They hit you," he said.

Jimmy felt drops of rain blown in by a sudden gust splash across his face.

"She'd better not hit you." Then he ran out of the shed and vanished into the rain, white into grey. The bell was ringing.

She didn't hit him. Michael was very careful. When the end of the year came round, she hadn't hit him, had barely spoken to him at all.

"We're going to have someone staying with us this Summer, for a while."

Michael was eating sausages, beans and chips, his favourite meal, and his mother was sitting at the table with him, drinking a mug of coffee. He liked cutting a piece of sausage and putting it on the fork with a few chips and beans, then putting the whole lot in his mouth. His mother said it was the proper way to eat.

"Your grandmother is coming over from America for a visit. Your father's mother."

Michael concentrated on his food. There was always something awkward and unspoken between him and his mother about his father, who'd died when he was too young to remember. She didn't talk about him, and Michael always felt embarrassed for her, and didn't ask.

"She wants to see you. She wants to see us."

Granny was a stranger, the most complete stranger he'd ever met. She looked out of place, because her clothes were funny, and the expression on her face. Her voice was weird, too. She gave him a big hug, making loads of noise, and gave him a bag full of sweatshirts and jumpers and t-shirts. They were all too big for him, but they were cool. They had buffaloes and indians and American Football players on them.

She talked with his mother for ages, then he was called in and sat in her lap, even though he was way too big for that. His mother went out to make coffee.

"Let me show you something," she said, and rooted in her bag. Then she held up a photograph of two boys, smiling. The photo was old, black and white. He touched it, gently.

"That was your father, there on the left," she said, "And his brother, little James. My boys. That was taken in the back-yard. We all used to live here together, you know."

He looked closer while she sighed and hummed a little tune.

"You're so like him," she said, "You've grown."

He took off his glasses and looked at the picture again. He got up off her lap, not daring to speak, holding the picture.

"Your Uncle James," she said, "I'll tell you about him when you're older."

He looked up from the picture and when she saw the expression on his face, she stopped talking and raised her eyebrows at him.

"Okay," she said slowly, "But don't tell your mother I told you."

He tried not to think about his last year in school. He hated it, even though all his friends were there, even though he played soccer and ran with Jimmy, even though the Master stayed hidden most of the time; he still hated it. But what was secondary school going to be like? How much worse? It was a foreign country for which he had no map, a dark and dangerous place.

"Will you be going to the same school as me?" he asked Jimmy, but Jimmy didn't answer.

That morning, before the first bell rang, they were around the back sliding on the ice, and J.J. was showing off his father's binoculars. All the lads were crowding around him, begging for a go.

"You can look at the tower with it," said Jimmy. The tower was a tall black speck standing at the highest point of the nearby hills, rising over the carpet of trees. It might not have been a tower; there was no way of knowing what it was, it was too far away, but Jimmy was obsessed with it. He'd drag Michael to the fence and point at it for him, all excited, tugging at Michael's shoulder and chattering about going there one day, finding out what it was, exploring it. Michael could barely make it out unless the day was particularly clear, since he wasn't wearing his glasses.

Jimmy snatched the binoculars from J.J.

"Hey!" said J.J., but he made no move to get it back.

"Jimmy!" said Michael.

Jimmy pressed the binoculars to his face and pointed them at the tower. As if for the first time, Michael noticed that Jimmy didn't seem to feel the cold, even though he wasn't wearing a jacket or even a jumper, and his breath didn't frost.

Jimmy made a frustrated noise and ran away around the corner of the boys' shed. Michael, J.J. and the others began to go after him.

"I can see it! I can see it!"

Jimmy's voice came to them from the roof of the shed. They all looked up, and there he was, jumping up and down with the binoculars covering his eyes.

"They're my dad's!" yelled J.J. "He'll kill me if you break them!"

"Jimmy!" shouted Michael, but Jimmy ignored them. J.J. looked at Michael, anguish in his face. Michael gritted his teeth, then ran round the back of the shed. He caught hold of the black drainpipe, feet scrabbling against the wall, and began pulling himself up. The pipe was so cold it hurt his hands, and his feet kept slipping, but Michael ignored it, refused to let himself think about falling, and kept going.

He went up fast, pulling himself over the edge onto the icy, tarry roof. Jimmy was gone, but the binoculars were lying there. Walking carefully so as not to slip, Michael made his way over to them and picked them up. He paused for a moment, then pointed them at the tower and looked through them. It sprang out at him, leaping through space to stand before him. It was a building. He could see windows, paint flaking off stone, a dead winter garden and a man in brown bent low under a holly bush. The man was sitting up, turning.

"Michael Riordan!"

He jumped, and nearly dropped the binoculars. The Master's voice cut through him like a sliver of ice.

"What are you doing up there? Get down here, right now!"

Somehow, he managed to keep his feet under him as he made his shaky way to the edge. He looked down at all the faces turned up towards him.

"Stay there," said the Master. "We'll get a ladder."

Michael ignored her. He sat down, legs dangling over the drop. He put the strap of the binoculars over his head. Then he turned, and lowered himself out into empty space. The soles of his feet slid down the wall.

"Michael! Michael stop!"

He could hear her shouting. Miss O'Mahony, not the Master. He kept going until he was hanging there, legs swinging uselessly. He felt sticky with sweat, but the roof scraped his hands and he just managed to keep his grip.

He let go with one hand and dropped. He grabbed the pipe and pulled himself into it. Then he forced his other hand to let go, and he started sliding down the wall, but slowly, holding to the pipe with both hands.

When he was about halfway down, the Master caught him about the waist and lifted him off the pipe and lowered him. She shook him hard, and he looked up at her, defiant, daring. Then he saw Miss O'Mahony, angry, but also scared, looking back down at him, and he thought of his mother. His defiance dissolved. She shook him again, asking him something he couldn't hear. His legs went weak and he felt himself fall, but she kept hold of him, grabbing at him to hold him up.

The first thing he felt was his head, bouncing when it hit the wall. A big, numb, dizzy thing caught hold of the back of his head, then a large block of pain shifted and settled, grinding like rocks. He was looking up at the sky, neck bent back, mouth wide open, and Miss O'Mahony said "Oh, Michael!"

"She didn't mean it," he insisted. "It was an accident!"

Jimmy just smiled, a white glow brightening.

"I know who you are!" Michael shouted desperately. "Leave her alone! Leave me alone! I know who you are!"

Jimmy skipped into the trees and Michael ran after him. The trees were suddenly full of kids, chasing after each other, and Jimmy somewhere among them. Michael stopped, clenching his fists, screaming.

"Jimmy!"

Then Jimmy was there, hurtling at him, grabbing him by the shoulders and Michael grabbed him back and they were pushing at each other, grunting and straining, kicking out. One of them gave way, and they fell on each other, punching and pulling, gasping, rolling in the icy grass, onto the red dust, into the knobbly roots of a tree. There were kids all round them, but they were silent, watching with wide eyes. They kept struggling and wrestling, Michael squeezing out his rage and frustration and pounding Jimmy with it, Jimmy returning it blow for blow. The bell rang, and none of the kids moved. Jimmy and Michael kept fighting until the teachers all came out to see where their pupils were and then they broke and ran for their classrooms, leaving Michael lying alone on the ground, tears coursing through the dust on his face, drying sweat making his body shiver and shake in the cold.

"Are we still friends?" asked Jimmy the next day. Michael looked at his feet, hands in his pockets.

"I'm sorry about the fight, Michael. You were really good. You're really strong. You could beat up anyone."

"You're strong, too, Jimmy."

"Not as strong as you. Bet nobody could get us together. We could beat up everyone in the school."

Michael nodded. Then he took off his glasses and looked up at Jimmy.

"Let's go play soccer," he said, and they ran to the back of the school.

He wasn't good at understanding things, he knew. All the teachers said he was slow, except Miss O'Mahoney. She said he wasn't stupid, he just couldn't take things in. He couldn't put things together. With Jimmy he had to. He had to try. He sat down and wrote to his granny in America. Where was the man? Where was the Brother?

"That man," she'd said, "that evil man who killed my son. Jimmy was wild but he didn't deserve to die, not like that, not at all. They hushed it all up, said it was an accident, spirited the man away somewhere. A peaceful retirement, an insult, a travesty. They didn't even have the grace to move him somewhere far away. That's why we couldn't stay in the end. Not knowing that evil man, that murderer was so close."

He waited for her reply, and tried to keep Jimmy happy, and tried to be good in class. Months went by, and the end of the year drew near. Spring rain battered against the windows and the old radiators clanked and banged as the pipes heated up. The rains grew warmer, and the leaves spread and flowers danced in sunny breezes. Days were long and bright, and months became weeks, and the summer tests came suddenly, and then it was days. The Master was gone, there was only Miss O'Mahony, he knew that now. Granny's letter never came.

Thursday evening he came through the door, dropping his bag, knowing it hadn't come. Tomorrow was the last day, a half-day. His mother called to him from the hallway.

"Michael! There's someone who wants to talk to you."

She handed him the phone.

"Michael?" said his grandmother. "Why do you want to know that?"

"I...I can't explain. I just need to know."

There was a pause.

"I've tried to put all that behind me. I've lost two sons and a husband, all gone like they were never there. I try not to let it destroy me but sometimes I feel so empty. You're all I have left of them, you know. Would you like to come visit me?"

"Yes," he said, "I'd really like that."

There was another pause.

"It's a place named Evergreen Lodge. The Order owned land up in the hills, but sold most of it to the forestry. They kept the lodge, though. He's still there."

Michael took a deep breath, then let it out in hiss.

"Thanks, gran," he said, "I'd better go."

"We'll talk again. Arrange your visit, okay?"

"Okay," he said, and giving the phone back to his mother, he ran out.

A shower had just passed. Thick white clouds shining brilliantly in the sun were falling over the horizon while darker clouds came creeping up from the other side. His bike swept through puddles, sending sheets of water flying. He barely noticed the ache in his legs as he climbed up into the hills, nor the smooth tar road giving way to rocky tracks. The trees grew close and thick, but they were young and short. The air reeked of pine resin.

He had a map of the hills with all the tracks on it and he followed it carefully, plotting a route to where he thought it most likely the lodge would be. Trees were taller here and the sun was starting to set. The shadows grew thicker. He stopped the bike and looked around, but there was no building anywhere to be seen. There was a gap in the trees, though, wide enough for a car to drive through. He swung off the track and followed the trail upwards. It grew darker.

Michael came out of the trees suddenly, the trail growing steeper than ever. He caught his breath. There was a wall, bigger than a man, with sprays of flowers flowing over the top, and rising like a tower, red in the light of the setting sun, the gable end of a house. He pushed his bike along the path until he came to a large metal gate, standing open. He left his bike on the ground and went through. There was a gravel driveway in front and flower beds on either side, all meticulously cared for. The house itself was run down, most of the paint gone, the windows all grimy, the wood of the door rotting.

Flowers rustled, and a man stepped out onto the drive. He wore a brown robe, stained and filthy and torn. Michael was wearing his glasses, so he could see him clearly. He was stooped and pudgy, bald, with fat, red cheeks and milky eyes. His chin trembled when he saw Michael. He was holding a small gardening fork which he pointed at Michael before he turned and lowered himself to his knees, using it to dig at the flower bed.

"I have to ask you something," said Michael. He walked over to the kneeling man.

"Hello? Listen, I have to ask you about something. I have to ask you about Jimmy Riordan. He was my uncle. I have to ask you about him. Please!"

The man ignored him. He just kept digging away at the soil with his trowel, pulling weeds and throwing them in a small pile.

"Please listen to me!"

But the man kept digging. Michael stood there, helplessly.

218

"Let's go exploring," said Jimmy. Michael was wearing his glasses, so he saw Jimmy, saw the young boy in shorts and shirt and untied shoes, saw the wavy hair and smile, straight out of his granny's photo. Saw him step up and hold out his hand.

"Come on," he said.

The kneeling man stopped digging and turned. Uncertain and hesitant, he took the boy's hand. His chin worked silently and he dribbled from the corners of his mouth as he got shakily to his feet, his face slack and childish, but with stark terror in his milky eyes. He was crying. Jimmy's smile was hard and bright, full of teeth. There was a bruise on his forehead. Blood began to flow down around his eyes, over his face, dripping onto his shirt. Michael backed away. He hadn't wanted this at all.

Jimmy started pulling the old man towards the house.

"Come on," he said. "Come on!"

The Brother went with him, walking jerkily, mouth opening and closing like a drowning fish. Jimmy, face red with blood, his head tilted at a strange angle, said, "I want to show you something!" Then he pulled the old man through the door, and Michael turned and ran and grabbed his bike and cycled home through the cold twilight as fast as he could.

He didn't sleep that night, and got up, shivering, at dawn. Skipping breakfast, he went straight out to the school to sit on the wall and wait. Birds sang, and the trees shook in the wind. He waited as if in a dream. Kids began to arrive, and he didn't move. Teachers drove up in their cars. Miss O'Mahony arrived, and still he didn't move. The bus came and spilled out a torrent of children. Watching them, Michael felt very old and distant and sad.

Finally, the bell rang, and he got up and walked through the gate and up to the doors. He wasn't scared. Jimmy wouldn't be coming to school anymore.

James White, born Belfast 1928, was one of Ireland's leading SF authors. His stories, full of wit, generally bypassed violence as a plot device. They often featured ordinary people and benign aliens, unusual in much early SF. He saw various occupations, from tailoring to department store management, and in his stories these experiences often saw use: the ordinary brought to life by the fantastic. Raised on Golden Age SF, he came to produce, with Walt Willis, the fanzines *Slant* (1948-53) and *Hyphen* (1952-65). His first sales (1953) were to *New Worlds*, to which he contributed regularly thereafter. 1957 saw his first novel, *The Secret Visitors*, and the appearance of the well-known Sector General Hospital series, with a novella in *New Worlds*. Alongside the Sector General novels and stories, Jim produced many fine stand-alone novels, such as *The Watch Below* (1966) and *The Silent Stars Go By* (1991). Jim earned a Hugo-nomination for his story 'Un-Birthday Boy' (*Analog*, 1996) and also for the story in this collection, featured in *Stellar 2* (1976), demonstrating his ability to make interesting even the most ordinary of settings. Sadly, Jim passed away in 1999.

Custom Fitting

James White

For many years Hewlitt had been in the habit of spending half an hour sunning himself at the entrance to his shop when the sunlight was available in sufficient strength. The period was determined by the length of time it took for the sun to clear the eaves of the buildings on his side of the street and to move far enough out to necessitate his pulling out the shop's awning so that the cloth on display would not fade. He spent the time watching the passersby - hoping that some of them wouldn't - and anything else of interest. Usually there was nothing interesting to see, but today was an exception.

A large, plain furniture van, preceded by a police car and followed closely by an Electricity Department truck, turned into his street from the main road. The presence of the police vehicle was explained by the fact that the convoy was moving in the wrong direction along a one-way street. When the procession finally halted, the removals van was directly facing him.

For perhaps a minute there was nothing to see except the reflection of himself and his doorway in the dark, glossy flanks of the van. It was the slightly distorted picture of a thin and rather ridiculous figure wearing a black jacket and waistcoat with striped trousers, a small flower in the lapel, and a tape measure - the outward sign of his profession - hanging loosely from his neck. The lettering on the door behind the figure was executed in gold leaf in a bold italic script and said, in reverse:

GEORGE L. HEWLITT,
TAILOR

Suddenly - as if some hypothetical film director had shouted "Action!" - everything happened at once.

Two senior police officers carrying traffic-diversion signs left their vehicle and moved in opposite directions to seal off each end of the street. The Electricity Department truck disgorged a gang of neatly overalled workmen, who quickly began unloading collapsible screening, a nightwatchman's hut, and a man wearing a well-tailored suit of dark gray worsted and a tie which was strictly establishment. He also wore a very worried expression as he glanced up and down the street and at the windows overlooking it.

"Good morning, Mr. Hewlitt," the man said, coming forward. "My name is Fox. I'm with the Foreign Office. I, ah, would like to consult you professionally. May I come inside?"

Hewlitt inclined his head politely and followed him into the shop.

For a few minutes nothing else was said because Fox was pacing nervously about the interior, staring at the shelves of neatly rolled cloth lengths, fingering the pattern books which were placed strategically on the polished wooden counters, and examining the paneling and crystal-clear mirrors in the big fitting room. While the Foreign Office official was looking over the premises, Hewlitt was studying Fox with equal attention.

Fox was of medium height, slimly built, with a head-forward tendency and prominent shoulder blades. From the small but noticeable lateral crease behind the jacket collar, it was obvious that he tried to correct the HF and PSB tendency by carrying himself unnaturally erect. Plainly Fox's tailor had had problems, and Hewlitt wondered if he was about to inherit them.

"How may I help you, sir?" Hewlitt said when his visitor had finally come to rest. He used a tone which was friendly but one with that touch of condescension which very plainly said that it would be Hewlitt's decision whether or not he would build a jacket around Fox's prominent shoulder blades.

"I am not the client, Mr. Hewlitt," Fox said impatiently. "*He* is waiting outside. However, this matter must be treated in the strictest confidence - kept absolutely secret, in fact, for the next two weeks. After that you may discuss it with whom you please.

"From our thorough if necessarily hasty inquiries," the Foreign Office official went on, "we know that you live above these premises with your wife, who is also your seamstress and a partial cripple. We also know that your work is competent, if a little old-fashioned as regards styling, and that your stock is remarkably lacking in materials using man-made fibers. For many years your financial position has not been good, and I should say at this juncture that your silence as well as your work workmanship will be very highly paid.

"The garment itself should present no difficulty," Fox ended, "since all that is required is a fairly well-fitting horse blanket."

Coldly, Hewlitt said, I am completely lacking in experience where horse blankets are concerned, Mr. Fox."

"You are being proud and unnecessarily stubborn, Mr. Hewlitt. This a very important client, and may I remind you that across the street there is a branch of a well-known multiple tailoring company which is also capable of doing the job."

"I agree," said Hewlitt dryly. "That company could do a pretty good job - on a horse blanket."

Fox smiled faintly, but before he could reply one of the workmen entered and said, "The screens are in position, sir, and the van is blocking the view from the other side of the street. Now we need the pole to pull out the sun awning. That will hide the shop front from the upper-story windows on the other side of the street."

Hewlitt pointed toward the recess behind the display window where the awning pole was kept.

"Thank you, sir," said the workman in the tones of a senior public servant who is addressing a lowly member of the public he serves, then he turned away.

"Wait," said Fox, visibly coming to a decision. "When you've done that, ask His Excellency if he would be good enough to come in, please."

The strict secrecy being observed, the Foreign Office involvement, and the type of garment required had led Hewlitt to expect some highly controversial political figure: an overweight person from an underfed nation who was intent on expressing his individuality and independence by wearing an English-tailored native garment. Such a person might well be frightened of an assassin's bullet and feel it necessary to take these elaborate precautions; but that, after all, was not any of Hewlitt's business. But when he saw the client. . .

I'm dreaming, he told himself firmly.

The creature resembled a centaur, complete with hooves and a long, streaming tail. At first glance the torso from the waist up resembled that of a human being; but the musculature of the arms, shoulders, and chest was subtly different, and the hands were five-digited, each comprised of three fingers and two opposable thumbs. The head, carried erect above a very thick neck, was made to seem disproportionately small. The face was dominated by two large, soft, brown eyes that somehow made the slits, protuberances, and fleshy petals which comprised the other features visually acceptable.

Apart from a large medallion suspended around its neck, the being wore no clothing. Its skin was a mottled pinkish-brown color, and the creature twitched continually as if to dislodge invisible flies. It was obviously male.

"Your Excellency," said Fox smoothly, "may I present Mr. George Hewlitt. He is a tailor, or maker of clothing, who will produce for you garments suitable for your stay on Earth."

Instinctively Hewlitt put out his hand. He discovered that his client's grip was firm, the digits warm and bony, and the way the lower thumb curled upward into his palm was indescribable but not unpleasant. For some odd reason he could no longer think of the being as an "it."

"The initial requirement," Fox said briskly, "is for a garment which will be comfortable and will keep His Excellency warm during the presentation ceremonies and socializing that will follow. The garment should be black, edged with gold or silver braid, perhaps, and should carry pseudo-heraldic decorations. No existing family crests can be used, obviously. He will also require a second garment, less formal, for use during sightseeing tours out-of-doors."

"A braided and decorated horse blanket, then," said Hewlitt, "and a plain one for walking out. But if you could tell me the kind of function His Excellency is to attend, I would be in a better position to produce something suitable."

Fox shook his head. "Security."

"I can, if necessary, work blindfolded and with one arm tied behind my back," Hewlitt said, "but I do not produce my best work under those conditions. However, if His Excellency would kindly follow me into the fitting room?"

With a soft, irregular thumping of hooves the client, accompanied by Fox, followed into the fitting room and stood looking at himself in the angled mirrors. Rarely had Hewlitt seen a customer more ill at ease. The other's hide was twitching and tightening along his back and flanks before Hewlitt had even laid the tape on him.

Without being obtrusive about it, Hewlitt studied the twitching hide, looking for insects or other evidence of parasitic presences. Relieved at not finding any, he thought for a moment, then switched on the wall heaters, which were never used during the summer months. Within a few minutes the room was uncomfortably warm and the twitching had stopped.

While Hewlitt went to work with his tape measure and pad, he asked, "I assume that my client's home planet is warmer than Earth?"

"Yes," said Fox. "Our weather at present would approximate to one of their sunny days in late autumn."

From small of back to root of tail, 63 inches, Hewlitt wrote carefully. He said, "In cool weather they wear clothing, then?"

"Yes, a form of toga wrapped around their bodies in a loose spiral, with - Oh, now I see why you switched on the heaters. I should have thought of that; it was very remiss of me. But His Excellency does not want to wear his native clothing for very good reasons, so he thought it better to suffer a little discomfort rather than to take the risk of your being influenced, even unconsciously, by his native dress. It is most important that he wear clothing which is made and styled on Earth."

From centre line back to foreleg knee joint, 42 inches, Hewlitt wrote. To Fox he said, "The requirement is for a blanket-like garment, but surely my client will require additional clothing if he is to feel-"

"Just the blanket, Mr. Hewlitt."

"If the positions were reversed," said Hewlitt patiently, "you would no doubt feel reasonably warm in a blanket; but you would feel much more *comfortable* if you were wearing shorts as well."

Irritably, Fox said, "Please follow instructions, Hewlitt. Your fee will be generous, regardless of how many or how few garments you make for His Excellency. Your attempt to drum up extra business is a waste of your time and ours."

"The majority of civilized people on Earth wear undergarments," said Hewlitt, "and unless climatic conditions, religious beliefs, or the dictates of local fashion rule otherwise, I should think that the same applied on other worlds."

"You are being argumentative, uncooperative, and you are introducing unnecessary complications into what is a very simple set of instructions," said Fox angrily. "Let me remind you that we can still go across the street!"

"Please do so," said Hewlitt.

Fox and Hewlitt glared at each other for several seconds while the alien, his features unreadable by virtue of their complete alienness, turned his outsize brown eyes on each of them in turn.

Suddenly a soft, gobbling noise issued from one of the fleshy slits in his face and, simultaneously and much louder, a pleasant baritone voice spoke from the ornament suspended from the alien's neck. It said, "Perhaps I can resolve this difficulty, gentlemen. It seems to me that Mr. Hewlitt has displayed qualities of observation, good sense, and concern for the comfort of his customer, myself. Therefore, I would prefer him to continue to act as my tailor providing he is willing to do so."

Fox swallowed, then said weakly, "Security, Your Excellency. We agreed that you would not speak to any member of the public until ... the day."

"My apologies, Mr. Fox," the alien replied through his translation device, "but on my world a specialist like Mr. Hewlitt is considered something more than a member of the public."

Turning to Hewlitt, he went on, "I would be most grateful if you could give the matter of my underwear your attention. However, for reasons which Mr. Fox would prefer to remain secret for the present, this garment must also be of Earth material and styling. Is this possible?"

Hewlitt bowed slightly and said, "Of course, sir."

"Not *sir!*" said Fox, obviously angered because his instructions had been ignored by the alien. "This is His Excellency the Lord Scrennagle of Dutha-"

Scrennagle held up one double-thumbed hand as he said politely, "Pardon the interruption. That is only an approximation of my rank and title. 'Sir' is sufficiently respectful and conversationally much less cumbersome."

"Yes, Your Excellency," said Fox.

Hewlitt produced a swatch of patterns and a style book from which Scrennagle chose a soft lambswool in pale cream which would not, the tailor assured them, react in any fashion with his skin. The style plates fascinated him, and when Hewlitt began to sketch similar designs modified to fit his centaur-like body, the alien was practically breathing down the tailor's neck.

Polite questioning had elicited the facts that Scrennagle insisted on dressing himself and that the area or skin covering the spine between waist and tail was the part of his body most susceptible to cold.

"If you wouldn't mind, sir," said Hewlitt at that point, "I would like you to advise me regarding the positioning of fastenings, openings for the elimination of body wastes, and so on … "

Scrennagle could twist the upper part of his body so that his hands could reach either flank as far back as the tail, although he could only see the lower end of his back. The undergarment which Hewlitt had to devise would have to be stepped into and pulled up on to the fore and hind legs in turn. It would be doublebacked and buttoned through, with one wide flap or cloth going over the back to the opposite flank and fastening there, while the other flap passed over the back in the opposite direction to button on the other flank - rather like a double-breasted suit worn back-to-front. Scrennagle said that the double thickness of cloth at the back would be very comfortable, the local temperature being what is was; and he found no fault in the more complicated flap and fastening arrangements for the fly and rear.

He was politely insistent, however, that his tail should not be even partially concealed. There were strong psychological reasons for this, apparently.

"I quite understand, sir," said Hewlitt. "And now if you will stand quite still I shall measure you. The dimensions and contour descriptions required will be much more complex than those needed for the blankets. Once I have drafted a properly fitting pattern for the garment, however, making additional ones will present no problems. Initially a set of four undergarments should be sufficient to -"

"Hewlitt-!" Fox began.

"No gentleman," Hewlitt said very quietly, "no matter how high or low his station, would undertake a major journey with just one set of underwear."

There was, of course, no reply to that; and Hewlitt resumed measuring his client. While he worked he told Scrennagle exactly what he was doing and why. He even went so far as to discuss the weather in his attempts to make his client relax bodily so that he would not shape the garment to a figure that was being held in an unnatural pose through tension.

"I intend making the leg sections reach less than halfway between the hip joints and knees, sir," he said at one point. "This will give the maximum comfort and warmth commensurate with

the length of the over-garment. However, it would assist me greatly if I knew something more about the purpose of this blanket -
what movements you would be making in it, whether or not you
are expecting to be photographed, the geographical or architec-
tural surroundings - so that the garment will not look out of
place."

"You're fishing for information," said Fox sharply. "Please
desist. "

Hewlitt ignored him and said to Scrennagle, "You can rely on
my discretion, sir."

"I know that," said Scrennagle. Turning so that he could see
Fox in the fitting-room mirror, he went on: "A certain amount of
curiosity is natural in these circumstances, and if Mr. Hewlitt has
been entrusted with the secret of my presence in this city, surely
the reason of my being here is a minor additional confidence
which should not overstrain his capacity for-"

"With respect, Your Excellency," said Fox, "these matters
must not be made public until all the necessary preparations have
been made."

Hewlitt wrote *Girth at forelegs, 46 inches.* Controlling his
exasperation, he said, "If the material, finish, and decoration of
these garments are to fit the occasion - an important occasion no
doubt - I really should be told something about it."

There was silence for a moment, then Scrennagle and his
translation device made noises which were possibly the equivalent
of clearing an alien throat. His head went up and he stood very
still as he said, "As the accredited representative of Dutha and the
Galactic Federation on Earth, I shall be presenting my credentials
at the Court of St. James with the usual attendant ceremonies. In
the evening of the same day there will be a reception at which the
Sovereign will also be present. Although I am officially only an
ambassador, the honors will be similar to those accorded a visit-

ing head of state. The reception will be covered by the media, and interviews will be given following the official … " .

Hewlitt was no longer listening to him. His sense of outrage was so great that no word could filter through to his mind with any meaning in it. Quietly he excused himself to Scrennagle; then to Fox he said, "Could I have a private word with you, outside?"

Without waiting for a reply he stalked out of the fitting room and across to the door, which he held open so that Fox could precede him into the hallway. Then he closed the door firmly, so firmly that the glass shattered and tinkled onto the porch tiling.

"And for this," he whispered fiercely, "you want me to make a - a *horse blanket*?"

Just as fiercely, Fox replied, "Believe it or not, I sympathize with your feelings. But this could be the most important event in human history and *it must go well!* Not just for Scrennagle's sake. What we do here will be the yardstick, the example, for embassies all over the world; and they must have no room for criticism. Some of them will feel that they should have had the first visit, and would welcome the chance to criticize. They must not be given that chance."

One of the Special Branch men in the too-clean overalls came onto the porch, attracted by the sound or breaking glass. Fox waved him away, then went on, "Of course he should wear more than a horse blanket. I know that as well as you do. But I didn't want you to know how important this is. Apart from the danger of a leak, a very small risk in your case, I didn't want you to worry about the job so much that you would go to pieces."

"At the same time," he went on harshly, "we cannot afford to have him appear ridiculous, to look like a cross between a dressed-up horse and tail-coated chimpanzee from a circus. He is far too important an individual, and this is much too important an occasion for our planet and our race, for us to risk anything going wrong."

More quietly he went on, "Scrennagle wants to make a good first impression, naturally; but we as a species must also make a good impression on him. So it is probably safer in many respects to let him wear a blanket, even though it lacks both imagination and dignity. But, Hewlitt, if you *want* to tailor something more elaborate for the first ambassador from the stars, it must be exactly right for the occasion. Do you want to take on such a heavy responsibility?"

Hewlitt's vocal equipment seemed to be completely paralyzed by a combination of extreme anxiety and sheer joy at what was the ultimate challenge not only to an individual, but to a member of one of the oldest crafts known to mankind. He nodded.

Fox's relief was obvious. He said, very seriously, "You are assuming a large part of the responsibility which is properly mine. I'm grateful, and if you have any suggestions which might help ..."

"Even if they are none of my business?" Hewlitt asked; then he added, "My *tailoring* business, that is."

"Go on," Fox said warily.

"We were discussing dressed-up horses just now," Hewlitt went on. "My client resembles a horse much more than he does a human being. He is too much of a diplomat to complain; but put yourself in his place for a moment and think of the effect on you of the pomp and pageantry, the transport arrangements and-"

"Scrennagle has already studied and adapted himself to the more personal aspects of our civilization," said Fox. "At meals he lies with legs folded underneath his body, allowing his erect torso to rise to a comfortable height for eating and conversation. Since he has no lap, the napkin remains folded by his plate. Where toilet facilities are concerned-"

"I was thinking," said Hewlitt, "of how he might feel about horses pulling him or their being ridden by human beings. I would suggest that a state limousine rather than a coach be used, and that the escort and guards be chosen from regiments other than the Household Cavalry or Horse Guards. There are several physiological similarities between Scrennagle and terrestrial horses. Not as many as those between an ape and a human being; but it might be better not to have too many animals around which closely resemble the visiting ambassador, wouldn't you say?"

"I *would* say," Fox said, and swore quietly, "somebody should have thought or that."

"Somebody just did," Hewlitt said, opening the door and motioning Fox to precede him over the broken glass and back to the fitting room, where the most important client an Earth tailor had ever had was waiting and gently stamping all four of his feet.

"My apologies for the delay, sir," said Hewlitt politely "but I now have a dearer idea of what is expected of me and of *you*, sir. Before I resume measuring, do you have any allergies toward certain materials, or any particularly sensitive areas, which might cause you discomfort?"

Scrennagle looked at Fox, who said, "We have investigated this matter in great detail; and there is a long list of items which could cause trouble - some of them serious trouble - if they were allowed to remain in contact with His Excellency's skin for long periods."

"The situation is this," he continued. "Extraterrestrial pathogens cannot live in human bodies, and vice versa. This means that we cannot possibly contract a disease from Scrennagle and he is likewise impervious to our germs. However, purely chemical reactions are a different matter. One of the things likely to cause His Excellency to break out in a rash or worse is the synthetic fibers used in clothing, virtually all kinds of synthetics. You see the problem?"

Hewlitt nodded. The ambassador's underwear, shirts, ties, and socks would have to be made from pure wool, cotton, or real silk; the suiting materials would have to be woolen worsted and, for the casuals, Harris or Irish Thornproof tweed. Bone buttons would be required and zip fasteners made from metal rather than nylon. Trimmings, the canvas stiffening, the wadding for shaping and softening the outlines would also have to be nonsynthetic; and the thread used to hold everything together would have to be the old-style sewing cotton rather than nylon thread. He could see the problem, all right, and like most big problems this one was composed of a lot of little ones.

"One of the reasons why you were chosen for this job," said Fox, "was that you were old-fashioned enough in your ideas to keep such things in stock. But frankly, I was worried in case you would be too old-fashioned to react properly toward an ... unusual ... client. As it happened, you showed no sign of xenophobia whatsoever."

"I used to read a lot of science fiction, before it became too soft-centred," Hewlitt said dryly. Then he turned to Scrennagle. "I shall require additional measurements, sir, since I shall be building something a little more ambitious than a blanket. And it will be necessary to draft patterns for the garments as I go along. Making up, fitting, and finishing will take time if the work is to be done properly. I shall therefore board up the broken pane and attach a notice saying that I am dosed for alterations ..." He looked along Scrennagle's extraterrestrial body contours and thought, *There will probably be a lot of alterations.* "And I shall, of course, work on this order exclusively. But I cannot see it being completed in less than ten days."

"You have twelve days," said Fox, looking relieved. "I shall have the broken pane replaced as soon as possible. During our investigation your shop front was photographed, so we shall be able to reproduce the gold lettering. After all, the breakage was indirectly my fault."

"I venture to disagree," Scrennagle broke in. "As the prime cause of the trouble, I would be obliged, Mr. Hewlitt, if you would allow me to replace the glass from material in my ship as a memento of my visit. The material is transparent and proof against both meteorite collisions and minor emotional disturbances."

"You are very kind, sir," said Hewlitt, laughing, "I accept." He wrote on the measurement pad, *From center back to wrist, 35 inches.*

It took nearly three hours to complete the job to his satisfaction, including a half-hour's discussion regarding the musculature and jointing of the limbs and torso and the provision needed to give comfort as well as style to the garments, particularly in the areas of the neck, chest, armpits, and crotch.

When Scrennagle and Fox left, Hewlitt locked the door and climbed the stairs past his first-floor stockrooms to the flat above to break the news to his wife.

Mrs. Hewlitt had been a virtual cripple since a street accident eighteen years earlier. She could walk about the flat for three hours a day without too much discomfort, and these hours she saved for the evening meal and for talking to her husband afterwards. The rest of the time she spent rolling about the flat in her wheelchair, tidying, cooking, sewing if there was work for her to do, or sleeping, which she did not do very well even at night. .

He told her about his extraterrestrial client, and of the necessity for keeping the matter a close secret for the time being. She studied his sketches and measurements with interest, working out the yardages of material and trimmings needed for the job. Hewlitt should be ashamed of himself, she said, for trying to make her believe such a tall story. She reminded him that in her youth she once had to make a costume for a stage horse. The reason for the number of costumes required, particularly the sets of underwear, was unclear, she said; but no doubt they were being used in a sophisticated pantomime or farce in which the stage horse was expected to partially disrobe. The detail required in the fly fastenings, she added disapprovingly, probably meant that it was a very sophisticated and *naughty* show.

"Not at all, dear," said Hewlitt with a perfectly straight face. "It will be more in the nature of a spectacular, and you'll be able to see the highlights, and our costumes, on TV."

Hewlitt, who had always held moral cowardice to be the better part of valor, noted her pleased and excited expression and said nothing more.

During the three days and for most of the intervening nights before Scrennagle was due for his first fitting, the pleasure and the sense of excitement remained with Mrs. Hewlitt, even though on one occasion she said that there had been a time when they would have refused such a gimmicky commission. Hewlitt replied by saying that the work required the highest standards of tailoring and finish, regardless or its ultimate destination, and that the work was the most professionally challenging as well as the most remunerative he had ever been given. But secretly he was becoming prey to self-doubts.

His problem was to design, cut, and build a suit which would not make a horse look like a man but like a very well-dressed and dignified horse. The whole idea was ridiculous, yet Scrennagle was much too important a personage to be left open to the slightest suggestion of ridicule.

As Hewlitt had expected, the first fitting was visually a disaster. The fore and hind trouser legs were unpressed, shapeless, and held together temporarily with tacking stitches, while the embryo morning coat looked even worse with just one sleeve attached and tacking cotton holding together the lapel canvas, fronts, and shoulder wadding. While he plied his needle, chalk, and pins, Hewlitt transmitted confidence and reassurance for all he was worth; but it was obvious that neither Scrennagle nor Fox was receiving.

The Foreign Office official looked desperately worried and unhappy, and the pattern of wrinkling and puckering on the ambassador's features was almost certainly the extraterrestrial equivalent of these emotions.

Hewlitt kept this own doubts to himself and did his best to retrieve something from the situation by producing the first two sets of underwear, both of which fitted perfectly. He explained that these were relatively simple garments made from material which stretched and clung. He ignored the hints dropped by both Scrennagle and Fox that it might, after all, be better to settle for the horse blanket over underwear idea, and he requested a second fitting in four days time.

Scrennagle's jacket was a large and structurally complex garment which covered not only the forward torso but the body back to the hind quaters. It was cut away sharply at the front, after which the skirt maintained a level line two inches below the point where the legs joined the body. But the jacket, because of the length and area of material used, made the trouser-clad legs look disproportionately thin.

Hewlitt apparently had been able to reduce the area of the jacket by introducing a set of false pleats running along the spine and dividing at the tail opening; and he had used a series of strategically placed darts to shape the garment at awkward body contours. But he had had to scrap and recut the original trousers, making them nearly twice as wide but with a neat taper to approximately double the hoof diameter at the bottoms. This meant redesigning the method of suspension across the back and modifying the crotch, but the over-all effect looked much better balanced.

During the second fitting Hewlitt was pleased to find that he had been able to cure a troublesome tendency to crease where the foreleg muscles periodically distorted the waistcoat while Scrennagle was walking. But the garments, to Scrennagle's and

Fox's untutored eyes, still looked like the proverbial pound of tripe. It was obvious that they were both coming to a decision - almost certainly the wrong one - and Hewlitt tried desperately to head them off.

"We are extremely lucky," he said, smiling, "in that a size 16 neckband shirt is a perfect fit on you sir, as is a size 8 hat. The hat will be carried rather than worn for the most part, likewise the gloves, which don't quite fit-"

"Don't you think," said Fox suddenly, "that you may be trying for the impossible, Mr. Hewlitt?"

More quietly, Scrennagle joined in. "This is by no means a criticism of your professional ability, and you may well produce the garments required; but wouldn't you agree that something in the nature of the blanket already discussed would serve as a useful standby? It would also relieve you of a heavy responsibility."

"I did not ask to be relieved of the responsibility," said Hewlitt. The responsibility was beginning to scare him sick. He really should take this easy way out - but he had too much confidence, or perhaps over-confidence, in his ability. He went on, "I have undertaken to clothe you suitably for the forthcoming social and formal occasions, sir, and you can trust me to fulfill my obligations.

"However," Hewlitt continued quickly, "I have a minor problem regarding foot coverings. The black woolen socks can be adapted and cut to fit, but Earth-type shoes would look out of place and would be difficult for you to wear with confidence. Would it be possible to use a non-toxic paint to color the osseous material of your hooves - glossy black for the formal occasion and brown for the walkabouts? They should also be padded, since hoof sounds might also be considered out of place." *It would make you sound too much like a horse*, Hewlitt said silently. Aloud: "And there is the matter of displaying the tail, sir. It is a long, luxuriant, and remarkably handsome tail-"

"Thank you," said Scrennagle.

"-but it is constantly in motion and likely to be a distraction to people holding a conversation with you. Mr. Fox tells me that these movements are involuntary. However, as I see it, your tail is analogous to the cranial and/or facial hair in an Earth-person. Those who have such hair frequently display it to the best advantage on formal occasions. It can be pleated, braided, decorated in various fashions, and combed or oiled to give it a richer texture. If you have no objections, sir, we might plait your tail, adding, say, a few lengths of white or silver cord, then coil it neatly and secure it with a retaining strap which I can add to the center seam?"

"I have no objections, Mr. Hewlitt," said Scrennagle. "We do something similar on Dutha."

"These are details, Hewlitt," said Fox. "Important details, I admit, which will apply to whatever type of garment is worn. But-"

"There is also the matter of decorations, sir," Hewlitt continued. "These are colored ribbons and pieces of engraved metal which indicate that the person wearing them has achieved some great feat, or that an ancestor has done so. The evening reception will include many people wearing dress uniforms and full evening wear to which are added the kind of decorations I have been describing. I would like you to wear some kind of decoration or award," he went on seriously, "but preferably one that has not simply been invented for the occasion. Can you suggest something which might be suitable, sir?"

Scrennagle was silent for a moment, then he said, "My race has no equivalent of these awards, except possibly the translator which is necessary to the performance of my work. There is a somewhat larger version, decorated with the Federation symbol, which is worn when more than one translation has to be handled at the same time. But these, also, are merely the tools of our profession."

"But it is not a common profession, surely?"

"It is not," said Scrennagle. The expression which twisted the alien features might have been one of pride.

"Would you have any objections to displaying this device on a colored ribbon?"

"No objections."

"Thank you, sir," Hewlitt said. He went on briskly, "The morning wear will be ready for collection before breakfast time on the day required, and the evening wear in the afternoon of the same day. Your walking-out suits and accessories, which will not be required until your list of formal visits is complete, will be much easier to make as a result of experience gained with the first garments-"

"Which will be," said Fox very firmly, "a well-cut and tastefully decorated blanket."

Hewlitt pretended to ignore him as he said, "You may trust me, sir."

"I am trusting you, Mr. Hewlitt, more than any other person on this planet ..."

Long after they had gone, Hewlitt thought about Scrennagle's parting remark. While his wife and he worked on the recutting and finishing of the first outfit, he worried. Was he being a stupid, self-opinionated, sartorial snob or did he really have the right to dictate to Scrennagle as he had been doing?

The ambassador was an extremely important being who was, in the way of all representatives of other governments, anxious to make a good impression. But he would also be receiving impressions, favorable or otherwise, from the people he was meeting. Being realistic about it, the latter impressions were the more important as far as the human race was concerned. In all probability Scrennagle was important enough to make the decision whether his world and the rest of the Federation maintained contact with Earth or left it strictly alone.

And this was the being that he, a conceited and impoverished little tailor, was going to dress for the most important occasion in human history. He was, of course, going to dress to the best of his ability; but the media were fond of poking fun at VIP's. Given half a chance, they would tear Scrennagle apart; and the ambassador would go away and neither he nor his friends would ever return to the place where the people lacked manners and where the Federation representative had been made to look a fool.

Many times while he was reopening a seam to remove an unsightly fullness or while giving the pockets the swelled edges that were his own particular signature on a suit, he thought about putting aside the work for the few hours necessary for him to make a blanket. He thought about it long and seriously, but he kept working on the job in hand while he was making up his mind. When he and his wife went to bed in the early hours of the following morning, and arose to resume work a short time later, he still had not made up his mind.

Producing a glorified horse blanket would be insurance against the dress wear turning out to be a sartorial disaster. But if he made the blanket he would simply be obeying orders and shifting the responsibility back to Fox. He would also be allowing a man who knew less than he did to tell him what to do.

Then suddenly the morning coat and trousers were finished, pressed, and hanging with their accessories on the form which Hewlitt had adapted from the limbs and torsos of one and a half window-display models; and there was no longer enough time to make a blanket because it was the morning of *The* day and Scrennagle was due at any moment.

The ambassador said little while Hewlitt was showing him how to fasten the shirt, knot the tie, and fit, among other items, the footless dark socks over his black-painted hooves. While fitting the trousers, waistcoat, and jacket the tailor talked about the desirability of moving slowly - sudden movements lacked dignity and looked bad on TV. He was aware that he was talking too much and that he was making himself sound ridiculous by punctuating every few words with a yawn.

Perhaps Scrennagle would not realize how nervous and unsure of himself Hewlitt felt because the over-all ensemble did not look exactly as he had envisaged it - and in his present physical and mental state of fatigue he did not know what it looked like.

During the proceedings Fox maintained the tightest-lipped silence he had ever experienced; but he tossed Hewlitt a copy of the morning paper and nodded worriedly as they left.

The news about Scrennagle was published as a Court Circular:

His Excellency the Lord Scrennagle of Dutha will be received in audience by the Queen this morning, and will present his Letter of Credence as Ambassador Extraordinary and Plenipotentiary from the Galactic Federation to the Court of St. James. A State Reception will be held in his honor at the Palace, during which sound and vision broadcast facilities will be available.

Hewlitt moved the TV into his workroom so that he could watch without disturbing his wife, who was still asleep, while he worked on the evening suit.

But the TV coverage was unsatisfactory. Apparently the Court Circular had been treated by the press as some kind of hoax. A tourist had been able to film Scrennagle's arrival at St. James', and he would probably receive a fortune for a few feet of badly focused film which did not give any indication of how well or otherwise the ambassador's suit fitted him.

Hewlitt waited for a couple of hours, then switched on his transistor radio to hear an excited voice saying that news had just been received from the Palace to the effect that Dutha was an inhabited planet circling a sun some two thousand light-years from Earth and that the Duthan, Scrennagle, was being accorded the honors of a visiting head of state as well as those of an ambassador. Whether the whole thing was a hoax or not, the voice went on, tonight's reception would be covered to the same extent as the early moon landing.

His wife heard the same news item. She looked dreadfully tired but happier than he had ever seen her for a great many years. But she was not talking to him for the time being because he had told her the truth and had deliberately made it sound like a lie.

Hewlitt's mind and fingers were so stiff and tired that he was almost an hour late in completing the suit. But that did not matter: Scrennagle did not call for it. Just two hours before the reception was due to begin, a uniformed inspector arrived to say that there had been unforeseen delays and that he would collect the outfit and take it to Scrennagle's ship. A few minutes later, a more senior police officer arrived to say that since there was no longer any need for secrecy they were removing the screens from his shop and that a couple of glaziers had also arrived to replace his door window.

"Can't it wait until morning?" Hewlitt asked, clenching his teeth to fight back a yawn.

"You look very tired, sir," the policeman said. "I would be happy to stay here until they've finished, and lock the door as I leave. I'll put your key in the letter-box."

"That is very considerate of you," said Hewlitt warmly. "I do need rest. Thank you."

"My pleasure, sir," said the officer, so respectfully that he seemed to be ready to salute.

The warm feeling left by the unusually friendly policeman faded as Hewlitt mounted the stairs. He thought about the probable reasons why Scrennagle had sent for his suit rather than collect it himself. The outfit he had worn this morning had probably been a mess, and this evening he would be wearing a horse blanket tailored on short notice by someone else. Being a diplomat and a considerate being as well, Scrennagle would not want to complain in person to Hewlitt, or to pass on the criticisms which had doubtless been made about his appearance. He would simply take delivery of the second outfit and say nothing.

But Hewlitt's misery was short-lived. As he slumped into his chair before the TV screen, a panel of experts were discussing the implications of contact with an extra-solar race, and pundits always put him to sleep.

The first few bars of the fanfare which opened the late-night newscast, especially extended to cover the visit of the extraterrestrial, jerked Hewlitt awake. Quickly he wheeled his wife in from the kitchen, and then settled back to see how Scrennagle had comported himself.

Unlike the amateur film taken at St. James', Scrennagle's arrival for the reception was covered in close-up, middle distance, and from every angle.

The ambassador was *not* wearing a horse blanket.

His jacket was a good fit at the collar and shoulders, but showed a tendency to wrinkle across the back when Scrennagle straightened after making a bow - something he had to do every few minutes. The trousers hung well, making the legs look neither too blocky nor too thin, and the black socks and dully polished hooves were elegantly inconspicuous. The tail was coiled and tied forward like that of some heraldic beast, and its occasional twitching were barely noticeable.

The only touch of color was the wide silk ribbon that diagonally bisected the white shirt front and waistcoat. It was pale blue with a thin edging of red and gold on which was centered the intricately decorated translation device which bore the symbol of the Federation. Although not the most impressive decoration there, it still managed to hold its own among an the Baths and Garters.

Scrennagle of Dutha, Hewlitt realized suddenly, looked *well* ...

Then the Duthan was making his speech, outlining briefly the purpose of his visit and touching on some of the advantages which membership in the Galactic Federation would confer in both directions.

It had been just over one hundred and fifty years earlier that one of the Federation's unmanned searchships found intelligent life and a rapidly developing technology on Earth. The long delay in responding to the situation, Scrennagle explained, was due to the fact that the searchships - which rarely found anything - were not fitted with power-hungry, ultimate drive because machinery, unlike Duthans, Earth-humans, and members of other intelligent species, did not age or become bored. The search ship had spent many years in orbit photographing, analyzing, evaluating speci- mens of flora and fauna, the written and spoken languages - the last being particularly difficult for its soft-landed probes to obtain because radio and television had not then been invented.

When the data had been returned to Dutha for study, several difficult decisions had had to be taken. There was, of course, no question that contact should not be attempted with the rich and varied cultures on Earth. But at the time the material had been gathered, many sociopolitical groupings were showing signs of imminent collapse while others were rapidly growing in power and influence.

At the time the British Empire, with its center of power and commerce in London, was the most important and influential grouping, but it, too, was showing signs of collapse. It had grown slowly, however, and its traditions and laws were deeply rooted.

The indications were that it would collapse not catastrophically, but wane slowly and disintegrate in a stable fashion. It was also thought that the manners and practices observed a century and a half earlier would not significantly alter in such a long-lived grouping...

"That is why I landed quietly in this country rather than in one of the others," Scrennagle continued. "I now know that the decision was the correct one. But we, too, have certain rules of behaviour in these circumstances. You might think that for a highly advanced Galactic culture we are surprisingly old-fashioned. But an acceptable code of behavior plays a vital part in dealings between species so widely varied as the members of our Federation.

"One of our strictest rules," he added, wrinkling his facial openings in what was undoubtedly a smile, "is that visitors such as myself conform to all of the social practices and customs of the host planet, even to the extent or wearing its clothing ..."

He concluded by saying that his intention was to make a round of official visits to heads of state on Earth. Then, later, he would return to take a leisurely, sightseeing tour of the planet which would enable him to meet people in more relaxed conditions. He added that Earth had been the first new world to be offered membership in something over four centuries, and he would be happy to answer questions on every subject under this or any other sun.

The next item was the TV interview, during which, at long last, the subject of Scrennagle's clothing came up.

" ... we will need much more time to consider the wider aspects of your visit," the interviewer was saying, "but right now, Your Excellency, I would like to ask a question, and also compliment you, on your clothing. Or perhaps I should compliment your extraterrestrial tailor?"

"You should compliment my terrestrial tailor," Scrennagle said, then went on: "On many worlds clothing is simply a means of giving protection from extremes of weather, while on others the fabrication, styling, and wearing of clothing has been raised to the level of a major art form. Earth is in the latter category and possesses at least one tailor who is capable of making an extraterrestrial. . . presentable."

The interviewer laughed and asked, "Who is he, Your Excellency?"

"I would rather not say at present," Scrennagle replied. "He and his wife have worked long and hard, and they deserve at least one night's sleep before fame descends on them. Suffice it to say that my tailor is relatively unknown but a craftsman of the highest order. He is also something of a tyrant in sartorial matters, a characteristic common to tailors throughout the Galaxy. He is not afraid to accept a professional challenge, as you can see."

"Yes, indeed," said the interviewer.

"No doubt there will be other challenges," Scrennagle went on, turning his face directly into the camera, but Hewlitt knew that he was not speaking solely to the interviewer. "My race was chosen to make first contact with Earth-humans simply because my people most closely resembled yours - despite what you must think are major physiological differences. Other races in the Federation have much more varied and interestingly arranged limbs and appendages; and to the uninitiated they may even appear to be quite horrendous. But ambassadors from all these species in time will visit Earth to present their credentials and their good wishes. And they will all require to be suitably attired for the occasion. They will be very pleased and reassured to know," he ended, "that there is an Earth-human tailor in whom they can place their complete trust ..."

The intense feelings of pride and excitement which should have kept him awake that night, but did not, were with him in undiminished intensity when he opened the shop next morning. His reflection in the store window opposite looked the same as always, but something different about the reflected picture made him turn around quickly.

The new door pane was not quite the same as the old one. It now read GEORGE L. HEWLITT, TAILOR, centered above a beautifully executed copy of the design which appeared on Scrennagle's translator - the symbol which represented all the worlds of the Galactic Federation - followed by the words BY APPOINTMENT.

David Logan lives in Co. Antrim, Northern Ireland. Over the years he has had fiction published in many small press magazines in Ireland and the UK. In addition to writing, David edited and published *Grotesque Fiction*, a long running and high quality A4 production. *Grotesque Fiction* ceased publication in 1996 to allow David more time for writing, but is still remembered for featuring some of the strangest fiction you're ever likely to read, often humorously reflecting the sometimes bewildering nature of human (or inhuman!) existence, along with entertaining reviews of other small press productions. The story that follows, winner of the *Albedo One* 'Best in Issue 9' Award, demonstrates that fresh blood can still be found even in the most tired of genres.

Emerald Isle, Ruby Blood

David Logan

Hard shades of green contrasted brilliantly with the stolid grey sky, both rattling past the window of his carriage like a promise delivered. The land was sparkling emeralds. The kinetic panorama captivated him in a manner that the lighter grey of rock, and duller green of shrub, through the cursed barren Carpathians, had never done. Ireland was the wettest country he'd ever visited. Its grass, its trees, even the brown brickwork of houses and black slate roofs possessed an exuberance he'd not encountered in New York, London or Paris. Those places boasted scores of people, highly strung and restive. In comparison this new country was empty; its substantive life was in the soil and vegetation, the things that didn't move or make a sound.

"I am Daniel," he thought, smiling beguilingly through the

rain-dotted glass. The name did not come readily to his tongue. It sounded best with a French accent, the second syllable pronounced and prolonged.

He twisted the blond rat-tail from under the collar of his tweed topcoat as the train slowed approaching urbanization. The wet green turned to damp plaster and concrete. Numerous passengers disembarked at Coleraine station, but few boarded.

As soon as the journey commenced its final stage, to his last-stop destination, Daniel intuited his quarry was near. Was she to be quarry or prize, victim or redeemed? Trella's stature was imprecise, even as his beloved. The fine hairs on Daniel's arms bristled, his heart beat solidly with expectation and desire. His sharp bruise-black fingernails scraped the lining of his pockets and the chilling of fast-flowing blood made him shiver.

The train did not gather speed, rather plodded like an old man mercifully near the end of his sojourn. Portrush was near. Through the open skylight wafted the smells of fish and candyfloss, faded photographs and stained bedsheets, tired old people and bored youths. Over the emerald green fields a band of dark North Atlantic ocean parted land from sky. The railway track bordered a park of holiday caravans and a golf course.

Portrush's wide bay came into view, a cliff at the far side, a large warehouse painted red and white like a barber's pole. The water's edge boasted a long, narrow strip of sand, the town standing above, tiered like a poor man's Monte Carlo. Daniel sat forward and, at that moment, the sun split cloud and shot its beams full at the carriage window. Daniel turned away swiftly and fumbled in his inside pocket for the dark lensed glasses that protected his sensitive eyes.

By the time he'd turned back to the window, the bay, the beach and Portrush were gone - over the glistening hillock lifeless until next summer's picnickers arrived. The train rolled ever more slowly and came to a standstill in a shelter with the walls painted grey, like the Irish sky.

As Daniel stepped from the train, onto the platform, several heads turned, casting glances of disapproval. 'A conservative land,' he'd read, 'steeped in the conflict of Christian religious traditions, a conflict exacerbated by the residue of British colonial domination. The Irish, in Ireland, are suspicious of outsiders.'

Daniel stood perfectly still, only his eyes moving behind the shades, and took his bearings. A pubescent girl looked at his face and blushed, walked on, then could not resist looking back at the tall, thin boy with the white skin, gypsy-hoop earrings and cropped hair but for the rat-tail. Daniel noticed her but paid no attention. He'd long ago lost his thirst for virgins and nubiles; women bored him too; men, boys and animals irritated and, more often than not, made him itch. His focus was single track; his *raison d'etre* depended on it being so.

Accommodation was available in The Eglington Hotel across the street from the station. From its facade Daniel deemed it to be comfortable enough for his needs. He entered via a revolving glass door and found a tastefully furnished foyer and a pleasingly dark, sparsely populated lounge. There were few guests this time of year.

He spoke to the young female receptionist who awaited his request with a practised smile. "I want a room, please, for one person for one week." His accent was unidentifiable; maybe continental European with more than a shade of American east coast.

"Certainly, sir. A single room?"

"With a good view of the street"

The receptionist frowned. "I'm sorry, our single rooms are at the back of the hotel."

"Then I will take a room at the front: single, double, triple or quadruple. I shall not require meals or room service, only solitude."

She cleared her throat and hit a computer key. "There's a nice family room, but it costs ninety five pounds per night; that includes breakfast of course."

"I won't require breakfast. The family room will suffice."

"Could I have your name please?" Her hands trembled now, waiting like little strangers over the keyboard.

"Daniel."

She typed it in. "And your second name'?"

"Only Daniel. That is the name I was given." Daniel removed a roll of notes from a pocket in his trousers. "I have sterling cash to pay in advance; or if you wish I can pay by card: American Express, Visa, Access."

"Cash is okay, Mr. Daniel; but you don't have to pay in advance, really..." She saw his fingernails and her mouth dropped in a frown. "Ah, I wonder if I could have your home address'?"

Daniel raised an eyebrow and she added, "Just for our records. You know, sometimes people slip out without paying, but I'm sure..."

"I understand." He returned the wad of notes to his pocket. "I have several addresses. It is best if I give you the Hotel Chelsea, New York." From a hip pocket he removed a black wallet and presented the receptionist with a Hotel Chelsea card. "You phone now and ask to speak to the manager. He will verify what I have told you."

"Oh, I'm sure that's not necessary."

"Go on, please phone. I have not time to waste."

The receptionist fluttered over the telephone before deciding to do as he asked. The direct call was answered in seconds.

"Hello. This is the Eglington Hotel in Portrush, Northern Ireland. Could I speak to the manager, please? - You are the manager! Oh, I'm sorry. I'm phoning to ask if you know a, a Mr. Daniel... Yes... He is? Really?" She glanced up at Daniel and blushed pink, then said goodbye and put down the phone, face beaming. "Well, Mr. Daniel, it's a pleasure to welcome you to The Eglington Hotel and I hope you'll enjoy your stay. If there's anything you need…"

Daniel sat on a child's swing where no children played today or had done since last the sun shone, and that was months ago. Breakers crashed against rocks behind him, beyond the short grass and the graffiti-scarred public toilet. Rain drizzled from the misty sky as it had drizzled since his arrival several days ago. He watched the tall houses that fronted the green. Most were guesthouses and a few remained open this late in the year. Accommodation in one of these would have been cheaper than the Eglington. Money, however, was not an object of concern to Daniel. It came and went, like the long nights and the tiresome days, all but worthless. Anyhow, to have stayed in one of these guesthouses would have been a mistake. Trella lived in the one called Belvedere and might have seen him. It was not time yet.

Cold, ruby blood bubbled in Daniel's narrow veins; blue lines rose like worms on his neck, forced the skin, sank away. His one lust, one purpose, was to reclaim that which mortality dictated he must lose time after time, life after life.

The small party left Belvedere dressed smartly for their hour of worship. The husband carried a black umbrella over his mother while the woman's husband took her arm and helped her down the steps. The wife closed the house door and followed them to the large family car, Trella at her heels.

Daniel sagged on the swing; moaned. He had to restrain his mind, which was already reaching towards her with a cry of longing. The drizzle and hazy air made the darkly dressed party a distant, indistinct water canvas; but Daniel didn't need to see clearly, and poor Trella's human eyes would not see as well as his own. He would be a blur, a mad shape sitting in the rain, if she noticed him at all. When the car doors closed, and the engine ignited, Daniel rose from the swing. He knew their church. The walk was not far.

The last of the Presbyterians shook hands with the elders, were handed hymnbooks at the double-door and went inside. The elders followed. Daniel's hair was rain soaked and matted. Water trickled down his fine features and the saturated coat hung heavily on his narrow shoulders. He crossed the road between parked cars and entered 'God's House'. The nature of the place meant little to him; his interest in Christianity, what there was of it, was historical and sociological, no more. He waited at the inner doors until the drone of the church organ ceased.

Then he opened a door, letting in a gust of cold air, and stepped onto the polished wooden floor. His boots were loud in the silence and necks twisted from pews to see who had arrived late. Only one woman gasped. Seconds passed and there were a few murmurs. When the minister took the pulpit he could not help but see the stranger standing, like a sentinel, at the back of the hall. He stumbled over the opening sentences of his prayer.

An elder approached Daniel. "Would you like to have a seat?" Daniel had located Trella and her family, near the front of the hall. They had not seen him. Trella, however, would surely have felt his presence. Daniel moved to an empty pew at the back and was given a hymnbook. When he removed a hand from his pocket to accept it, the elder was reluctant to let go, then drew his hand sharply from the demonic fingernails and retreated to whisper his tale.

When the service ended the minister went to the door, passing Daniel without looking at him. The congregation left - those at the rear first. Daniel moved along the pew, away from the people, and watched Trella with a heart so wounded he was next to tears.

She was beautiful, of course; she was always beautiful; a boy no more than sixteen. She wore a dark blue suit, white shirt and blue tie. Her black hair was short and neat, parted at the left side. Her face was her own: delicate, enchanting, vulnerable; no incarnation ever changed her face. She was so small and frail.

The other boys at her school must make her life hell. Daniel felt hurt. He would kill for her; kill to ease her pain. He had been powerless to help her in the years she had been growing up and they were necessarily apart. The only solace was that now it was almost over.

She moved gracefully up the aisle, behind her mother, chin high, not reflecting all the mockery and abuse she had lived her life with. Her eyes were drawn to Daniel and she watched him - as he watched her - all along the aisle. Her tender but pale lips were fractionally apart. The spell over her only snapped when Daniel forced himself to break eye contact.

Daniel was last to leave. He looked at the cross on the wall without its Jesus. 'The crucifix is infinitely more eloquent,' he reflected. 'Humans have no imagination. They need to see Jesus suffering, that's why Protestantism is vacuous.' He turned to the door and welcomed the chilling seaside wind, curative from the threat of born-again salvation. Daniel smiled and, seeing this, so did the minister who had steeled himself for the encounter. He shook Daniel's hand without looking at it. "It's always nice to see a new face in church on a Sunday morning. I'm Reverend Hastings; how do you do. I trust you enjoyed the service Mr. ...?"

"Daniel. It was interesting; not what I'm accustomed to."

"Ah! I see you're not from these parts. Let me guess; German?"

"More or less."

"And may I ask, Mr. Daniel, what it is you are accustomed to?"

"Discernment."

The Reverend's amicable face collapsed. Daniel was amused to watch him dither, no doubt trying to decide if he had been insulted, or was it no more than a linguistic difficulty. "Quite," said Hastings, blinking heavily as though something was caught in his eye. "Mr. Daniel, tell me, are you a believer?"

"In?"

"Do you believe in the Lord Jesus as the one true Saviour?"

"Unequivocally."

Hastings was taken aback. "Good. Splendid. Praise the Lord. Tell me..."

As Hastings spoke Daniel moved away, ignoring the fool. Trella and her family were entering their car.

He returned to his hotel invigorated. She had been drawn to him. Daniel had known she would, but that did not lessen the thrill. In his room he drew the curtain and slept.

The young woman lit a cigarette in the dark space between the lamp-posts, hidden by the parked cars that belonged to residents. Her blood red lipstick smeared the filter. The gold lighter was a gift to herself only she knew about; the cigarettes were secrets too. She returned the packet to her leather shoulder bag.

Mark Street was a cemetery: two nursing homes, a brood of boarding houses with barred doors, icicles on window ledges, ice patches on the broken pavement flags. She could relax here, now that she was off Main Street, where night owls still flew and one might see her for what she was. She inhaled deeply, like a sigh, and fingered the silver clips that held her hair in an unaccustomed right side-shade, swept back off her pale forehead. A touch of her mother's blusher powdered her cheeks but it was hardly notice-able in this light. The blue eye mascara and silver nail polish she'd bought in a cheap shop made her a child's doll, someone to toy with; she'd never been this deviant before.

The steps to Kerr Street sparkled with frost until shadow over-took them a quarter way down. She held onto the rail in the cen-tre and stepped carefully, her heels higher than she was used to on boy's shoes. On such heels it was impossible to be as graceful as she wanted to be; like everything else she wanted, grace was beyond reach. Living is hard when you're made to do what makes you uncomfortable, and forced to be what you're not. Being out of the closet for the first time felt like walking into one, or walking into the belly of Hell, as the shadows consumed her. She slid her hand along the rail, not daring to let go. In her other hand the cigarette burned, a mere prop. She remembered and inhaled for bravado. She looked high, over the ocean horizon between two dark walls, and blew out a stream of poisonous smoke. The orange streetlights of Kerr Street extinguished the shadow. She descended the last steps and wondered if he was watching, if he thought she looked ridiculous, if he was laughing.

Daniel watched; he did not laugh. The moisture in his eyes was there because of profound sorrow. That mortals should have to live in such ignorance and anguish was the folly of nature; that they should have to suffer it life after life was the great absurdity; that his Trella should be so cursed was Daniel's agony and despair.

Satisfaction was close. For Trella it would be complete, the climax; for Daniel it would be enough, until next time. As Trella was cursed with ignorance, he was cursed with knowing. He watched from the corner wall of the street; to his right a footbridge over the harbour's narrow inlet, to his left Trella's silhouette, uncertain which way to turn, or if turning back was best, or if she should run away for ever. He would not disclose himself yet; rather let her settle. She must suspect... like a small bird led to a trap because all it knows is that it must eat.

He watched Trella cross the road to the ocean side and, still undecided, stand there, coat-tail quivering in the icy wind. 'The harbour, Trella,' he called in his mind, touching her. She moved towards him like a ghost on air, towards the far end of the harbour where she left the street and disappeared from sight. Daniel went to her.

She was sitting on a low wall. When Daniel appeared she looked up, clearly not surprised, but her slack mouth suggested she was afraid. He approached her slowly, hands in pockets. She remained seated, her hands in her pockets against the cold. She was a summer daisy plucked from her meadow and cast on a violent street; yet she retained her loveliness; it was innate and could not be taken away. Her perfect mouth moved with half a thought, or maybe a vague question. Why? Daniel had seen her like this before, defenceless, lost. Being this close to her again, after so long, all the things he had rehearsed to say would sound wrong. Should he tell her everything now, or at all? She would be overwhelmed. He'd told her on other occasions, but she'd been a different person then. The person she was this time would not easily accommodate the truth. Yet maybe she could accommodate parts of the truth as fantasy. Or, should he simply enjoy her? It would not much matter in the end.

"I've waited a long time for this reunion," he said. She didn't understand and was lost for a reply. Daniel spoke kindly, reassuringly. "We've been together - in past lives."

Trella turned her head aside and there were tears in her voice. "You're making fun of me. You're all cruel, but I don't care."

"Look at me."

She did.

"You're wrong. Look into my eyes and tell me I'm lying."

She looked into his eyes and there was only honesty. Her tear-wet face smiled.

"What does it mean? I've always known there would be someone like you who understood."

"I understand, better than you know." He strolled around the wall on which she sat. At the other side a flight of stone steps sank into the water of the harbour. "I've something to show you." The tide was high. Rowing boats and vessels of various sizes bobbed very gently.

Daniel crouched at the bottom step and stroked a hand through the water, which was orange because of a nearby streetlight. The water rippled and Daniel looked up at her. Trella watched, a faint smile and peace on her pretty face for the first time in her youth. She waited patiently for what he had to show. Daniel waited for her to see; when she did Trella's smile faded and died. The stone steps, boats moored to the shore, red and yellow buoys, all cast shadows leaning away from the source of the light. Where Daniel's shadow should have been there was none, just orange water.

Daniel returned to her side. She said, "Who are you?"

He wanted to tell her, but did not. "Someone you need. Someone who can release you and let you experience happiness - and love. Kiss me. Please kiss me."

She stood and craned her little neck up towards the moon. Daniel bent to reach her, took his hands from his pockets and rested them on her hips. Their kiss was sweet, soft and long. When their mouths parted Trella's eyes were glass. Daniel touched her angular chin with a fingertip; she opened her mouth wider and took it in.

The receptionist at the Eglington Hotel, the same one who had welcomed Daniel less than a week before, stopped writing and watched over the desk top. Her jaw hung like the muscles had died. They were soaked and miserable. Daniel, hands as ever in pockets, led Trella from the revolving door, across the foyer and up the stairs. They looked ahead and there was no-one to see them but the receptionist who now, perplexed, bit her thumb nail and decided the matter was not her business.

The window curtains were closed, as Daniel had left them. Trella stood in the center of the dark room and let her coat be removed as though she no longer possessed a mind of her own. Daniel cupped her cheeks. "You were born a boy," he said tenderly. "That's funny after its fashion because it has never happened before."

"Why did it happen this time?" asked Trella, dreamily, partially understanding him, wholly trusting him because no-one had ever been so kind before.

"I don't know, I can only guess. The planet is changing faster than ever because human beings have tampered with that which they should have left to their own mechanics. The air is different than it should be by nature, the water has lost its purity and the creatures that live in it, and in the earth and on the land, can no longer survive and multiply without mutation and adaption." Daniel paused to resume an even tone. This was no time for anger. "It seems that you and I must adapt also, sweet Trella. The food of the land grows in soil fertilized by unnatural elements. The animals slaughtered as food are made plump by chemicals created in scientific laboratories. It is all so tiring... and Trella is a boy."

"I'm sorry."

He laughed, his first for a long time. Apologetic, gentle, delightful; this was his Trella. If only he could enjoy her company as equals. "There's no need to be sorry," he said.

"Don't I disappoint you?"

"You could never disappoint me; not in eternity."

"Are," she hesitated. "Are you homosexual?" I don't know what I am."

Daniel tasted her lips. He said, "Peel back physiology and you have souls naked, then you can't tell one from the other just by looking at mere flesh. Sexuality is such an opaque thing. I surrendered mine a long time ago in favour of pleasure and ambiguity."

They kissed. His fingers and thumbs caressed where breasts should have been and nipples should have stood erect. The boy in Trella responded. Daniel unbuttoned her skirt and slipped it over her narrow, boy's hips. He kissed a cheek, an ear. Trella touched him and asked, "Will you make me like you?"

He said, "I can't do that. You are what you are." He kissed her neck. She leant aside to give it. Daniel put a hand inside her pants. She shuddered, sighed, stiffened, cried, went weak in his arms. Her legs gave way.

Daniel laid her on the bed, removed his coat, touched her immaculate throat.

The morning train left Portrush bound for Belfast. The day was chilly but bright. The winter sun was freezing. Daniel wore his dark glasses and sat at the shaded side of his carriage. At Belfast he would change for Dublin, then fly home, to kill more endless days and eternal nights. At least, in the mountains, relaxation would come easier. Now that his hunger was satisfied he could read and reflect, try to think of a way he could make it different next time, different for all the next times so that Trella would not hurt so.

By now the chambermaid might have found the body, no longer Trella, pierced and dry, inside and out. The corpse would be smiling. Daniel smiled too. It was ironic that giving and taking should cancel each other, amount to the same sum.

Police officers might stop the train. If so he would cooperate fully, until night fell and he could melt from their grip like the Portrush ice

The train stopped at a small rural station and an elderly man entered Daniel's carriage. He wore a sandwich board that said, 'Vengeance is mine, says the Lord' on one side and 'Ye must be born again' on the other. He removed the board and sat down

260

with a great sigh. He looked at Daniel, all the demons in Hell seething from the old man's eyes. "An' what about you, young lad. Have you been washed clean by the precious blood of the Lamb?"

"Unequivocally," said Daniel.

John W. Sexton (born in London of Irirsh parents in 1958) is a widely published poet and author. He was nominated for the Hennessy Literary Award. He is the scriptwriter of RTÉ's children's radio serial 'The Ivory Tower', which ran for over one hundred episodes. His books include the short collection *The Prince's Brief Career* (1995) and the YA Fantasies *The Johnny Coffin Diaries* (2001) and *Johnny Coffin School-Dazed* (2002). He has also released an album, *The Sons Of Shiva*, with Stranglers frontman Hugh Cornwell. He lives with his family in Kenmare, County Kerry.

This elegant vignette shows that it doesn't take much to change the world (now does it?).

On a Planet Similar to Ours, the Virgin Mary Says No

John Sexton

Between the space of two traffic lights emotion gets confused with thought, inevitability with despair, and she becomes a drunken half-suicide. The tiny foetus in her womb is too unformed to plead, and her problems become obliterated, blurred beyond recognition, by the simple process of acceleration.

As Mary loses control of the car it begins to spin free of the road, its left side wheels lifting themselves from the surface. The car rotates twice on the pivot of its own velocity, and then hurtles forwards into the plate glass window of a dry-cleaners. In the retarded seconds of the crash, she can see the reflection of herself accelerating towards herself in the car. As the window shatters she is shattered into thousands of pieces, and her mind begins to break free into fragments of memory.

As the car comes to a final halt with the dry-cleaners, its metal body grafted onto the bodies of the dryers, Mary's head is knocked backwards against the headrest, and before losing consciousness she sees a final reflection of her bloodied face in the round window of one of the drying machines. Confused as to what has happened, she wonders for a moment why she can see herself inside the machine, and then the machine starts its cycle, and she begins to revolve into a vortex of unconsciousness.

Inside her womb, Christ, barely budded from the egg, is swaying gently in his amniotic bubble. The pulsing coral of his brain is infused with light, but contains not a single thought.

Momentarily coming to, Mary is back inside the chaos of the dry-cleaners. Racks of coats are spilling against the windscreen of the car, shards of glass are everywhere, tucked into Mary's hair, embedded in her skin, and she thinks, dizzily, that she is the shattered mirror in her bedroom, that she is the wardrobe burst open and vomiting its stomach of clothes. A great pressure is beginning to build up suddenly inside her head, and she thinks yes, yes, I am the bedroom exploding with clothes, calling out to be worn, to be given life. At that moment she is aware of a blue light revolving through the fission of her expanding consciousness, and she is stretched beyond the confines of the crumpled car and into infinity.

As Mary's body is being cut from the wreckage, her spirit is leaking into the anarchy of the heavens, where antimatter cancels matter, non-thought cancels thought. By the time she is taken into the ambulance, whole galaxies have unwound, their demise a fading photograph of ancient light.

But the thinning thread of Mary's spirit is still connected to her ruptured body. The world is not yet severed from eternity: nurses walk softly through darkened corridors. And the owner of the dry-cleaners turns in his sleep, a premonition of blood disturbing his dreams. The telephone rings.

Sam Millar was born a Catholic in Belfast in 1955. Growing up through the Troubles, he was 'the first Irish nationalist to appear in front of the infamous non-jury Diplock court' in 1973 and got three years in the Maze prison. He served a second stint of seven years for being part of a Belfast bombing campaign. He has written about his life in the North and the USA in his autobiography *On The Brinks* (2003). He also wrote a short modern-day horror novel, *Dark Souls* (2003), is winner of the Brian Moore Short Story Award and a runner-up in The Cork Literary Review Awards. He is married and has three children.

'The Barber', collected here, gained an honourable mention in Ellen Datlow's annual *Year's Best Fantasy & Horror*. It is a story that will leave you scarred, as it proves the pen is mightier than the scissors.

The Barber

Sam Millar

From his house, the boy watched as snow fell in thick leaves, swirling tightly in a rage at the base of the old shop across the street.

He had always loved the solitary feel of the old abandoned shop with its fearful loneliness avoided by others.

He had always loved it, but now he hated it.

It had always been derelict; at least as far back as he could remember. Pigeons made their home in it, as did rats and the stray, wild cats that spat at you and chased the dogs, leaving their snouts a bloody mess.

He remembered - hating to remember - how he had climbed in through the back window, searching for something that he knew couldn't be there. The dark drew him in, seducing with its magnetic pull, knowing the weakness of curiosity that the young possess.

The smell of human waste was overpowering, as he entered, almost a living being.

As his eyes adjusted to the cobweb-filled interior, to his horror the shop was carpeted by the carcasses of dead birds, their fragile bones gleaming like hulls from tiny ships caught in the rocks, blending wickedly into an origami of shadows and repulsiveness.

The ever-skilful rats had been proficient in stripping the flesh. It was a massacre, a feasting of the dead, and he was baffled how creatures of flight could have been captured so easily.

Only when he stumbled on the two birds, each crucified to the beams, their necks twisted into grotesque, feathered question marks, did he realise the rats had only played a meagre part in the bloody pantomime.

A shudder iced his spine. What if the killer was still in the shop, watching him this minute, knife in hand? No one would know. They hadn't seen him enter. The killer could leave him dying in his own blood, just like the ugly birds pinioned to the mast, staring at him in disbelief, at his stupidity in remaining.

Then the rats would come, finishing the job...

The shop's acoustics echoed behind him in the darkness, making his heart thump, his face swell with rushing blood. He wanted to ask who's there but feared it would expose him, so he moved slowly across the room, as if swimming in a morass of sand. If he could only make it another few feet, freedom would sweep him away to safety, away from whatever lurked there, watching him.

Suddenly, the sound of feet crushing glass made his hair tight, burning his scalp. Liquid was flooding his brain and he could no longer think. Was it *his* feet, or someone else's that had made the sound?

He heard a laugh, so soft it was almost silent, meant for his ears only, sinister and deliberate.

Not thinking, not caring, he took a chance and ran. He had only one thought and that was to escape. He wouldn't die, not here with the dead.

It was funny how John Wayne always made it look so easy, jumping through windows of a saloon as the bad guys shot at him. But he was no John Wayne. He was a failure, and the perfect casement of glass suddenly became a kaleidoscopic pattern, all in slow motion, as he tumbled to the ground watching his blood hit it before he did, the shreds of glass following him, piercing every inch of skin.

Afterwards, he could only remember the pain as he drifted in and out of needle-induced nightmares, screaming for water to be thrown on his face, stop the burning heat that came from it. People with masks floated above him, surrounding the face of his mother.

Scarred for life, he remembered her voice whispering, contradicting the specialist, sitting there in his fat leather chair, manipulating the shadows on his face, obscuring clarity of expression. "They will fade," he said, his voice a politician. "Given time, he'll hardly notice them."

But four years had passed and there had been no fading, either of scars or memory. If anything, the opposite was true.

He would have gone insane had it not been for his plastic models of the *Werewolf*, *Dracula* and *Frankenstein* with whom he found comfort and friendship.

The plastic monsters were the only therapy he needed, not doctors. They sustained him, building his confidence as he meticulously attached each intricate and tiny piece together, shaping them, giving life to them.

At night, with the lights dead, they would glow eerily, like a lighthouse bathed in fog, guarding him against the completeness of isolation.

Just as he was about to close the curtains of his window, his eyes captured a small blue car coming into view, its loneliness augmented by the starkness of the deserted street.

It stopped at the entrance of the shop and an old man emerged to stand at the doorway, nodding to himself in a world of his own.

Every now and then he would quickly scribble something into a tiny pocket book, wetting the pencil with the carpet of his tongue, staining it black.

"What was he doing?" said the boy, out loud to no one but his monsters, as he watched the car disappear into the snow, its liquorice tyre marks chasing it.

A feeling came to him at that exact moment but he quickly erased it, as he had done many times before, not wanting to set his hopes high.

If the shop were to change, be transformed into something - *anything* - perhaps he would change and it would no longer have the power to make him wince with terror each time he saw it.

If he were a good boy, he would have whispered a nice wee prayer to God. But he wasn't nice, and God didn't exist.

Months passed and the old shop remained unused. Then one Saturday he watched as men with tools piled planks of wood outside the shop, talking loudly to each other.

His heart skipped a fraction. *It was happening*, he told himself. *Don't look at it. You'll jinx yourself. They'll disappear.*

Expectation began to swell in his chest, but doubt, heavy as an anvil kept it firmly in place.

Normally, he hated Saturdays. All the other kids in the street loved Saturday, but they didn't have to endure all the nonsense that he had to handle. He would much prefer staying in his room, putting the finishing touches to *The Mummy's Vengeance*.

At least it was raining outside, he told himself, plus he had the added advantage of being up while most people in the street slept. No one would see him, he hoped.

First on his agenda were the boxes of apples from his mother's trees.

As he approached the fruit shop, he stopped to watch the horses utilised by the local glazier. They stood in unison, eating, pissing and shitting. They never stopped, their arses perpetually pushing out fist-size boulders with slivers of undigested straw protruding from them like burnt cacti. Kamikaze sparrows darted in and out between the horses' legs capturing the spillage.

Sometimes his mother made him scoop up the dung to fertilise the trees, much to the amusement of the kids in the street. He had wanted to poison the horses, burn down the trees, make his mother eat her precious dung, and even though these were only thoughts, they became at times so tangible he could taste them, boring deep down into his skull, as if searching for oil.

He took a deep breath before entering the fruit shop, before having to deal with Richardson, the greengrocer from hell.

"Ah! Young Gary!" exclaimed Richardson, crowbar in hand. "Good to see you're not like the rest of the dirty dogs, sleeping in their beds on a beautiful morning like this." It was still pissing outside.

Dead, supine flies lined the window of the store like a contiguous military convoy debilitated by superior forces, while their air-borne comrades struggled above, stuck on dusty flypaper.

Gary stared at the adhesive, fascinated by its struggling victims trying, in vain, to detach themselves from the sticky graveyard. It always reminded him of the currant buns sold next door in Mullan's bakery. He had never eaten one in his life.

Richardson squeezed the teeth of the crowbar between the lips of the banana crate and with a slight movement of his elbow, popped the wood asunder.

"How many, young Gary?" asked Richardson, a giant with tight clothes. The man's large stomach had sheltered too many beers for its own good.

"Fifty, Mister Richardson," squeaked Gary. He hated this part, the barter of apples.

Richardson handled one of the apples, rubbing his thumb against the texture, smelling it with his giant nostrils.

"Four cabbages. Howsabouthathen?" He said this as one word.

"My ma said *five* cabbages, four carrots and a stone of blue spuds."

Gary wished Richardson would speed it up, in case one of his schoolmates came in for a toffee-apple, witnessing his humiliation.

"Ha! Yer ma's arse is out the window!" laughed Richardson, who was now juggling some of the apples, like a clown, into the air, winking as he pretended to allow them to fall. "But you've caught me in a generous mood. Four cabbages. And here's some carrots as well."

Gary was not in the mood this morning, so he didn't argue.

As he left the shop, Richardson handed him a pear. It was badly bruised and had teeth marks in it. "Here, that's for you. And tell yer ma she's gotta get up early to catch me!"

Gary could still hear the laughter halfway down the lane and he knew his mother would look on the exchange with disdain.

"That's all?" she asked as he entered the living room.

Tiny needles of pain began to burn his skull.

"Why didn't you go yourself, then?" he answered, watching her face flush. A few weeks ago he wouldn't have answered her back, but she was becoming just like the trees: hateful.

Suddenly, the pressure on the edge of his skull began to ease into an acceptable throb. Pleasurable, almost.

A week later and the old shop had been transformed into the new barber's. It would be a godsend for the men in town who traveled at least three miles, on foot, to have their hair cut.

A few days after the initial opening a 'Help Wanted' sign was placed in the window.

Gary stared at the sign from his room. It was teasing - *no, torturing* - him, whispering for him to return, to be friends.

But he knew his mother would not permit him to take the job and he was more than surprised when she said she would consider it.

Then surprise changed to anger.

Consider it? How could she allow me to enter that place after all I have gone through? Had she being doing her job as a so-called mother, perhaps I would not have these scars for the rest of my life, nor her crocodile tears.

But he said nothing, simply smiled at her, like a fox hiding in the dark of night.

Yes. You do just that. But while you consider that, consider this, also: one day the oil is gonna come bursting out, like a geyser, all hot and sticky. There were times when he tried - and succeeded - to keep these terrible feelings for her consecutively, allowing each a life of its own, each dominating the other in equal periods. But most times the darkness ruled, bullying out the decency that he knew he possessed but hated for its weakness. He thought the darkness like ink seeping destructively into bread, destroying all that was good in him.

Stop, he admonished himself. *You're not to blame. She is.*

So... you've come at last?" said the old man, scissors in hand, clipping perfect shapes from the flawed head of a customer.

"What do you mean? Am I not allowed to come in for a haircut?" said Gary, indignantly.

"Of course! Of course! Silly me. I thought you had come for the job - at least for the summer, get some money in your pocket. But not to worry, I believe another boy is interested." Both the barber and customer smiled at their reflections in the mirror.

A stone of fear moved in his stomach, sliding downwards like acid.

"Did I say I wasn't interested?"

"Are you?" smiled the old man, knowing the answer.

Gary started that afternoon, sweeping puddles of hair, making tea and reading the comics. Occasionally, he wiped the mirrors on the wall, keeping his eyes glazed, as if in a trance, not seeing his face. It had been over two years since last he saw his face. He doubted if he would ever look at it again.

As time went by, Gary started to love the shop. It was an emporium of treasures so delicious they hurt his heart: sweets harboured in jars lined the groaning shelves; towers of American comic books piled haphazardly, waiting to collapse; shrunken, rubber heads dangled ghoulishly from the nicotine ceiling. Religious paraphernalia sat incongruously with magazines of half-naked women, decapitated corpses and Mafia rub-outs - appropriately enough - in barber chairs.

A *Brylcreem* poster of Denis Compton, cricket bat in hand, proudly proclaimed: *Perfectly set for the day.*

This is home. This is what it should be all about, thought Gary as he watched the barber wield his magic on a customer.

The old barber, razor in hand, quickly attended the soapy face, making a swathe in the air before resting it on the man's pliable throat and protruding Adam's apple the size of a robin's egg.

With a slight, invisible movement, the old man removed the soap, leaving the customer's cheeks gleaming a pink red, not unlike a baby's bum.

Power, thought Gary, watching the stubble vanish. *To make something disappear, with such ease, is true power.*

The old barber broke his thoughts. "One day, Gary, you will be able to do this. You will become the best barber the town has ever known. They will remember you forever…"

The crackling static of an old Bakelite wireless nipped at his neck as the classical music of Puccini's *Madame Butterfly* floated abstrusely about the shop, appreciated by no one except the old barber who prayed for the last pangs of day when he would sit, upstairs, listening to his beloved music.

Once, not too long ago, Gary had slipped up the stairs, hiding in the shadows and watching as the old man prepared supper, listening to the tragic love story of Mimi and Rodolfo in *La Bohème*, tears rolling down his face.

The young man was fascinated. How could music make you cry? He could never remember having seen anyone cry. Not even his mother cried when she witnessed his destroyed face.

Have… you gone mad?" said his mother jokingly. "Wouldn't we look the proper fools sitting here covered in soap, you with your plastic razor trying to shave a couple of my hairy moles!"

"But it's the only way I'll prove myself to the barber. I know I can be the best."

She laughed out loud, stopping suddenly, seeing the hurt on his face. "I suppose it would do no harm," she said, relenting.

He warmed the towel at the fire.

"Must do it right."

"Watch you don't burn it," she almost said, before holding her tongue. She had upset him enough today.

"And how are you today, Mr McCarthy?" asked Gary, taking on the role of the old barber.

The mother was laughing, now. "Don't be expecting a tip

from me, young man, unless you do a good job," she said, her voice hamming a masculine throaty gruff.

"Oh, no sir! You will never forget this shave. Like a baby's bum."

"Gary! Now watch your language," said his mother's muffled voice from beneath the hot towel.

Gary, watch your language, mimicked a snide voice somewhere on the oil rig. *Gary, pick up all that horse shit, rub it in those scars of yours. That'll take them all away, all on a summer day.*

The hedgehog's voice was laughing now, blending seamlessly with his mother's. He felt his fingers tighten on the towel and something bubbling in the hollow of his stomach.

"Gary! You almost suffocated me! Enough of this nonsense!"

"No! Please, mother. I'm just nervous, that's all. I want to get it just right. Please…"

She shook her head then sat back in the chair as Gary applied the shaving brush, gently but firmly to her face.

"What's that music you're playing?" she asked, the soap tickling her nose. She felt a sneeze coming on.

"Opera. *La Bohème*. It tells the tragic love story of a poor poet, Rodolfo, who falls in love with Mimi, a seamstress."

"I didn't know you knew opera, son?"

He smiled: *There are a lot of things you don't know about me.*

He found his mother's skin not unlike the naked chicken he practiced on. It was withered, beyond care and he wondered if the consumptive-ridden Mimi's skin was as horrible.

Her skin may be withered, sneered the voice in his head, *but at least it isn't scarred.*

He watched as his mother's eyelids became heavy, listening to the softness and adagio of the music.

Why should I have all the scars, he thought, as oil moved faster and faster, pumping in his brain.

273

It was strange and powerful how a tiny nick could create such a forceful release of fluid. Her clothes would be ruined, but it was a small price for freedom.

She hadn't even stirred, lost somewhere in the music of dreams and failed hopes.

He made another nick - a fraction wider - to the left of the original.

She moaned, but he held her hand tightly, giving her strength, the strength he had needed all the years of his isolation.

Somewhere outside, nightlights came on, accentuating the darkness in the room. *La Bohème* came to a crackling end leaving only his soft breathing in the room.

He looked back at her, before closing the door, thinking how she resembled one of his models: stiff yet life-like. He tried to think which model, but the tiny hedgehogs had returned, biting at his brain.

It was only later in bed - as he closed his eyes, squeezing in the night and feeling his lids flicker as if housing angry ants - did he agree with himself to tell the old barber that the time had now come. He was a real barber now...

Fred Johnston was born in Belfast in 1951 and has published seven collections of poetry, three novels, three plays and a collection of short stories, *Keeping The Night Watch* (1998). With Peter Sheridan and Neil Jordan, he founded the Irish Writers' Co-operative in the mid-seventies. In 1986, he founded Galway city's annual literature festival Cúirt and more recently, he founded The Western Writers Centre. He has also recorded two traditional folk albums with the group Parson's Hat in the early 'Nineties. He received a Hennessy Literary Award in 1972 and was writer-in-residence to the Princess Grace Irish Library at Monaco in September 2004.

'Bolus Ground' is the other side of the coin presented in Mike McCormack's opening story of this collection, showing that there's no artist without an audience....

Bolus Ground

Fred Johnston

"There are hundreds of other gifts of painting which are not at all involved with moral conditions . . . ."

- John Ruskin: The Unity of Art

There is music in the way water bubbles in gutters and drains. The sort of music one finds in paintings, sometimes. No, not paintings of musical instruments, not like that. Natural and fixed. You know what I mean.

It was raining heavily, my pork-pie hat, my trademark to some, was drenched. Little globules of silver water had formed their own universes on the fabric. I'm a familiar figure. The odd wave here and there. The clubfoot is what they see first, or rather, my up-down hobble. The cane's for show.

There's been a lot of unnecessary, in my view, fuss, about this Bacon business. I knew him. Spent hours pissed in that refuse-tip mews kip; squatting, leaning, nothing to sit on. Brushes in butter bean tins, tripping over his enormous VAT 69 carton while he fondled his miniature *David* to illustrate some point or other. He was reading Nietzsche and trying to teach himself German to read him in the original, which I thought was daft and said so: *German for Adults.* He'd borrowed from me a rather heavy book on Velasquéz, whom some said he imitated, though I never could see it. I thought he'd leaned a bit much towards Picasso. The recurring naked light bulb motif is out of *Guernica.*

Sometimes we'd just sit and listen to his transistor radio. He liked music. Once he told me that all his paintings were about himself. The light bulb was about illuminating the horror of our lives, he said. The false, fake Apollo casting his limp light over a catastrophic world.

Some say my style apes his. I dispute that, though of late I've begun to concentrate even more on the human form. This new show, for instance, is about human form and what happens to it. Corruption, if you like.

The good days in London didn't last long, more's the pity. London: the Grail, for some. And there was talk, a cottage in Cornwall, Goldsmith students. I think there was some idea of creating a second and decidedly half-arsed Camden Town Group, Lord help us, but there was too much drink and messing about. I ignored the gossip, let them get on with whatever they got on with. There were many crude attempts to discuss Francis' art back then. And mine, which wasn't as fiery or as mad. The head and sides-of-beef thing, though, had given some of them the opportunity to say he'd tied himself to outmoded notions about trauma and the last world war. Bollocks. His paintings are all about himself, even when they're not.

I don't think he was fair to those who loved him. I think he hated himself for this but was unable to do anything about it. Hence, the self-rage in his work. Anyway, if you want to hear any more about him and those days, read my memoirs.

I crossed this bridge once and asked a begging child if I could draw him. He asked me for money. I told him to piss off. He knocked the spontaneity out of it for me. Cheapened the business.

I remember when, underneath, the black Guinness barges blew thick brown smoke up into your face and the air was full over the river and the bridge of the homely smell of hops. Things have changed. *I've* changed. Can't chase anymore, can't run after anything or anyone. When that dies out of life, life implodes, like they say a TV set does. I long for the days, not always but now and then, when everything we did was illegal. Added spice.

Now it's all young shaven-headed pretty boys dressed in black acting the artist for the columns of Saturday newspapers. No life, no violence, left.

You have to have a nail in your soul, the heart snagging on a rusty wire, as my old friend, bless him, John Noble, once said to me. John was a teacher, a good one, having done the decent thing and given up art when he couldn't do it well. I held his hand as cancer dissolved him. He didn't complain. He faded into the bed-clothes and disappeared. It's a long time ago now. The room was full of the sweet smell of flesh decaying, I remember that.

My scarf, wrapped around my neck, has become saturated with rain. It feels like a snake trying to strangle me. The light is beginning to go, the sky is the colour of tinned salmon. I've often thought of plunging headfirst into the old Plurabella. Tell me the man who hasn't. Now I give the river a passing glance, as it were, a kind of side-of-the-eye regard. It's often been a comfort to me that I could take my own life.

Now some say that this sort of melancholy has taken root in some of my pictures. I hate the word root, it reminds me of illness, things going deep down and killing. There is, let me be clear, no room for sentiment in painting. At least, not any more. The age of sentiment is long passed. Perhaps it ended after the First World War, who knows, and I could drag up the names of painters, but I'm not going to bother. What I paint now is the most unsentimental subject you could imagine: the revenge of life on the body, the way we decay, all stops out, all systems go, over to the worm. In a way, that's what Francis painted; the gape-mouthed dissolution of the body and the soul. Under a naked light bulb. Everything liquifying. Nothing solid, certain. He took out a plastic lighter once, a green one, and held the flame up to my face. He could be frightening. In a loving sort of way.

No, I was never a lover *there*, not me. Perhaps could have been, I was a drunken Irishman like himself and he liked pissed Paddies. I remember a certain leprechaunish playwright whom I met, starkers, in that kip of a flat. Sings *shtum*, nowadays. Someone else mentions this in a book. I think he could fall in love but a painterly insanity made him break the love up into bits he could paint with. I'm only mentioning my preferences, as they're called, because they're old news anyway.

I'm walking now towards my doom. I'm always nervous at an opening. People have come to expect a certain darkness about my work and I sincerely hope they'll not be disappointed. But there's something extra in these works. The *Table IV* might make some-one throw up, but that's all right as long as nobody compares me to Francis.

˙ Traffic at this time of day. No manners. There's a rush on this city that's not good for its heart. I hobble clubbily between cars and feel the heat come off the engines and out of the eyes of their drivers. I feel like a target. I've never driven, just as well, maybe. Terry offered to have someone pick me up, and I should've taken the offer, but that's me. What I'm worried about right now, even as I see the yellow square of light from the big front window of the gallery reflecting, doing marvellous colour work, on the wet street, is to have some decent press. Critics I loathe.

One in particular, and he's here, naturally.

I open the glass door, a drenched Claudius, remove my porky. The beetle-black tailored back of a decent critic shifts itself and he offers me his hand. More hands materialise, it becomes a Beckett play. The noise is conversation and music from the walls: Allighiero's *Artemis Concerto*, First Movement, followed by Lotti's *Crucifixus* and then Gesualdo's *Tenebrae factae sunt*. All looped, as I've asked, the lighter Allighiero blending subtly with the darker others. There's canapés and white and red plonk and pinky things on sticks. Redfaced men in various degrees of sweat smile and kiss the cheeks of women of a certain age who smell, as I squeeze past them, of talc and the process of drying out. Or is it *up*? All this is not for the young. Old age is not for the young, is it? Well, then. Neither are the painterly rantings...

My hand shoots out like a predatory bird.

"Harry. Good of you to come."

Harry resembles something by Beatrix Potter. His fat shape is cast in a Plaster-of-Paris-toned suit that clings to the fat folds of his legs and arms. He has charcoal eyes and a lizard's mouth, always wet and red. Harry emerged from some hatchery in the Yank mid-west, did no good in a nameless university, ended up here and whipped onto a newspaper as a critic before the ink's dry on his passport-stamp. As if the Yank drawl is what post-revolutionary Ireland respects in place of Oxbridge. You loathe Harry because he knows nothing about art and gets paid to ladle this vacancy back out to you. A dangerous nothing, let me add, because it's a black and dark negative that can do damage. You may suspect, from the anger in his reviews by times, that he didn't get on with his Dad. Or perhaps got on too well.

But it's my opening and I shake his hand wetly. He's cradling a gin and tonic. A soft-ground etching of a human being.

"Wouldn't like to wake up to one of those on my wall."

"You won't, dear boy. I promise."

I enjoy falling into the sad old queen routine for people like Harry. They expect it. It gives them a tale to tell.

"Bringing home the Bacon again?"

"Schoolboyish, Harry. Are we going to act the cunt tonight? Excuse me."

I move through the sweat and talc. Give them what they want, John, bless him, used to say. Terry comes over. So thin. I think he was born sickly looking. Every time I shake his hand it's like saying goodbye. But he's the best. His thin grey face shatters into a smile of enthusiasm. His handshake is firm and he can look you straight in the eye.

"This is very good work."

A camera flashed beside us.

"I hope I flog one or two."

"Give me your hat. And the scarf. And the stick"

"The stick's my prop, Terry."

But sure enough, a red spot had appeared on a frame across the room. The only sort of red spots a painter wants to see - now who said that first?

Terry busies himself chatting people up. He's good at that. You have to allow for his abrupt comings and goings. It's the business end of things and it's very necessary. I meanwhile hoke through the catalogues. The reproductions are decent. The Gothic print is a bit over the top, but there you are: *The Arrogance of Flesh.* So, I turn and view my own work, try to stand outside it, as it were.

The *Table IV* is a set of five humanesque figures, redly disembowelled, emerging tortuously from a dark background or space, all on unprimed canvas. There's not much to be said about them beyond that, from my point of view. They never look quite so large hung as when they're snug on the easel. But they are attracting red spots, or perhaps, growing them. *Attitude* is a tall work, virtually devoid of human shapes, but you can see them, as it were, bleeding into the bright foreground if you stand back a bit. *Reclining Mask* is a lovely macabre little thing, with two head-shapes, skulls more correctly, leering out, mouths open, from a dark background. Nasty young things in an alley? Scumble. I'm not a great acrylics fan, really. The effect is to make the skulls almost go in and out of each other, and the glazing is very light. *Resurrection V* is one of a series I'm doing, and I thought it would do no harm to bring out a finished piece here. The body shape, armless, split, is doing a chiaroscuro stretching trip upwards, imitating religious painting of a certain type that calls itself visionary. Now the background is not shaded, but deeply blued and greened, suggesting growth and emptiness, using the optical mixtures routine, so that it's almost pointillism but not quite, though nothing much can be gained from the work by standing up close to it. The human figure is drawn first and I've left the drawn lines visible; they have become like whisps of smoke around the torso. I'm particularly happy with *Christ Seized*, a sort of yelling head with thorns dissolving behind bars. Bacon there, fair enough. But it's a homage. The flesh-tones fade, my handling . . . .

"Ladies and Gentlemen, if we could have hush for one moment..."

Terry does the needful. Great em-cee. I'm squaring up to a bulbous G *agus* T and finding my form. Terry, back frail as the skeleton of something lying a long time underground, addresses the audience and sings my praises. A factotum turns off Lotti. I'll add a few words. Do the needful. From nowhere appears an image of gentle John Noble, dying. I feel something swelling in my throat, seizing my voice. A cancer of loss?

"I'd like to remember a dear deceased friend in this show," I say. "A great teacher and artist in the real sense, John Noble. Thank you."

Terry *hear-hears*. He knew John. Terry's wife came over to London when John was dying. John and I were not lovers, as some suggested, but we were friends from the Goldsmith days. He was the first artist I'd ever watch die, but not the last. I had thought we were immortal. Funny how the passing of years sometimes does not diminish some things, but rather enhances them.

"Bravo," Terry says, and pats me on the back. "A lovely gesture. Is it his anniversary or something?"

"No, nothing like that."

"Bravo. Well done."

He moves away. I'm left, for a moment, with my thoughts, which have turned a nasty shade of grey. I feel old, suddenly. Well, hardly suddenly. But I feel what it means now, its weight. The passing of something irretrievable. An energy going out of you, more than physical. A coming to terms which is a refusal to come to terms. Perhaps it'll be quick, for me. Or slow, like John, silent, wordless, floating backwards and backwards until you fall off the earth with a sigh. You reach an age and you know you'll die. You don't know that at twenty. But at my age, you do. It's all you have left to look forward to, in some ways. The end of all this, whatever it is.

I can't remember sitting down, but I'm sitting down when old Harry drawls his way over. He stands over me fatly. I fake a grimace.

"Tell me you aren't just doing your Bacon thing here. I need to know. *Really*."

"Is this a recent Americanism, Harry, to say *need* when you mean *want*?"

"What? Tell me."

"There's nothing to tell. You see what you see, Harry. It's not up to me to guide you around my paintings."

"I see Bacon, is what."

"So you keep saying. Interminably. God forbid, you risk becoming a bore."

A yelpish woman's laugh cracks over the room. A photographer is scribbling names in his notepad. Terry is pouring wine. Drunkenness is taking over. The buying hunger is fading.

Harry won't go away, he's a tad unsober himself. His drawl is sheathing about my nerves like a disease. He moves closer. Intimacies, Christ? I can smell his aftershave, see the red welt where his white shirt is digging into his fat neck. A shirtmaker's name; same place our better-class fake politicians go. It's all fake now, a voice in my head, probably John Noble's, tells me. Harry has taken up another gin and tonic and begun to sweat. I think of the last time I read his column, two brick-shaped lines of type under his grinning postage-stamp photograph. It reminded me of the images of the dead under glass I'd seen in village graveyards in France, the South, land of the Cathars, the sky blue and the earth yellow and the vines grey and sturdy-looking. A Toulouse hotel in the old red-light district; a woman, too old, in fishnet stockings scratching a Lotto card with a cognac in her other hand. The great walled towns, the heat, the coffees in the open air; *en pleine air.* Days painting life and light and colour and music down by the Garonne, in the reeds, naked sometimes. Slumbering heat. The train station at Toulouse with its iron raftering, its tracks running on and on so very lonely.

I'd come back that summer to a Dublin grey and torturous and the old crowd had asked me where I'd been, like mother hens. A photograph of Francis and John taken outside a bookshop in London that's now a bloody take-away. Round-faced Francis, slightly sad always, cravatted. Sainted Francis-of-a-Cissy, as some adolescent giggly toilet-filth scrawled on the jacks of what pub was it? The rage in Spain, the illustrator whose work depicting Lope de Vega in a whorehouse had caused Franco to ban him from ever working in the country again. The rage, the anger, the

holy violence of love-making. Lovers among the Arab boys in
Paris. The rue de Rivoli in the heat, shimmering like a glaring
shovel of concrete shoved into the furnace of the city. Too young,
under the flowers and the sun, ever to think of death, ever to paint
death of any kind or watch it paint over a loved life. Oh, I told
them of the heat and wine and the gouts of energy and the paint-
stained fingers scrawling over your wet back...

"Can you just, like, elaborate your obvious need..."

He'd made a move for his notebook. This was official Harry. I
hated him, the sound and shape of him. Anger grew up in me and
it had a salty taste. Had we painted our arses off to end up here
under the Judgement of Harry? I'd actually bitten my tongue: was
I taking fits now? Maddened, wounded, fed up, I shouted.

"I'll elaborate all over your face, you fat little pork-plumber.
Do you know, dear Harry, that we used to fuck Yank sailors in
London in the good old days just to keep our hand in, so to
speak?"

Knew I shouldn't have said it, of course. Harry smiled, as he
might well have done. I'd raised my voice, risen to his bait. But I
was angry, for God's sake. Rightly so. Though I didn't want to
acknowledge to myself that I'd faded in and then out of something, I'd been far away from Harry and the gallery and everything, drifting off somewhere. Terry was watching us.

I stood up, shakily, but with enough energy to have Harry
step back a pace or two.

"You haven't lived, Harry. You've seen nothing, been educat-
ed to nothing. Your arse-wipe newspaper needs you for show,
everyone else has a Harry. Can I buy you in kit form?"

I'd lowered my voice, but Harry's smile had disappeared.
Dried up, I should say, it was rather like that. I hadn't meant at all
to say what I'd said, but there was no residue of guilt, thank God,
no feeling that I should apologise or retract anything. I saw the little fat boy no one would talk to in the schoolyard pull his soiled

Yankness over his head and his Mom said night-night and tucked him up. Harry wilted visibly, head down.

"Rude and vulgar," he trailed after him. "The slip is showing."

I barely heard him, I was drowning in my own shame.

The crowd was dispersing. I suppose I'd helped them along, come to that. The old crip getting stroppy again, time to leave. I huddled a bit myself, behind a dodgy damp canapé and a fresh big iced gin. Harry was talking to someone, keeping his dignity rather well, I should have said. I was a *disgust* - John's use of the word. He used to describe Francis as a *disgust*, coining a noun, when in his more Bachanalian episodes. I felt, absurdly, like crying. Whenever I felt like this, painting helped. I wanted - Harry would no doubt have said *needed* - to get back to my studio. Terry was wandering around, happy with himself. I tapped his shoulder.

"Give my regards to your good wife."

"Are you off? I thought we might have dinner later, a few..."

"No thank you, Terry. I'm plunging rather nastily into my cups. Another time. And thank you most sincerely for everything. Wonderful."

I held his hand and shook it vigorously. Terry knew me long enough to let me off when I wanted to go. I looked around and saw a generous rash of red spots. Terry said, looking with me:

"You've done well already. Will you come in during the week and we'll run over some things?"

"I hate business, Terry. But I will, of course. I should say something to him, Terry, shouldn't I? I insulted him, lost it. He hasn't lived. Not like me, is it? Or is it?"

Terry, like the gent he is, didn't play stupid and act as if he'd seen-no-evil-heard-no-evil. He raised his eyebrows. He looked like a brush handle with a worn layer of bristles on top. His breath smelled, oddly, of mint.

"He's not the most loved, I know that. But he's young."

"Maybe that's what I dislike about him. He'll call me a prick in his column. I'll sue."

We both laughed. But I couldn't rid myself of a gnat-like itch, an irritation of spirit, call it what you will. I shook Terry's hand again and did the sort of social choreography that had me out on the street in the chill dry river wind alongside Harry, God love him, both of us goodnighting Terry with waves.

Porky on pate, Laocoon-ed by my damp scarf, stick conducting traffic, I stump-legged my way across the street almost by Harry's wounded side. I walk fast. Harry wasn't going my way. At length, I had to stop, pull myself up to a lopsided height and shout after him. An elderly queen shouting after a fat young man in a street gorged with sex-shops, as it happens. *Very* nice, visually.

"You have my apologies, Harry!"

He kept going. This was too ridiculous. Then he turned.

"Have a drink with me," I said. Heads turned in the street. Very silly, all of it. But Harry hadn't lived. That was all, curiously, I could think of. He walked back to me, rather tight-lipped and prissy, I might add. But he walked back.

"I was unconscionably rude," I said. Harry, being American, would have trouble with *unconscionably*, I thought. I stuck out a hand. The cold air was full of fat white seabirds that should have been in their beds. Some of them circled us like angels and barked. Harry looked very small and lost.

"I don't believe in keeping a grudge with artists," Harry said. Nice of him, I thought, very uncharitably. "It's not the first time someone's taken a shot." He was game, I'll give him that.

We shook hands. That's what gentlemen do. I offered him the drink again. He looked at me as if I'd propositioned him. Then I could see little gears cogging up behind his eyes, little men running backwards and forwards across his retina carrying messages, or votes perhaps, one way or the other. He'd boast that old whatsizface had tried him up. You know, the painter. Queer as a three-pound. Quasimodo, with a cane. Paints Bacon lookalikes and says he doesn't. Him. Good for a tea-break giggle with the girls in the canteen, or wherever Harry sits at trough. He might even call in the rag's brief and see if it'd be kosher to call me a queer. Which it wouldn't these days. I hate the word Gay, myself. Makes it appear that all of us are happy. Which we are not. Harry yawned. He'd made a decision, or the little scuttling men had.

"Where?"

"My place," I said, and saw him wince. You really must see the Minotaur's lair, Harry, I thought maliciously. Do some living. Besides, it's a story. The artist's garret.

"The spider's web," Harry said.

"Something like that."

"Are you inviting me back to your place?"

"You make it sound like I've just shown you my prick, Harry. No, actually. I want you - need you - to see my studio. I want to show you where everything takes place, as it were."

That was different. Harry could see what was what, he's not stupid. I wanted him to see what I believed about the human figure, blah-blah, and so on. I explained all of this as we walked. His notebook flagged out of his arse pocket like a rent-boy's menu handkerchief. He actually helped me down and up some quaintly Georgian steps. We cruised along the quays in slow motion. Or so it must have appeared to the rest of the bustling younger world. Dying is merely getting old very fast, John used to say. When he could still speak. On the way, we collected cigarettes, a bottle of plonk.

My door. Big and pompous with knowledge of its preservation order, my Georgian castle towers over our demolished street. The sound of African music one side, the odour of Chinese cooking the other, and always a Gauguin of colourful women walking up and down carrying bags and small children. They chatter and laugh and show big white teeth. Now and then an African in an expensive suit and immaculate white shirt will stand and look up and down the street. The women know me. The Chinese keep to themselves. The grandmother speaks no English, a wizened doll of a woman drying like vellum in the back room, you can see her every time the door to the kitchen swings open. I remember the Italian chippers with their Pope pictures and the sound of new chips when they'd crash into the boiling fat. Changes. The odour of hashish drifts like a gas on the wind.

I fiddle the majestic useless key in the lock. The big door's paint is peeling like strips of blackened skin. The knocker, brassy smooth, reflects every light in the street.

"After you, Harry."

Harry is carrying the bags like a good boy. We enter the catastrophe of my room and I turn on the light. A naked bulb, of course. There are my familiars, my wrecked couch, my crushed armchairs, the drink-sodden Turkish carpet, the retreating wallpaper. I indicate the couch to Harry. If he only knew the celebrity arse that's snuggled down there, he'd be grateful. More for the column. But knowing things isn't really living, is it? There's more.

Over the plonk from relatively clean glasses, we create little damp patches of silence. Harry's eyes wander around the room, going off on their own. I let them. I watch Harry. I study the tightness of the fabric of his pants over his fat knees, the way, I suppose, Michaelangelo studied the folds of fabric in his day. Not that I like Harry's fat knees, God help us. Harry takes everything in. He reads the spines of my few books by tilting his head. He spots the book, coffee-table size, on Velasquéz.

"That's from the Bacon set-up. The reconstructed flat."

"No, that's the original."

Tipsily impressed, Harry actually went over to have a look at it. That was the loneliest, the saddest thing I could ever have imagined him doing and I didn't give him credit for much. He was like a curious child. A man-child. A living ambiguity between maturity and childhood. Ideas for a study formed in my head. Then Harry leaned up and away from the book, which I'd bought, as it turned out, for fifty pee out of a basket a month back.

The silence, as Harry turned around and around like a figure in a music-box, was a colour all of its own. A texture, too. Like sandpaper. The old irritation came back. I wanted Harry to be more curious and then I'd show him what he wanted - *needed* - to see. Sure enough:

"And where, like, do you work?"

"Back in there," I said carelessly.

"I really would like to see the studio."

"Your-eyes-only status, Harry. Have I your word?"

Harry was hooked. He reached round for his notebook but I nodded my head seriously like a teacher who'd received the wrong answer. He understood, or the child in him did. I stood up wearily. How much, after all, can you expect another to understand you?

Behind a heavy red curtain, mottled at the hem with rat munchings, I opened my studio door. Another naked light bulb blew out upon a long room full of paints, brushes in tins, bottles of turps, easels, clothes, rolled paper, big housepainter-sized brushes, empty wine bottles, objects under white sheets. There were no windows, which was just as well of late. At the shadowy end of the room was the fire escape door, which also did for deliveries at all hours.

"Funny smell," said Harry.

"Paint and things. The usual."

Harry planted himself awkwardly on a paint-mottled rickety stool. I put on an apron. I steadied a large canvas on its legs. Harry got up, as I knew he would, and took a peek.

"Part of my *Resurrection* series, Harry. Driving me ga-ga. It needs life, the human shape rising from the earth sort of thing. Won't be a tick."

Harry nodded and grunted. The dark tones of the work so far revealed very little. But the hint was there, a mass of tissue rising agonisingly from the earth itself. I might just chance something with this one, I thought. I might let it flow a little. Like water.

"Definitely," said Harry. He was getting just a tad tipsy now, our Harry. He flunked his big tumorous arse across the little round stool. It disappeared up inside him. Billy Bunter wrapped in Old Glory. He slugged his wine back and peered about him again. I leaned into the canvas and pretended not to look at him. In fact I couldn't keep my eyes off him now.

"What sorta life?"

"I don't know, Harry. Something natural. Just a hint of movement. A gesture."

Harry didn't understand, and indicated this with a lardy frown. It made him look even younger. I'd conveyed the impression that I was using him as a model and that made him drunkenly smug. This was fame indeed, for Harry; how the coffee cups would chatter now! He began to straighten himself up, as clearly he thought a good sitter should. Harry was, quaintly, Old School, if you follow.

"You're obsessed with the human figure," Harry said. I suppose it was a question. By now I had angled myself in towards the canvas like a truly inspired painter should. Harry, watching me, would have seen that. He found it difficult to sit up straight and hold his glass in his hand. The wine was spilling, though he didn't notice it. Dark red, on cream white.

"It is all we are, Harry. That absurd pronged image. Then it disintegrates. Symbol of time itself. Loosen yourself a little, Harry."

I didn't make sense even to myself. But that was unimportant. Harry was hypnotised. Every word I said now, every gesture I made, would sit like a jewel in the rubbish-heap of Harry's critical mind. I felt inexplicably sad. Are all critics merely lonely children no one'll play with? Is art itself such a sad thing? Am I someone's fretful lost child?

A lump formed in my throat, a tightness that seemed to rise out of my chest. As the lump grew, it pulled its energy from my hands. The brush slowed, got stuck in its own paint. I stood back from the work. I took a depth breath. Harry was staring at some point on the floor. I recovered myself. Whatever had hovered round my soul had flown.

"Must have models," I heard Harry say. He smiled, but it was like a great toothachy thing, bending his face. "I really liked your work tonight. It's just like, well, I guess we're kinda all Bacon-ed out..."

"The models are all around you, Harry. Pull off one of those drapes. Carefully, now."

I'd paid enough for them, God knows. And they wouldn't last. I'd end up having to pay to have them taken back. Dark doings at the back door. So I had to make as much use of them while I . . . .

Harry screamed. Well, a loudly amplified rat's squeak, if you can imagine. A sound as if his very soul were being dragged across a bed of nails. His hands in the air like that, the expression on his face as his flabby mouth opened, the glass tumbling over and over in the air, spouting wine like blood everywhere as if he'd been shot, his body arched backwards and upwards from the waist. You couldn't ask for better.

I worked quickly, filling my head with a sort of snapshot, a still, of Harry's St Vitus' hysterics. The human figure repelled him, obviously. Headless, armless and legless it was broken down to its workable minimal centre, the focus point from out of which emotion was drawn, shaped, angled; but you couldn't explain that to Harry. I don't like too much whiteness, it hints at leprosy, and the effect of darkening and withering to indicate decay, an eating away, is achieved by pouring a little petrol, an eggcupful, over an incision in the flesh and then setting it alight. The flesh will crisp and darken. Takes a while, and it's smelly, but it works. I felt confident about the *Resurrection* pieces. Harry's little agony would pass, but I'd captured it, at least in the rough. I could touch it up. The vomiting I most certainly did not need.

Or is it *want*?